PURPLE ORCHID

A NOVEL

BY

S CUNLIFFE

Purple Orchid Blues

S Cunliffe Press

ISBN 978-1-7385502-2-7

Chapter 1

Atlanta, Georgia

"Not being heard is no reason for silence" (Victor Hugo)

The arraignment of Barry Watkins for aggravated assault and battery took place on 1 March, 2023. The previous week on 23 February in South Atlanta, Georgia he had beaten Eric Senser, the owner of Big Daddy's Burger Bar to within an inch of his life. Barry was a 33-year-old Black man who worked at the Amazon depot and had lived in South Atlanta all his life. The court had appointed Public Defender Gavin Gates to act on his behalf, owing to his low-income status.

When Gavin and Barry met before the arraignment, Gavin encouraged Barry to plead guilty as the case against him was overwhelming and there was no apparent reason for the attack.

"No Sir. I was defending Song when that motherfucker Senser tried to rape her," said Barry.

Gavin looked at his notes "Who is Song again?" he asked.

"We were together" said Barry "She was in my bed when I was arrested. Ask her."

Gavin looked through the reports. "There is a Chinese woman who was at your apartment and was taken to an Immigration Detention Center in Atlanta mentioned in the report. But she was at your apartment, not at the burger bar."

Barry was getting angry "She worked at the fucking burger bar." He said: "Senser tried to rape her."

"But no-one has come forward to say they saw her at the burger bar. The only mention of Song is that she was at your apartment when you were arrested. No-one saw a woman in the alley at the burger bar where the assault took place." Gavin looked carefully at the police report and then said "According to the police report the assault was called in by a woman who worked in the burger bar named Sonya. She went outside to look for Senser when he had not returned from taking out the trash and found him lying in a pool of blood and you stood over him. She said you ran away when you saw her. Who are your witnesses who report seeing Song there?"

The thing was no-one had come forward to speak up and say they saw Song at the burger bar. No-one had spoken in Barry's defence. Where were his friends, he wondered. He had never felt more alone and as if his voice was not being heard. He was stubborn though.

"I am not guilty. I acted to help Song. If I hadn't Senser would have raped her." he said.

Nothing Gavin Gates could say or do, would cause Barry Watkins to change his plea. It was not a motiveless attack and Barry knew that was the truth.

Barry pleaded not guilty, and as he could not meet the conditions of bail, he was returned to prison waiting a trial.

Background to the arrest

At first sight Big Daddy's, a burger bar in Atlanta, a private university in Los Angeles and the Purple Orchid, an upscale nail salon in a small city in the southern states would have little or nothing in common. However, the arrest of Barry Watkins for aggravated assault and battery wound the fates of all three of them together with shocking and unforeseen consequences. Barry said he was acting on behalf of a Chinese woman, Song, and she was in fact, the link that joined everything together.

Song Zhang had been sent by her father, Professor Xingping Zhang, to study at an American college. She was Chinese and, not by any stretch of the imagination, academic. She loved dressing up, makeup and painting nails. However, her father was Head of International Programs at his university in China and he wished Song to have an academic career. Using his influence he was able to secure her a place at an American university in Los Angeles called Highbridge College.

After a few months at the college and finding the academics too difficult Song ran away with her friend, Lily. Song now needed a job and forging qualifications she took a job as a manicurist at the Purple Orchid. Her immigrant visa only allowed her to work on the campus of the university making her employment at the Purple Orchid illegal. By the time the owner of the Purple Orchid, Jinni, a Thai lady, found this out she had already fallen in love with Song and allowed her to stay.

A couple of months later hearing about a potential raid by the Immigration Services, Song went on the run again. This time to Atlanta, Georgia where she began work at Big Daddy's burger bar. Her next door neighbour in Atlanta, was Barry Watkins, who also fell in love with her. Eric Senser, the owner of Big Daddy's had a reputation for employing illegal immigrants, paying them in cash and treating them badly.

One night Eric asked Song to take out the trash to the alley behind the burger bar. There he attacked Song attempting to rape her. Barry Watkins came to her assistance, beating Eric Senser severely.

Song and Barry escaped the scene in the alley to take refuge in his apartment. It was at the apartment that Barry was arrested and Song was taken to an Immigration Deportation Centre as she could not show the relevant papers.'

Song's father had employed a lawyer and private detective to find her. They met first with Jinni at the Purple Orchid and then moved on to the Detention Centre. The lawyer was able to present a petition to have Song's academic visa reinstated. This involved stating that she had been ill with stress and this was why she had missed college for a number of months. A doctor agreed to sign the petition.

It was now very important for Song's future academic career in the USA that there be no mention that she worked at either the Purple Orchid or Big Daddy's burger bar. Her presence at these places was effectively wiped away by her father's lawyer.

Yet, a man was awaiting trial for defending her and was potentially facing years incarcerated without her testimony.

This story takes place in the time leading up to the trial of Barry Watkins and the immediate aftermath of the trial. The ladies of the Purple Orchid nail salon are at the centre of the story but the story also follows what happens during this time in Atlanta and Los Angeles.

It is the story of a trial but it is also a story about how ambition and greed can clash with justice and the pursuit of personal happiness. At its heart this is the story of people who seem to have no voice but who dare to speak up and make their voices heard.

> "It's not about finding your voice, it's about giving yourself permission to use your voice." (Kris Carr)

Chapter 2

The Purple Orchid Salon

At the beginning of March 2023

February 2023 had been a challenging month for the Purple Orchid salon. The Purple Orchid was an upscale nail salon in the fashionable Walks District of the city. Up until very recently it had been "the" choice of nail salon for those in the know. It was always "Hair by Raymond, beauty by Siva Spa and nails at the Purple Orchid." Reviewers of the salon raved about the innovative nail art and beautiful surroundings. Walking through the door, was to be greeted by a display of white and pink lotus flowers. These were a beautiful sight in themselves but looking around there would be even more flowers, orchids and jasmines, in pots on the window sills and a display on each manicurists station. Customers commented that the sights and scents from all these flowers was almost intoxicating.

The salon was owned by Jinni, a Thai lady, who always employed manicurists who were nail technicians with a license from the state's board of cosmetology. The atmosphere was upscale and luxurious.

This was until January 2023 when the salon was raided by the Immigration Services. Although they found nothing wrong and all manicurists in the salon on that day had the relevant paperwork, this scandalised the customers who were there that day. These customers of course, told their friends, or posted on social media.

"Jinni is foreign. Where is she from? Does she have papers?" mused one customer "Or is she illegal? Why would the Immigration Services raid her if all was in order?"

Suddenly customers remembered Song, the beautiful Chinese girl who had worked there and suddenly left at the end of 2022 and wondered if this had anything to do with her.

Of course, no-one said anything directly to Jinni. But it was a topic for gossip for a number of weeks. Although no-one had said anything to her, Jinni had guessed there would be gossip and intrigue. She had seen anonymous posts on social media . On 1 March 2023 there was a cryptic post on the Facebook community page for the shopping district.

> "Are our local businesses employing illegal immigrants? The government have made this a criminal offense – employers can go to jail for up to 5 years. Do your duty and report anyone employing illegal immigrants."

Jinni knew that customer numbers were down, she didn't have to consult the accounts to know that. Yet still there were loyal customers who had been coming for years. Very few of the customers knew that Song did not have working papers. In fact Jinni had only confided in Ellie, an Englishwoman and her American husband Kevin. Ellie and Kevin worked at the state university – Ellie taught first year students and Kevin was a professor. However, had it been a wise decision confiding in Ellie and Kevin? Could Ellie be trusted to keep quiet? Ellie had flirted with scandal herself by making her views public and getting involved in online arguments on a variety of subjects including Meghan Markle and Prince Harry and their claims of racism that drove them from the British Royal Family.

Issues of illegal immigrants and her business aside, Jinni had always worries about her immediate family. She loved her brother Somchai very much. However, he was a hopeless alcoholic and womaniser. At present he had left his wife to live with Randi, who tended bar, at the Black Cat.

Jinni always tried to please Somchai and on his advice had offered Randi's sister, Lila a job as a receptionist at the Purple Orchid salon. She only worked part-time at busy periods, but Lila was a larger-than-life woman who completely took over given half a chance. Jinni had never known anyone as ambitious as Lila for her husband Ronnie's band "The Brothers of Swing". Lila had brought a new dynamic to the salon.

So at the beginning of March although to the casual observer everything seemed fine, underneath all was not well in the Purple Orchid. There were tensions and secrets that could potentially surface with disastrous effects.

Chapter 3

Jinni

Worries about the salon...

Sometimes I dream of Song. I can feel her fingers gently massaging my tired shoulders and I am happy again. When I wake and I know she is gone I am heartbroken.

I have never felt like this before about anyone. I never felt love like this for my husband. I would do anything for her if she were to come back and be with me. I have no reason to believe that this will ever happen, but I am obsessed with her.

She is such a beautiful young woman and, in many ways, very naïve and trusting. I am a serious businesswoman. In the years before I met Song, my business was my whole life. I started out as a manicurist in a City centre salon and then I leased a small shop front in the suburbs. This was so successful, that I was able to move to my present premises in the Walks shopping district of the City. This is a very upscale area, and my salon fits well into the area. It is decorated beautifully, and I usually only employ qualified manicurists. I would never employ an illegal immigrant......that was until Song came along.

Why did I not ask her to leave immediately when I found out she did not have papers to work in the USA? I will never know the answer to that question. She was Chinese and was supposed to be at a private university in Los Angeles on a student visa but had run away. In retrospect, I believe her story about how difficult she found academics, and how her Chinese family had pushed her to go to college. It seemed her father, Professor Xingping Zhang, was Head of International Programs at a university in Guangzhou. He was involved in setting up links with the USA for Chinese students to study here. He wanted his only daughter to also study in the USA and to become an academic like him. The truth was that Song had no interest in academics. . I truly believed she only got a place at university because her father was able to pull strings and open doors for her. She could speak English but found it difficult to write in English. She loved gossip, makeup, and fashion. She had fit in so well at the Purple Orchid working as a manicurist. She did a fantastic job cutting, filing and painting nails. She also worked out some great new designs which she put onto nails. Also, and very important, she loved chatting to the customers and making them feel welcome in the salon.

My heart is broken and I have so many memories of Song. I remembered the evening when she first started to massage my shoulders and I had felt an overwhelming desire for her. When she stopped, I turned and looked into her eyes, and then she had kissed me. I had never been kissed by a woman before. There had been no reluctance on her part, and I felt she desired me as much as I desired her. Our lovemaking had been special. I had felt cared for and loved.

Song told me she loved only me. She confided that she had no desire for men. Yet a few weeks later when she was found by the police she was in Atlanta in bed with a man. She was also involved in a scandal which would be very dangerous for my business if it came to light.

My gut instinct was screaming "Jinni, you had a lucky escape. Song is like a child who will use people to get what she wants" and my heart was saying "But I love her more than life itself."

Maybe I had never been in love before, but if this was love, it was agony. I felt tormented, even though I kept a brave face for the customers in the salon.

Just as I was leaving for the salon on Saturday morning after yet another night of vivid dreams, my cell pinged that I had a message. It was from Harry Zine, the attorney representing Song in her petition to have her educational visa reinstated. Harry was based in Atlanta, but he requested a meeting with me. Apparently, he was happy to talk on Zoom.

I messaged back that I would be busy in the salon today but could speak to him when I returned home after the salon closed. We arranged a time and he said he would send me a link to log on to Zoom.

The thought of this meeting worried me. Of course, my first instinct was to protect my business, but I was obsessed with Song and what would happen to her. I am Thai and although I have working papers, I am always mindful of the fact that I am an immigrant in the USA and I should abide by their rules. In the case of Song, I had broken rules.

I tried to keep a smile on my face all day in the salon, but this was difficult.

Lila was on reception, and I could see the customers liked her friendly joking manner. I knew this was good but to be honest I found her loud and overbearing. I was not sure why I had hired her, other than on the recommendation of my brother as she was his lady friend's sister. I hoped I would warm to her as the weeks went by.

When I closed the salon at 4pm (it was Saturday and the salon closed early) I hurried home and set up for the Zoom meeting. Harry Zine came on the screen looking casual in a polo shirt. I guessed he was in the study of his home rather than at the office. He was friendly, but I was very nervous, and I think he may have picked up on this.

He started out by saying he wanted to bring me up to date on the immigration case. The college in Los Angeles had agreed to say that Song had been absent from class for 4 months due to sickness. Harry explained that if a student then takes up their place again within the 5 month period the visa can be reinstated. A doctor had been involved who had issued a certificate to say Song had been suffering from stress which had affected her ability to attend classes and study. The college had accepted that the stress had prevented Song calling into her tutor to tell her that she was too ill to attend class. It was now on her record that she had been on sick leave for the autumn term. It was looking very likely that Song could be reinstated at the college.

"That is good news, yes?" he said.

I knew that what he was saying was true as Kevin, Ellie's professor husband, had checked it out for me. The timings were such that Song could still be reinstated. However, under an F-1 visa students could only legally work on campus or at college approved activities. If it came out that Song had been working, then that would stop her visa being reinstated.

I nodded because I didn't know what to say. It was so wrong. Song had run away in the first place because she found college very difficult and had no interest in academia. Why reinstate her? It would just make her miserable. It was all because her father wanted her to have an academic career like his. What was the point in arguing with Harry Zine, he would just do what he was paid to do – and that was to get her back into the university. The college was a private university charging $44,000 a year in fees. An enormous sum of money it seemed to me and they were not included in the rankings of prestigious universities. Maybe this college did not have scruples.

“Is Song happy?” I ventured.

“Of course,” said Harry “and we want you to be happy too, Jinni”

He lent towards the camera looking sincere “I know this has been very difficult for you. After all you are an immigrant too” he said meaningfully “this is why I feel that there is much that happened over the last few months that should now be forgotten and not spoken of anymore.”

I was a bit slow, but I was beginning to get the message.

“So, Song was sick and although she did not attend class in Los Angeles, she stayed there being cared for?” I said.

Harry smiled widely now and took up the story: “Yes that is right, Jinni. Until such time as she felt better and went to visit a Chinese friend in Atlanta. This was an ill-advised trip but she was only in Atlanta for a very short period of time”

Of course, she never worked in my salon or Big Daddy’s burger bar in Atlanta – if that came out it would ruin her visa reinstatement. A clever expensive attorney like Harry Zine could engineer a cover up.

But isn’t that what I wanted? I did not have to worry about the Immigration authorities coming to my salon again accusing me of employing someone without papers. I faced a criminal prosecution and a fine and jail sentence if the Immigration Authorities found out I had employed an illegal immigrant. With the help of Harry Zine, I was in the clear.

I knew what had happened in Atlanta as I had accompanied Professor Xingping Zhang and his lawyer to the Detention Centre where we met with Song. I wondered how he would explain her presence in the alley at the rear of the burger bar. But he was a clever man, and I am sure that could be covered up too.

After saying goodbye, I went and poured myself a large glass of SangSom and sitting in my favourite chair began to drink. I felt sick and dirty for my meek agreement to the lies and plotting of Professor Xingping Zhang and his attorney. What a pathetic person I was. I sat there for a very long time...

Chapter 4

Ellie

On a new mission....

At the beginning of March 2023 when Ellie Watson went to the Purple Orchid for her manicure she was aware that the salon was not as busy as in the previous year. "Perhaps there is a new trendy salon and this is competition for the Purple Orchid" she said to herself. But she knew the reasons behind the loss of customers was most certainly something else. Jinni had confided in Ellie and her husband Kevin about Song and the issues around her student visa. This was because she saw them as academics. Ellie and Kevin both worked at the State University.

Looking at Ellie today is to see a tall, full figured woman in her mid-thirties. Her hair is blonde and piled on top of her head in a messy bun. She is an English woman married to an American academic. In fact, it was in England that they had met while Kevin was doing research for his PhD. They had lived many years in England and Ellie taught at a college. When Kevin's father died in America they had moved to the states to be near his mother. Kevin who had a PhD and publications easily got a position as a professor at the State University. Unfortunately, Ellie did not have a PhD, which was the qualification for a permanent teaching position in the USA. It had not been as easy for her to find work. She had been working as adjunct faculty at the State University and a small Catholic University. This was education's equivalent to the gig economy. She was paid only for the hours she worked, and her hours could be cut at short notice. At the end of last year, she was told her hours (and those of other adjunct faculty) were going to be cut in the new year. This put the couple in a poor position financially.

Ellie had joined the Union who had tried to negotiate with management on behalf of Adjunct Faculty. When this had not worked, the Union had asked them to come out on strike until the situation was resolved. In February, the Union made an agreement with management where they were awarded more beneficial contracts. These meant that adjunct faculty had more job security, and their hours could not be cut on short notice. The awarding of this contract also paid more money across the year. Of course, this was good news but at the time Kevin had commented.

"You are so lucky to have been in the right place at the right time Ellie" he said "all part time lecturers deserved better contracts and the Union has convinced management of this fact. Yet, you so very nearly spoiled everything for yourself with your activism in the fall and winter. Why you would go on YouTube and get into arguments about Meghan Markle and Prince Harry and their claims about racism in the British Royal Family is beyond me. Also, your YouTube video about fat shaming. I still feel it is suspicious that you didn't even get an interview for the job at the Palmer Institute. I really wonder if they found out about this side of you and it stopped them from employing you? Thank goodness your contract was confirmed by senior management at the State University."

Ellie knew he was correct, and that she did not get an interview for some part time work at Palmer Institute even though she was qualified for the work. She also knew it was not wise to go online and talk about public figures and controversial subjects and become involved in arguments. Yet somehow it rankled her. As she told Kevin "If we all shut up and did not comment on current affairs and what we felt was right what would happen to the world?"

Today, Kevin and Ellie had a secret they had not shared with anyone else. Ellie was pregnant and the couple was thrilled. There had been times when they thought they could never have children after a devastating miscarriage when they were living in the UK and then right out of the blue it happened.

In many ways they were a very fortunate couple. Kevin's mother, Jennie, they were sure would help with childcare when the baby was born. Kevin's career seemed to be going well. He was writing a research paper with Dr John Strickland from Georgia State University and was due to present this at a conference in Hawaii in the summer.

Ellie knew she should have been happy and looking forward to the future. The problem with Ellie is that she just could not stop interfering. Her gut instinct said to her that she should take a step back and start looking forward to being a mom later in the year. But Ellie never listened to her gut instincts. Instead, she could not get Song, the Chinese manicurist from the Purple Orchid salon out of her mind.

Sitting in the chair while Jinni worked on her nails Ellie could not help but ask her about Song. She felt comfortable asking about Song as in February Jinni had confided in Kevin and Ellie about Song dropping out of university in Los Angeles and working in the salon illegally. Then things took a turn for the worse when Song had run away and got into trouble while in Atlanta.

In February Jinni had asked for advice from Kevin. It turned out that Song's father had employed a lawyer who believed that he could reinstate her educational visa. Kevin had done some research into the situation, and it seemed that it was correct.

After they had spoken, Ellie was shocked by what she heard. She then had asked Kevin "Why would a Chinese student want to run away from university and work as a manicurist? Surely someone who had got a place to study in the States would be grateful for that opportunity?"

Kevin had smiled "In China until recently the government had the one child policy. Parents are very ambitious for their only children. They will pay agents to get them into American universities by whatever means possible. In the case of Song there were two things. One, her father was Head of International at a Chinese university in Guangzhou. He would be responsible for setting up links with Highbridge University in Los Angeles. He would be able to work out a good deal for his daughter. Second, Highbridge is not a university that ranks highly in the US system like Harvard or Yale or Stanford. However, it is a private university with high fees and it can accept whichever students it wants"

This seemed more shocking "So what you are saying, I think" Ellie said "Is that even if Song is not very academic and there would be a good chance she could not do the work she could still be offered a place to keep her father happy and also because she would be paying high fees."

Kevin had smiled "Yes, the fees are $44,000 a year there. It's a good chunk of change. They need students to keep the college alive. I doubt that Song's father paid any fees for her to attend, or indeed, if she had sufficient qualifications to merit a place on the degree. The university would give her a place on the back of her father sending them other Chinese students from the university where he was Dean of International. These students would, of course, pay full fees.""

All of this had been horrifying to Ellie in February. Today Jinni confided something far worse. After her nail appointment was finished Jinni asked Ellie to come to the back room of the salon where it was more private. There she confided in Ellie about her recent trip to Atlanta. Song had been found in an Immigration Detention centre. The story was that Song had been working at Big Daddy's burger bar, a place in South Atlanta – illegally of course. Eric Senser, the owner of the burger bar had tried to rape her and Barry Watkins, a neighbour of hers, had defended her beating Eric to within an inch of his life. It seemed Harry Zine, Song's fathers lawyer was trying to cover this up.

"If this can be successfully covered up will she able to get her visa reinstated?" Jinni wanted to know. "Please could you ask Kevin to investigate, I am so worried about her?"

"I will ask Kevin" Ellie promised.

It was all very shocking to Ellie. All Jinni seemed to care about was the visa reinstatement. Yet the whole thing was sleazy and sordid and, of course, illegal, and it started to not sit right with Ellie and she could not leave it alone, her instincts told her to find out more …

Chapter 5

Lila

A new job and a new beginning...

Lila Oswald was the new part time receptionist at the Purple Orchid thanks to Jinni's brother putting a good word in for her. He was having an affair with her sister at the time.

When Lila started work part time at the Purple Orchid she already had two other part time jobs. Lila was 48 years old and had married Ronnie Oswald in the previous fall. To say she was madly in love would be to put it mildly. She adored Ronnie and the ground he walked on. She would tell anyone who would listen he was everything she had ever wanted in a man and to find love like this at this age was beyond her wildest dreams.

Lila had previously been married to Kyle, a man she met when they were both at High School, and with whom she I had two children, Peter and Josie. They had never been happy. Harry liked a drink or two or three. When he was sober, he was quiet and taciturn. She told friends "We may have been lovers, but we were never friends."

Over the years they had drifted apart and decided to divorce in 2013 when Josie the youngest was 18. Since then, until her marriage to Ronnie, Lila had stayed in the family home. At first there were Lila and the children and then Peter had left to marry Renata in 2016 and in 2018 Josie left to live in New York.

After they left there were times when Lila was very lonely, but she had never really wanted to get into the dating scene. She had nights out with girlfriends and took up various hobbies including line dancing and weightlifting! However, there were no other men in her life. This was until one night in 2022 when Lila went with some friends to the Albion bar in town where the "Brothers of Swing" were playing. Lila adored Ronnie from the moment she saw him. He was handsome and my word could he sing! There were three men in the band, Ronnie, Niall and Pete and they sang mainly Dean Martin and Frank Sinatra covers. Lila felt this was not really her scene but she certainly enjoyed listening to them. After their session finished, she went over to congratulate them, and felt an instant attraction with Ronnie.

Lila found out where they were playing the following week and made sure she was there. This time they had a drink together after they had finished their session and Ronnie offered to drive Lila home. Even though it was way out of character, Lila made up her mind to ask him in.

After years of sitting alone at home, Lila was very nervous inviting a stranger into her home, but after a couple of drinks sitting in front of the fire Ronnie made her feel relaxed and happy. She leaned over and started kissing him. "You are so beautiful, Lila" he said. Then she stood up and taking his hand led him over to the bedroom....

Lila would tell anyone who asked if she was happy "I see myself now as two people. The person I was pre meeting Ronnie and the person I am now. Pre meeting Ronnie I was dowdy, middle aged, ignored, sexually frustrated, and dead inside. Now I feel loved, cared for and I have come alive. I even wear clothes I never would have dared to before in bright primary colors. How wonderful is that to be 48 years old and like a new woman?"

Their marriage in the fall of 2023 was modest (this was Ronnie's third marriage and Lila's second) but beautiful. They held the reception at the Bay Tree, a hotel just outside of the city and the Brothers of Swing did a set. Ronnie got up and sang a song that he had composed specially for Lila. There was not a dry eye in the room by the time he finished the song.

Ronnie and Niall had composed several songs and these are available for streaming or you can buy them on a cd. However, even with that and the gigs they perform they still do not make enough money to support themselves. The Brothers of Swing have so much potential and should be making much more money in Lila's opinion.

Ronnie still worked as a delivery driver for 'Brentons' a local market, however, this did not pay much either. Newly married and in love, the new couple were short of money.

For years Lila only worked part time as a cleaner for Welcome Maids a cleaning service in the Southern Hills. However, with all the added expense from her marriage, she now added two more part time jobs. The first was at the Institute for the Blind and Visually Impaired. Lila cleaned the classrooms there two afternoons a week.

The second was the part timer receptionist at the Purple Orchid on Friday and Saturday.

Lila found she enjoyed being in the salon and would dress up for the occasion. It was different to being a cleaner where she worked behind the scenes and at first, she was grateful to Jinni for giving her this opportunity to be customer facing. Lila knew nothing about Song working in the salon, but even if she had she had other things to concern her.

So here was Lila sitting on reception at the Purple Orchid at the beginning of March, happy and in love, and determined to help the Brothers of Swing become the most famous band in the southern states ...

Chapter 6

Ellie

Just can't stop being involved...

At the beginning of March when Ellie was about 3 months pregnant, Kevin and Ellie shared this with Jenni, Kevin's mother but had decided to not share with other people until the pregnancy was more advanced. While living in the United Kingdom, Ellie had suffered a miscarriage and after that they had been worried that they would never be able to have a child of their own. They were excited but tried to keep their excitement contained until they felt more confident that the pregnancy would continue to full term.

The doctor had assured them that all was fine so far. It was an exciting time and they were looking forward to being parents later in the year. Driving to and from the state university they talked about all nature of things including the baby. Today the conversation turned to the weekend.

"Your mom has invited us to a show at the Ritz Bar and Diner on Saturday night where the "Brothers of Swing" will be playing." Ellie said cautiously. She knew how Kevin felt about their concerts! Niall, Jenni's partner, and Ronnie and Pete sang mainly old classics to a backing track.

"I suppose we had better go" said Kevin reluctantly. "Whatever happened with Niall joining that Union?" he said "I don't think they make any money whatsoever from the band. It's just a hobby really. Niall is a financial drain on my mother. He is a money grubbing toyboy. I know she was lonely when my father died but I think Niall takes advantage of her. "

Ellie always stuck up for Niall saying "I think Niall loves your mother. What does it matter that she is older than him? They seem really happy together. Also he is making a success of the Brothers of Swing. They seem to get local gigs and they even got a play on Spotify this week"

Kevin set off laughing "Oh wow!" he said "and how much did that pay? Honestly Ellie you are as bad as my mom about that man. What a waste of space he is."

Ellie mentioned how she thought it was very unfair how much musicians like the Brothers of Swing got paid by Spotify. It was literally cents. Compare this to the few musicians that get big money.

"Actually Kevin this has reminded me to ask Niall about the United Musicians and Allied Workers Union that he had joined, and what if anything they had done for them."

Kevin grunted and that was the end to that conversation.

During the day, Ellie was busy with students and teaching but still had time in between classes to spend time on the internet looking up some of the issues she was concerned about. One of these issues was what had happened to Song. Surely if a student was in the USA on an educational visa there was a requirement that the student attend class? Ellie looked this up and of course there was such a requirement. The visa lapsed if the student did not attend class. However, there was a loophole that if a student had been absent from classes for less than five months then it could be reinstated if there was a good reason. So the university could agree to say that Song had been sick and that was why she had not been attending class. This would satisfy the Immigration Service and she could have her visa reinstated.

Ellie also looked up Highbridge College. It was an expensive private university near Los Angeles. Sitting sipping her drink she nearly choked when she saw the fees. Kevin was correct it was $44,000 per year just for tuition. In addition, it was not featured in the rankings of American top universities. Ellie guessed that Song's father, the professor, would have worked out a good deal for her to go there.

Reading about the university Ellie found out that it had recently relocated to new premises in Thousand Oaks. The new campus was quite extensive and the buildings looked beautiful.

In the car going home, Ellie brought up the subject of Highbridge college.

"I get the impression that the university has either received a lot of money from donors or is in a lot of debt." She said

"You may very well be correct," said Kevin

"It looks like a beautiful place, yet Song still ran away and ended up first at the Purple Orchid and then working at a burger bar in the south side of Atlanta. Why would someone do this? It almost seems unbelievable and shows me how unhappy she must have been. I wished now I had tried to talk to her while she worked at the Purple Orchid. Perhaps I could have helped her."

"Ellie" said Kevin "leave well alone. She would not have welcomed your interference when she was at the Purple Orchid. She wanted to keep it quiet that she did not have papers."

This effectively killed the conversation but that evening when Kevin had gone to the gym, Ellie's mind flipped over to the attempted assault and the violence in the alley behind the burger bar. If Song's father was trying to have her reinstated at the college, Ellie knew that without a doubt that would be covered up. But what would that mean for the man who came to her aid?

Ellie checked out the Atlanta news. There did not seem to anything about the case. However, Jinni had said that the police had come to Barry Watkin's apartment and caught the pair of them there. Ellie started with the TV stations and then went to local newspapers. Atlanta is a big city, and she could not find anything in any of the news releases. Ellie then went on to the internet to find out if the police file reports of arrests that the public can see. Finally she found this short report.

Aggravated assault and battery at Big Daddy's Burger Bar.

> At midnight on 23 February Eric Senser, 52, the owner of Big Daddy's Burger Bar, was attacked and beaten when taking trash out to a dumpster in the rear alley. The attack may have been motivated by an earlier argument in the burger bar. The perpetrator fled when onlookers hearing a loud commotion entered the alley. One onlooker identified the perpetrator as a local man living at an address near to the burger bar. Police visited the address later the same evening and interviewed the perpetrator who has been identified as Barry Watkins, 33. Watkins admitted being in the alley

but alleges that he was provoked into the altercation. Watkins has been arraigned waiting a trial date. Witnesses to the altercation are encouraged to come forward.

Sitting alone at the laptop Ellie shouted “This is a pile of bullshit!! This is not what happened!” What happened to Barry defending Song? There was no mention of her. To someone reading that short write-up Barry appeared as a thug. Ellie was very angry now. How could this have been written without Song being mentioned? It looked like, Song’s father and her lawyer had somehow managed to wipe her presence at the burger bar out. But she was the cause of the fight and, of course, this left Barry in a very bad position.

Although you may be thinking that this was none of Ellie’s business and she should keep her nose out of it, Ellie did not think like that. She said to herself “Let’s be honest if we all did that then things will never get better will they?” So she could not keep my nose of it – she had to interfere …

Chapter 7

Atlanta –

Public Defender's Office

Gavin Gates, Public Defender, was a very busy man. He had precious little time to take calls. Of course, he would always speak to a member of the public who had good information or new evidence on an ongoing case. So, it was that he agreed to speak to a woman who had rung in with information on the Barry Watkins case.

"Good afternoon, ma'am" he said "I understand that you have information on the Barry Watkins aggravated assault and battery case. I represent Watkins in this case".

The woman on the line went ahead without introducing herself - she said "Can I be guaranteed anonymity by speaking to you?"

Gavin was a bit taken aback by the woman's accent. She sounded British, but she spoke so quickly it was difficult for him to understand her.

"You want to be anonymous?" he queried.

"Yes, that is correct" the woman said.

"An initial call can be anonymous" Gavin said "however if your evidence is given in court and we wish you to act as a witness then of course we cannot guarantee anonymity".

"That is fine" the woman said "I have information that Barry Watkins was acting to defend a young woman in the alley. It was not an unprovoked attack. He is a hero rather than a thug."

Gavin's ears pricked up at the mention of a young woman.

"A young woman" he said "go ahead, tell me about her."

"She was a Chinese woman working illegally at the burger bar. She was, sorry is, a beautiful young woman and as I said was in the States illegally. When Barry saw that Eric Senser, the owner of the burger bar, was attacking a young Chinese woman he jumped on Senser to protect her. Will you be providing evidence of this in the trial?"

This woman was making Gavin nervous. She was saying the same things as Barry Watkins but there was no evidence from the police reports that any of this was true.

"Can I stop you for a moment?" Gavin said "how do you know Barry Watkins again?"

"I have never met Barry Watkins and I cannot reveal my sources, but I am aware of what happened that night." the woman said

"You are making some very serious allegations. How do you know this? Are you sure you are not repeating rumours and gossip? Have you some evidence to prove what you are saying?" said Gavin "this does not reflect what is shown in the police reports"

"At the moment I do not have evidence, but I can try to gather evidence." Said the woman "I wondered if you had spoken to the attorney who is representing the Chinese woman. I believe that his name is Harry Zine, and he has an office in downtown Atlanta."

Gavin knew of Harry Zine. He had been up against him in a recent trial and had lost. Zine worked for an old money law firm and only took on clients who could afford his high fees. It did not make sense that he would represent the Chinese woman. Gavin wanted to know more.

The woman continued . "The father of the Chinese woman has employed this person, Harry Zine to defend her and to make sure that she is able to regain her immigrant status as a university student in the USA. The last thing he will want is for her to be involved in the fight at the burger bar which could affect her immigrant status."

Gavin thought about this. It did make some sort of sense. However, Barry Watkins had not mentioned a concerned father and expensive lawyer. It seemed so farfetched, what was the daughter of a wealthy man doing in South Atlanta working at a burger bar and then in bed with a man in a cheap walk-up apartment block?

The English woman was carrying on talking "The Chinese woman came to the States to attend university but had skipped out of classes to be in Atlanta. If this was known to the immigration authorities, she would lose her study visa. This is why her presence is being covered up. Barry Watkins is being used as a scapegoat."

Gavin was very interested by what the woman was saying, however it seemed she had no evidence to back up her claims.

"I can certainly follow up on the information you have given me today." He said "the trial date has not been set yet, usually a date would follow within 60 to 90 days of the arraignment. I have an enormous workload, and so I have precious little time to do this and without any hard evidence or proof that the Chinese woman was there, and Watkins was acting in her defence it would seem that a custodial sentence will almost certainly be given."

The woman seemed very anxious "this is so wrong" she said "please do all you can to defend Barry Watkins. It is so unfair that he will go to prison for trying to protect someone. I will also try to find you evidence and will call back if I can find anything out."

With that the caller hung up. The caller had said she had never met Barry Watkins. Yet so much of what she said corroborated Watkins testimony. Watkins had told him that he was protecting a Chinese girl who was really beautiful. She had been working in the burger bar and Watkins had additionally said it was common knowledge that Senser had a bad reputation for hitting on beautiful young girls who worked in the bar. Watkins had been sitting eating a burger when he saw the Chinese girl go outside the bar and was followed very soon by Senser. He had a bad feeling so had gone into the alley to check all was okay and had found Senser with his hands all over the young girl and her fighting him off.

Two people had said the same thing, but it did not make sense. What on earth was a young woman whose father could afford to employ Harry Zine doing working in the less than salubrious location of the burger bar? Why was she not in university? He found it hard to believe that international students were reduced to living and working in such sleazy surroundings.

He decided he should speak to Harry Zine, but he was conscious of the fact that he only had a limited amount of time before the trial and a mountain of work to get through. He rang Harry Zine's PA to set up an appointment. The following Tuesday he was able to arrange a call with Harry Zine.

They exchanged pleasantries and then Gavin Gates asked Harry Zine if he represented a Chinese student who was at Barry Watkin's apartment at the time of his arrest.

"I represent her father" said Harry "This is, as I am sure you understand, a delicate situation. Song, the student in question, had been on sick leave from the university. Unknown to her father while still convalescing she went to Atlanta to visit an American friend who lives in Buckhead." Here Harry Zine paused for effect. "Yes I know you are wondering what she was doing in South Atlanta if she was supposed to be in Buckhead! Yes a very good question indeed."

Gavin Gates had not spoken.

Harry went on "Well you know what students are like – they went out partying and ended up at a club in the south of the city. There she met Barry Watkins and ended up back at his apartment."

Gavin thought about this. "Did they stop for something to eat at Big Daddy's burger bar?" he queried.

"Where is Big Daddy's? Is this in South Atlanta? I seriously doubt it" Harry said and laughed "Unless she was seriously slumming!! Her father is a very rich academic from Guangzhou in China. I think South Atlanta would have been a big shock for her – so I doubt she ate there."

Gavin was none to convinced by Harry's comments. However, how to prove that Song had been at the burger bar, if in fact she had, now that would be very difficult.

Sitting in his office looking at the papers piled up and the amount of work he had to do Gavin felt momentarily overwhelmed.

He would do his best for Barry Watkins but unless a miracle happened and someone came forward it looked like he was going down ...

Chapter 8

Lila

Becoming more involved...

Meanwhile back at the Purple Orchid on Saturday Lila had a full day tending to customers' needs. In the evening, the "Brothers of Swing" were due to play in the evening at the Ritz Bar and Diner and Lila had a full day working as a receptionist at the Purple Orchid salon. Lila woke early and went to shower. The thing Lila loved about being married to Ronnie was that he often followed her to the bathroom and surprised her while she was showering. Today was no different and Lila spent a blissful time in the shower. She couldn't believe her luck being married to this man , he was sexy, funny and loving. She was over the moon until she looked at the clock and panicked. "OMG" she screamed "I am going to be late for the salon." Dressing quickly and driving off with her hair still wet she skipped breakfast.

When she arrived, the salon was open, and several people were already having manicures. She met Jinni's stare. She did not look happy. "We open at 9 am Lila" she said "I do expect you to be here before 9 am to help open up"

Lila apologised though she knew her apologies sounded hollow! She was determined to make up for my tardiness by being extra diligent all day. So she smiled and made polite conversation and did her best to sell the well-being products.

On that Saturday a lady came into the salon who Lila knew. Lila cleaned her house in the Southern Hills. It was a beautiful, large house and the lady and her husband had recently moved there and employed the cleaning firm she worked for.

"Hello Janine" Lila said "nice to see you. How are you today?"

Janine seemed a bit surprised to see Lila at the Purple Orchid but once she got over her initial surprise, they had a nice chat.

At the end of the day, Jinni asked Lila how she knew Janine. Lila explained she also worked for "Welcome Maids" and cleaned her house. Jinni said "You have to respect distance at the salon. You need to be careful not to appear too friendly with the customers. Do you understand?"

Lila nodded to say she did, but inside she felt this was very old fashioned and over the top. Perhaps it was because Jinni was Thai and might have different views to those here in the US.

Lila had to admit that she was enjoying working at the Purple Orchid (especially the extra money) so knew she would have to go along with Jinni's wishes.

She couldn't wait to go home though and get changed for the evening at the Ritz Bar and Diner.

When the "Brothers of Swing" have a gig one of them always goes early to set up their equipment. They have a laptop, a stereo DI box, a small mixer and of course cables!! Tonight, it was Pete's turn to go early to set up. Lila and Ronnie did not have to arrive much before the music was to start.

When they arrived at the Ritz it was already busy with most of the tables around the small stage taken. Although the Ritz sounds grand it was in fact a small bar with only about 8 tables, each seating 6 people. Seeing Jenni and Niall sitting at a table near the stage they waved and went over. Niall asked them to sit down, and he introduced Kevin, Jenni's son, and his wife Ellie who were with them for the evening. Lila recognised Ellie as another customer from the Purple Orchid. Pete had set up the equipment and Niall and Ronnie went to talk to him in a small room behind the stage.

Everyone chatted while they waited for the performance to start. Tonight, the Brothers sang Frank Sinatra classics in the first session ending with a rendition of "New York, New York". It seemed like everyone was up dancing and singing along. There was such a good atmosphere.

During the break between sets Lila started to feel relaxed. Maybe this was the after effects of a couple of drinks or it might have just been she had been enjoying the music. She started chatting to Ellie, who asked how she enjoyed working at the Purple Orchid.

"It's my first time working in a customer facing role and I'm still finding my feet. Sometimes Jinni can seem very distant and strict" Lila said.

Ellie nodded and said, "Jinni is a good sort but recently she has had a lot on her mind which may affect the way she comes across to people who do not know her well."

Lila wondered what was wrong. Out loud she said "I hope that Jinni was okay and does not have serious problems."

Ellie told her there were issues that related to Jinni's personal life and were quite serious, but she had been sworn to secrecy. She said she did not feel it would affect the future of the salon, but for the present it was affecting Jinni's wellbeing. Ellie said " the best way to deal with it was to act as if you did not know Jinni was dealing with personal problems and to keep bright and focused during the day".

When they got home Ronnie and Lila talked about the set. The "Brothers" had been doing the same act for years. They were good, but it was in some ways limiting.

"I feel you could be more adventurous" Lila said "the songs of Dean Martin and Frank Sinatra are entertaining and people love your act, but it might be fun to include something different."

Ronnie agreed "I love Ellie Fitzgerald" he said and put Ella Fitzgerald on singing "It's a lovely day today" which was beautiful, what a voice she had! He then played Louis Armstrong singing "What a wonderful world". Ronnie wondered if the "Brothers of Swing" could start to add more songs to their current range? Talking about this they both started to get quite excited thinking of the possibilities for the future.

It was only when Lila was undressing ready for bed that she started to think about Jinni. What was wrong, she wondered. Ellie telling her that it was personal problems had only piqued her interest. Of course, her thoughts immediately went to Somchai and Randi. Lila remembered a recent conversation she had had with Randi. This was after she had received a text from Randi to ask if Lila would meet her for coffee and a chat.

They sat in a small outside area of the coffee shop. Lila started by talking about her interest - the "Brothers of Swing", Randi nodded politely and then she said: "I need to ask a big favour"

Lila knew where this was leading. They had been here so often in the past.

Randi went on. "I need a little loan just to tide me over. Things are really bad. Somchai has had his hours cut at work. It's fucking unfair. They pick on him because he is a foreigner. He is smart, you know, really clever, but they don't want to know. Nobody cares about Asians. He gets treated as if he is illegal."

Lila bit her tongue as she didn't want to get into this with her. "How much are you short?" she said

Randi got a tissue out and blew her nose. "About a thousand a month" she said.

Lila stared at her and gulped "Randi, that is a lot of money. I will talk to Ronnie and we may be able to help you short term, but we can't help you in the long term. We have just bought a new house and we have a mortgage. We don't have much left over. I am working three jobs." Lila realised she was going on and on trying to defend not giving her the money.

They both sat quietly for a couple of minutes.

"Is Somchai looking for work to fill the gap?" Lila eventually asked.

"He is trying, but people are fucking prejudiced. They see a Thai man and don't want to know. People treat him like shit."

Lila hated the way she used profanities and she wanted to say stop treating him like a victim. Instead, she said "I'll speak to Ronnie tonight and let you know how much we can let you have."

They said goodbye and Lila stopped by the bank on my way home. She checked the balance on her personal account and the Teller told her she had $3,000. She drew out $1,000 in cash.

That evening Ronnie was at a rehearsal with the Brothers. In his absence, she drove over to the Black Cat bar. Somchai was sitting on a bar stool and Randi was tending bar. They both greeted her, and she ordered a beer. When Randi brought the beer over, Lila passed her a brown envelope with the money in it. She spent a couple of hours with them, drinking beer and shooting the breeze. Somchai seemed cheerful.

"There is work coming up at the chicken plant outside of town." He said "My friend Roy works there. You work on a production line. The chickens are cut up and then they need people to package them. Easy work."

“You have to handle raw chicken?” Lila said “rather you than me.”

Somchai laughed “Perhaps Ronnie will let me sing in that band of his.” He said.

Lila sincerely doubted that, but they both laughed and chatted. Randi kept filling Somchai’s glass up. He was drinking vodka neat. His voice was slurred and his eyes looked bleary. When Randi was down the other end of the bar serving he said “You look beautiful tonight” and toasted Lila before downing his vodka. Lila knew when it was time to leave. She said goodbye to Randi and set off to drive home.

Driving home Lila mused.

“Money is so tight at the moment and I know it was mad to give 1/3 of my savings to Randi. I had bailed her out so many times over the years when she had got involved with men who had lied to her, cheated on her and used her. I didn’t know if Ronnie would understand why I had done it.” She decided as it was her money and she would keep quiet for the time being.

When he returned from rehearsals Lila had opened a bottle of wine and they curled up together on the sofa and chatted about their days. Randi and her troubles were never mentioned. Lila briefly wondered if they had been touching Jinni up for money and that was the reason she was upset. She instinctively knew she couldn’t mention anything to Jinni about her brother. She knew that she would have to be careful in the future about what she said in the salon that was for sure …

Chapter 9

Jinni

The messages keep coming…

After I had spoken to Harry Zine I felt worse instead of better. My business would be safe now I was sure of that, but that did not alter the fact that I still loved Song. I yearned to be with her. My business suddenly wasn't the most important thing in my life. I wanted to run away and go to Los Angeles and be with Song. But then my sensible side would take over. I would order new supplies, work on manicures and pedicures and smile for the customers.

Today a new post about illegal immigrants appeared on social media. This was again on the community Facebook page:

"Keep illegal immigrants out of our city. Report businesses that employ them. Put the owners in jail."

This was posted by "Dknite". The same person who made the other post. Was I being paranoid imagining that this involved me?

I had confided in so few people. When I returned from Atlanta I had talked to Kevin and Ellie about what had happened there. Kevin seemed to think it would be the end of Song's university career in the US. I think he was very straight and played by the rules. He probably could not imagine the lengths Professor Xingping Zhang would go to. I could not imagine them gossiping even though I knew Ellie had posted on Facebook previously and had had her own YouTube videos.

I decided to talk to my brother Somchai. He had left his wife, an American woman Barb, a few months earlier to live with another woman, Randi. Barb was by all accounts very bitter that Somchai had left her. In addition, their daughter Amara who had been working in the salon as a manicurist was now living and working in Thailand at an orphanage for a couple of months. I had been involved in setting that up and I knew Barb was resentful of this also.

Somchai came to my apartment to visit with me that evening. I immediately asked about Amara and if he had heard from her. Somchai said she had made a call the previous week and she seemed happy and like a new person since she had gone to Thailand.

"It was a really good idea, Jinni" he said, "she is beginning to think about her future again and seems much more positive."

I asked if he had spoken to Barb, and it seemed he had and Barb was quite positive. She had a new man in her life. An actor called Danny who had been staying with her while he was "resting" between projects. He had now left to return to his own home as he was filming a new series of a soap opera.

"She is moving on" he said "I am happy that she has a new man. Danny is not living with her now, but I believe they parted on good terms. Now there is some doubt if she can afford to pay for the upkeep of the house." He covered his face and looked down "I could not bear it if she had to leave the home, she loves because of me" he said "I will do all I can to help her."

I knew Somchai felt guilt at leaving Barb and that he really meant it when he said he would help her out. But how was he going to do that? He was not a wealthy man. I did not think that he would go back to Barb, so this was just talk.

I decided to move on with the conversation and so I mentioned the Facebook posts about illegal immigrants. Somchai was naturally concerned about them but felt that Professor Xingping's attorney had covered everything up so well that no-one would suspect that I had been involved.

"You don't think it's someone we know who is making these posts, do you?" I asked

He looked at me strangely. "Of course, not" he said "try not to be too worried. You were not the only person to employ illegal immigrants. The Black Cat bar do it all the time. I have heard rumours that there are illegal immigrants working at the 'Happy Trails' coffee shop on First Avenue. There are lots of rumours going around."

He put his arm around me "and your salon has not been mentioned once. So I would put it behind me if I was you and move on. Weren't you thinking of leasing another store in the regeneration area?"

He was correct. I was planning to lease another store in the regeneration area but had put this on hold with the upset over Song. I should go ahead with it and stop being paranoid. I had a bright future ahead of me and should stop worrying so much.

We poured another drink and then he told me that his hours had been cut at work.

"I have been offered more work. I can do an evening shift at Mercers, the chicken plant outside of town." He said "It is easy work on a production line packing chicken pieces. The chickens are cut up, then workers pack them. I saw people standing there putting chicken legs into a pack. What could be easier than putting 6 chicken legs into a pack? It pays good money too."

I was not sure it would be easy work, but I did not say anything. He would be at his regular job as a delivery driver for a DIY store now three days a week and then he was picking up shifts on four evenings at the chicken plant. It was a lot for him to do and I hoped he would be able to cope. I worried he might turn to drink if things got difficult, but I was not his mother I had to let him live his own life.

"Keep in touch" I said as he left. "Come see me on the weekend when you are not working and bring Randi."

He kissed me and promised to come and see me. I watched him as he walked to his car. I hoped all would work out for him.

Chapter 10

Lila

At the Institute for the Blind and Visually Impaired...

The week following the "Brothers of Swing" gig Ronnie and Lila continued to listen to and talk about music. They were also considering a weekend trip to New Orleans to listen to the music there. It was a very busy time for both of them.

On Tuesdays Lila went to the Institute for the Blind and Visually Impaired to help clean the classrooms. The Institute had advertised for cleaners on the community Facebook site. Lila had answered the ad and was able to get a couple of afternoons a week work cleaning classrooms after school finished for the day. The Institute only opened in January 2023 to much fanfare. It is in an old factory building near to the downtown. The whole area is zoned for regeneration and other buildings are in the process of being refurbished. The area around the Institute is messy and work is being carried out on several buildings, but once inside the building is beautifully put together. When she started, Lila was taken on a tour of the building by Regina, who was in charge of Estates at the Institute.

At the rear of the building in what used to be the factory yard is now a sensory garden. The garden has been planted so that the students can smell the different fragrances – jasmine, violets, freesias, lilacs and sweet peas are just some of the beautiful plants in the garden. There are also large floral displays from the garden in the entrance hall and the scents of the flowers and plants in the Institute are so beautiful. Anyone who ever visited the Institute would always remember the lovely scents even they lived to be 100 years old.

The classrooms and the library have been designed to make it easy for the students to get around and have tactile fitments and places where the students can work on learning braille. Also, as blind people have other senses that are heightened, the fitments and flooring had been designed to absorb sound so that other sounds were dampened down and did not assault the students' senses. The decoration inside the building is also very bright with loud contrasting colours. This is for the students who have partial sight and who can see very bright colours. The main staircase is painted in blue, but the edges of each step are painted in yellow. Classrooms are painted in bright primary colours. Lila loved the yellow classrooms on the second floor which always appear bright, warm and welcoming.

Today she was told to clean Classrooms 1 to 4 on the top floor. This was new as she had not cleaned on this floor before. She took the elevator up to this floor and began to clean classroom 1. It was light and airy up on this floor and there was a view over the city. When she went into the corridor to move on to classroom 2 she heard music. Someone was playing the piano and the song resonated with her as it was one of the songs she and Ronnie had discussed the Brothers of Swing could add to their repertoire. "I'm in the mood for love" by Nat King Cole. It was a beautiful tune and this was followed by "Smile" also by Nat King Cole. This time someone sang the lyrics. It sounded so beautiful Lila was almost in tears, and she forgot all about the cleaning.

She went down the corridor to find where the music was coming from. At the end of the corridor there was a classroom 5 that she had not been asked to clean. This is where the music was coming from. Lila stood outside listening and then to her horror the door suddenly opened, and someone walked straight into her before she had the chance to step back! It was a young girl about 17 years old, carrying what looked like a trumpet. They both jumped and apologised at the same time. The door was now fully open, and Lila could see into the room. It was much bigger than the other classrooms and did not have desks. It was set up so that people could play music. There was a grand piano dominating the room, and a student was sitting there. There were a few other students playing other instruments plus an older man who seemed to be the conductor. They were all turned in the direction of the door where the commotion was coming from. The older man was staring, and Lila got the impression he was sighted.

"I am very sorry" she said "I know I am interrupting your practice. I couldn't help listening to your music though, it is so beautiful!"

The older man smiled and said "Well of course it is, this is our very talented musicians playing together – no wonder you wanted to stop and listen! You are always welcome to come and listen to us practice."

Lila laughed and said "I would love to come and sit and listen to you practice. Sadly, I have to get on with my work though – I am just the cleaner."

"What is your name?" asked the man "I am Bruce, and this is the Institute jazz band."

"I am Lila" she said "it has been a pleasure to meet you all."

Lila left then to get on with my cleaning, but could still hear them practising as she propped the door open.

How did they play together when they couldn't see, she wondered. How did they read the music? How could the conductor guide them? One thing was for sure, she couldn't wait to tell Ronnie about them.

When she got into her car at the end of my shift Lila queued up Nat King Cole on the streaming service and listened to the most beautiful music on her drive home.

A crazy idea developed as she was driving – she could see Ronnie, Pete and Niall singing with the Institute band rather than having a backing track.

"Wow" said Ronnie when she told him later "that is ambitious Lila.

One step at a time darling"

He had that right: Lila was ambitious, and she had big plans for the "Brothers of Swing"! She was going to make them one of the biggest acts in the southern states.

Chapter 11

Ellie

A wrong has been done…

During the following week Kevin and Ellie went to an appointment where they got to view a scan of the baby, and all seemed well. They couldn't wait to show the pictures to Jenni and Niall on the weekend. They were going to Jenni's house to a barbeque on Sunday. However, they decided not to tell anyone else for the time being until the pregnancy was further advanced.

Ellie couldn't wait to find out if the public defender had followed up on their meeting. She had decided not to share her worries about Barry Watkins with Kevin who she believed would have called her obsessed and "needing something to think about".

Ellie had looked it up and found out that court rulings in the USA are made public and that anyone could find out what had happened at a trial. Barry Watkins had not had a trial yet; however, he was arraigned in prison waiting for a trial date to be set. Originally when Ellie had looked at the news there had been nothing on this case. However, this week when she tuned in to an Atlanta news station, she saw there was a short piece on the incident in the alley.

The news station reported that there had been a violent beating at a burger bar in South Atlanta. The owner was taking the trash out at the end of the evening and was jumped and attacked in an alley. It appeared to be a motiveless attack. The defendant, Barry Watkins, was arraigned in prison awaiting a trial date to be set.

The District Attorney for Fulton County was shown on camera, and he made a short speech

"This result of this trial is important to help us in cleaning up the streets of South Atlanta. We will not tolerate senseless, motiveless violence and we will prosecute to the highest extent possible until we make it safe for decent, law-abiding businesspeople to be able to take the trash out at the close of business".

Ellie screamed out loud! It was a good thing Kevin was at the gym! The whole thing was so wrong.

It was at this moment that she decided she could not let this drop. It seemed that the Public Defender she had spoken to either was still following up on the information she had provided to him or if he had followed up, had not been able to get any evidence. No-one was speaking up for Barry Watkins. All he had been doing that evening was protecting Song. She had not even thanked him and had now had her presence at the scene wiped out by clever lawyers! It was absolutely unfair!! Ellie knew that there was going to be a guilty verdict passed unless he could get some very good attorney to represent him. Someone who could get to the bottom of what really happened. Someone who was just as good as Harry Zine. This would be expensive she was savvy enough to know that – so it would require deep pockets to fund a good attorney. As Barry had used a public defender, Ellie guessed he would not be able to afford this. Her mind was working overtime. She had to be able to find a way to help, he couldn't be allowed to sit in prison taking the blame for this.

These thoughts were first and foremost in her mind over the weekend. However, she didn't know anyone she could talk to and share her thoughts with. They were due to go to Kevin's mothers house on Sunday for a BBQ but Ellie didn't think she would understand either. She would query why Ellie would be interested in a poor black man who was standing trial in a different city for defending Song. In fact, Ellie thought she would act rather like Kevin, saying "You need something else to think about. Mind your own business" and "Keep out of it, it is none of your concern." Ellie knew this was true, but if she felt if we all behaved liked this then no-one would help anyone anywhere. These were injustices and it needed someone to care. Surely that was how change was effected by someone who cared standing up and making a lot of noise about a perceived injustice. Ellie would not stop. She would find a way to help. However, for now she kept her thoughts to herself although she felt lonely and silenced.

On Sunday Kevin and Ellie drove over to Jenni's house. They had a good afternoon sitting in the yard chatting with her and Niall. They shared the scan of the baby, and they talked about the future for a while and how Jenni was looking forward to being a grandma. Then Niall turned the conversation around to the "Brothers of Swing" and the last gig they played at the Ritz.

"You met Lila didn't you at the gig last weekend?" Niall said "Ronnie's wife."

They nodded and Ellie mentioned she also worked at the Purple Orchid as a receptionist.

Jenni said "Remember Amara who worked in the salon?" Ellie nodded and she went on "Her father is Jinni's brother. He left his wife, Barb, who is Amara's mother for a woman who works in the Black Cat bar last fall. Her name is Randi and she is Lila's sister apparently. That is how Lila was introduced to the Purple Orchid.".

Niall went on: "Ronnie and Lila feel we should branch out more with our act. We should do covers of more traditional jazz swing numbers. Lila feels we would be more successful if we had live musicians to back us up. We should have our own band." Niall continued.

"That sounds fine, but how are you going to find a band to play with?" Ellie said.

Kevin carried on "how much would that cost? You would have to share the money you received from each gig with several other people. Would it be even worthwhile doing a gig if you had to do this?"

Niall admitted that these were good points, and they were just thinking along these lines at the moment. Lila had mentioned something about musicians from the Blind and Visually Impaired Institute. Apparently, Lila worked as a cleaner at the Institute and had heard the musicians playing.

"They are only teenagers" said Kevin dismissively "they might be able to play at a church event or a bar mitzvah. However, you must be careful with children under the age of 18 years. You can't just take them to bars and the usual venues you play. Also, how good are they? The Institute has only been open for a few weeks; I doubt they have had time to put together a band of musicians yet."

Niall nodded and said he agreed, "Lila is a powerhouse though" he said, "and a big influence on Ronnie so it will be interesting to see what they come up with."

Ellie vaguely remembered Lila saying something to her about Jinni being strict and distant and her trying to put her at her ease during the evening they were at the gig. Ellie remembered she had not wanted to share about the issues with Song which she suspected were still in Jinni's mind. However, with this new information Ellie wondered if Jinni also was regretting hiring a woman who was the sister of the woman who broke up her brother's marriage. It seemed a strange thing to do. Ellie dismissed the subject as she felt Lila could stand up for herself and she did not want to interfere further. So as they drove home, Ellie had put Lila and the Brothers of Swing out of her mind and turned her thoughts back to the mess Song had left behind in Atlanta and how she was going to try to help clear it up…

Chapter 12

Jinni

Catches up with Amara and has a meeting with Barb.

Here I sit in my comfortable chair with the laptop on my knee getting ready for a Zoom call with Amara in Bangkok. I do miss having her in the salon. She is my niece, but she was also a very good manicurist. I knew that she was not happy though. She had dropped out of UCLA and it must have been very difficult living with her parents, my brother Somchai and his American wife Barb. They had been unhappy for years, with Barb putting Somchai down because he did not earn much. Yet when Somchai left her for another woman, it turned out Barb found it difficult to manage financially.

I saw Amara's face appear on the screen. She looked happy and relaxed. She was working at an orphanage in Bangkok for a couple of months.

She said "Sawasdee kha", which means Hello in Thai and then "Sabai Dee" (how are you?).

We chatted for a short time using the basic phrases she had learned in Thai, then reverted to English. She was enjoying her job working with the children. "I love working with children" she said "I think this is what I would like to do when I leave here." She was also enjoying exploring Bangkok.

"I want to thank you, Auntie Jinni" she said "for giving me this opportunity to come to Thailand. I love it here and am beginning to get more of a sense of what I want to do with my life in the future. When I dropped out of UCLA, I had no idea what I wanted to do with my life."

This comment made me very happy and I smiled and nodded.

Amara then went on to say she had spoken to her dad who seemed "the same" but she also spoke to her mother regularly. "Her man friend Danny left last week to start filming the next series of "Grangemouth". Keesha is also in the new series. This means that Danny has had to move out of mom's house."

I had never watched Grangemouth – the program was utter rubbish in my opinion, so I could not comment on the filming or if another series had been made.

However, this meant that Barb was on her own.

"How is your mom?" I asked.

"Not good" Amara said, "she will struggle financially with Danny gone and may have to take in a lodger to be able to keep her house."

We chatted for a little while before ending the call and promising to speak again soon.

It was very hard for me to feel sorry for Barb who I saw as a hard, white woman who had inherited money from her father and should have been able to manage. The problem was she had bought the biggest house she could with her inheritance money. The house was in the Southern Hills and the size of a mansion with beautiful views over the city. It seemed from what she had said that without Somchai she couldn't afford the upkeep.

I struggled to sleep that night as I realised, I was sitting in judgement of my sister-in-law and although I was the owner of a very successful business, I had not given her any money or tried to help her.

I was also aware that deep down I had suspected her of putting the messages about illegal immigrants on social media. There had been another message this week:

"Boycott businesses that employ illegal immigrants. We should stand together to stop these people"

I was still worried about these messages. The next day as I went about my business at the salon, I could not get Barb out of my mind. During a break between appointments, I sent her a message:

> "Due to your continued patronage of the Purple Orchid, you are a lucky winner of our luxury mani-pedi package for free. Book your appointment now by responding to this message. Offer valid for next 7 days."

I knew Barb couldn't resist a free beauty appointment and, true to form, she booked an appointment for Thursday evening at 6 pm. I knew she would come straight from her job at the local TV station where she worked in admin.

When Barb walked into the salon she looked very much the same: Blonde, overbearing and with hair teased into an inch of its life. I welcomed her and began her mani-pedi. I knew she blamed me for

Amara going to Thailand and also, she felt I had influenced Somchai to leave her for another woman. We were superficially polite, but I had things I wanted to say and I knew this was going to be difficult.

"How are things at home?" I asked, and waited for a possible explosion.

Instead, she seemed calm. "As you know your brother left me in a bad place. However, I have moved on. I have taken in a lodger" she said and laughed "I seem to gravitate towards foreigners. Jihuau is a Chinese woman who is studying for a PhD at the university. She is very quiet and no trouble at all. She is also a very good cook and makes me a meal most evenings. Amara is also due to come back in another month or so."

This was news to me. I wondered if Somchai knew? I was relieved that she seemed to be managing and moving on.

It was a relief when she left, although we were perfectly civil with each other. I felt guilty imagining that it was Barb who was leaving the messages on social media. But if it was not Barb who was it?

Later that evening I stopped by the Black Cat bar on my way home and saw Somchai sitting on his usual bar stool while Randi, his new woman partner worked. I gave him 2,000 dollars with the request that he pass some of it on to Barb implying that it was from him.

I slept well that night, I felt I had gone some way to managing problems in my family....

Chapter 13
Lila
Plans an event...

Lila was a very busy person as she had three part time jobs. One of these involved cleaning private houses for Welcome Maids. This week she set off to drive up the narrow, winding road into the Southern Hills to clean Janine's house. She is the lady who is also a customer of the Purple Orchid salon. Janine's house is on Southern Springs Lane and is very large and expensive. Lila told herself that she and Ronnie would live in a house like that when the Brothers of Swing were famous. She decided to play some music as she drove along and put on Luther Vandross. What a voice that man had. Lila first listened to "A House is not a Home" live from a concert he did in London, and this was followed by "Dance With My Father". Lila found this song to be very emotional. After the first few lines, the tears started rolling down her cheeks and so there she was driving and crying!

As she approached Southern Springs Lane, Janine was jogging along the side of the road. Lila pulled alongside her and asked if she wanted a lift. She shook her head to say no and indicated she should drive on, although she seemed a bit concerned seeing that Lila was crying.

Lila arrived first and started cleaning and then Janine came into the kitchen.

"Are you okay Lila?" she asked.

Lila explained she had been listening to a sad song and they both laughed. Lila asked about her jogging.

Janine said she had been doing "The Couch to 5k" program with her granny and her granny's friend Amy. This program took people who had previously been "couch potatoes" and set out how they could go from that to being able to run a 5k (3 mile) race. The three of them were going to take part in a race in the downtown at the end of March. There would be different levels at the race – a 5k run, a 10k run, and a half-marathon.

Lila said it was brilliant that her granny and her friend who are in their 70's were going to take part in the race. Janine said she was very proud of them and the progress they had made.

She laughed and said "there will be prizes for the best in each race, but we don't expect to get a prize. We will be happy if we just get round the course!"

Lila asked whereabouts in the downtown this would be held and Janine said in Gent Town park. "Doesn't this park have a reputation for not being very safe? I have heard stories of robberies and drug dealing."

Janine said "It will be okay on the day. The mayor is going to be there to present prizes and there will be a concert as well."

This got Lila's attention – a concert. Lila asked if she knew which musicians were playing in the concert. Janine didn't, but she said to ring the mayor's office and someone could help if Lila wanted to know more about the event.

After Lila had finished cleaning and was driving home, she couldn't get the idea of the concert out of mind. What a brilliant opportunity for the Brothers of Swing. A race like that in the city would be well attended and even if the band did not get paid much, they would be introduced to a much wider audience! She couldn't wait to discuss this with Ronnie to find out if he would be interested to take it further.

Later Ronnie said he felt it was a good idea but surely the musicians for the event would be booked by now? Lila volunteered to ring the mayor's office to find out and she did this the next day. She was pleased to find out that they were very enthusiastic in the mayor's office. They told her that a band had been booked to play after the mayor had presented the prizes and they would be playing in the park. During the races, the local radio station would also be playing in the park.

"But" said the mayor's assistant "it might be good to have a band playing at a key point along the course. This would not be in the park at the finishing line, but perhaps at Delaren Boulevard where the runners disperse to go different directions depending on the length of their route.   However, we only have a small budget, so I can't promise a large sum of money and the musicians would be expected to play for at least 3 hours. If you are interested, can you give us a play list of their music – remembering that it is intended to motivate the runners, so upbeat music is needed."

Ronnie and Lila put together a play list which was different to their usual act – it was much more upbeat.   They included tracks by

Bruce Springsteen "Born to Run",
Jason deRulo "Take you dancing",
Harry Styles "Watermelon Sugar"
alongside old classics that the Brothers normally sang such as "Oh Marie" and "Pennies from Heaven".

They sent this to the mayor's assistant.

True to her word she did get back and she suggested the "Brothers of Swing" play for three hours at Delaren Boulevard where the runners dispersed. The payment was very small, but at this moment in time she was looking to expand our audience so Lila felt the band should accept it.

Fortunately, Niall and Pete agreed and so it was agreed that the Brothers of Swing would play on race day in the city …

Chapter 14
Ellie
Interferes at Big Daddy's Burger Bar

Ellie taught on four days of the week and she did administration on the fifth, which is Friday. This week Kevin was going to Atlanta on Friday to do a presentation at Georgia State University with Dr John Strickland on their research. What an opportunity! Thought Ellie. She immediately asked if she could come with him. She wondered if her going to Atlanta and meeting with people involved in the case would have any effect.

During breaks from classes Ellie had been looking up the law on cases like this. It appeared that Barry Watkins had a defence if it could be proved that he acted in the defence of another person and it was not an unprovoked attack. Her goal was to be able to help him provide this defence. However, she had no money of her own to spend on this and she had not figured out yet how she could get him legal representation even if she found the evidence. This would mean they would have to rely on Gavin Gates, the public defender.

"One step at a time" she said to herself as she applied makeup before leaving for the airport on Friday morning. Being British, she was still not used to living in America which was such a big country and where people took a plane to go to meetings. Kevin had told her that the flight would take one hour and was due to land in Atlanta at 10 a.m.

Kevin was spending the morning with Dr Strickland planning their talk. Ellie contemplated how she would spend the morning. She had promised Kevin she would come along to his presentation in the afternoon. She had researched visiting Barry Watkins in the prison and found out that would be difficult. An inmate had to place you on their visiting list and you had to be cleared by the Prison for visiting. Barry Watkins had no idea who she was, and also it seemed cruel to get his hopes up when at present she could offer him nothing expect her support for what that was worth. So instead, she decided to visit Big Daddy's Burger Bar to see what she could find out there. She saw herself being able to make a difference by going there.

When they arrived in Atlanta they caught a taxi to the university. When Kevin got out of the taxi he told the driver to take Ellie back to the city to the shopping district. After they had been driving for a few minutes, Ellie leaned over and gave an address to the driver. "Please take me to this address." She said.

The driver gawped at her through the rear view mirror. "I think you have made a mistake ma'am." He said, "You don't want to go there."

"Isn't it the address of Big Daddy's Burger Bar?"

The driver indicated that it was, "but" he said "it is not a place where nice young ladies go. Are you sure you want to go there? I can take you to Peachtree Center. Beautiful shops there."

"Sir" Ellie said "I want to go to Big Daddy's Burger Bar and I will pay you my fare to go there and for you to wait while I am inside. Please just take my money and do as I say."

"Wow that is some accent lady" He said, "Are you British?"

Ellie indicated that she was and she knew this was going to lead to him telling her that she was a fool to go to that area of the city. She was a foreigner and didn't know what she was doing. They went back and forth for a while, but then Ellie could see that after they turned off the freeway by the state of the neighbourhood they were now in that he was taking her to Big Daddy's. It was now 11 a.m. and the streets were quite busy in the poor rundown area they were driving through. He pulled up in front of a block of shops which had seen better days. The middle shop had a sign over it which said "Big Daddy's Burger Bar". OMG it was far worse than Ellie could have imagined.

"There you are ma'am" said the driver "do you need me to come in with you?"

Ellie told him to wait in the taxi and getting out she closed the taxi door and slowly walked across the sidewalk to the door. She pushed the door open and, oh my, what a sight greeted her. The place smelled of fat and grease and the furnishings were tired and old. There were cracked tiles on the walls, which she thought may have once been white. A large overweight black man sat at one of the tables next to the window chewing down on a burger. Song gave up a place at a private university for this, was the first thought that ran through Ellie's mind. She wondered what on earth was going through Song's mind?

An older dark skinned and dark haired heavy-set lady was sitting by the till sucking on a coke. Ellie went straight up to her.

"Hello" Ellie said "I would like to speak to the owner or his representative, please."

The lady stared "Huh?" she said "what did you say?"

Ellie repeated herself and then the lady asked "who is asking? What is this about lady"

To use British understatement she was not friendly at all! Ellie very nearly lost the will to go on, but then she remembered why she was there.

"I want to pay my respects to Eric and to ask if he is feeling better after the attack in the alley"

The woman then softened slightly. "Are you a reporter or a lawyer?" she said eyeing Ellie up and down.

"No just someone who cares" she said. "I am Ellie, an interested person."

This seemed to placate her and she said she was Sonya and she talked about Eric and how he was making a slow recovery. He hoped to be out of hospital in the next week and then would return to work in another couple of weeks.

Ellie then dropped a bombshell. "I also wanted to ask about the Chinese girl who worked here at the time of the accident."

Sonya visibly stiffened and suddenly the atmosphere changed. Her tone became hard "what Chinese girl?" she said.

"A beautiful girl named Song who had ran away from university and was in a position where she needed money and a job".

"Who are you again?" she said "what right do you have to come in here asking these questions. We don't employ Chinese workers here. This is a decent place. I want you to leave now."

She was not very subtle and it was very obvious she knew Song.

"You know don't you that Barry Watkins was protecting her when he attacked Eric?" Ellie rushed on like a bull in a china shop "but it is being covered up. Please tell the truth."

Ellie knew then that she had gone too far and said too much. She could see that Sonya was furious and the overweight black man turned round and got up from the table. He stood and eyeing Ellie said "Are you okay Sonya?"

Ellie didn't know who he was, but one thing was for sure, she didn't feel safe. Her heart was beating wildly and her face had gone bright red. She started backing out of the room. The atmosphere was poisonous and the man was moving towards her slowly but surely. Sonya was also on her feet now and coming towards Ellie, but she was moving quickly.

It was at this point that Ellie realised that she had messed up the whole meeting She had not been subtle or encouraged Sonya to change her mind. In fact, she had just stirred up things that had gone quiet after the trial.

"Get out of my fucking café and don't come back" shouted Sonya.

"The fact you are so defensive proves something to me." Ellie said "I truly believe Song worked here and she was attacked and Barry Watkins tried to save her. I believe it is all being covered up to save your sorry ass."

Sonya screamed "Fuck off lady" and waving her arms around "Get out of my fucking shop now or I will call the police on you."

The black man had been slowly moving towards Ellie and was next to her now

"I think the lady has made it clear she wants you out of her café. Go now." He said "Fuck off and don't come back here."

“That is right” agreed Sonya “You are banned!”

The overweight man lunged towards Ellie in what seemed to be a threatening manner.

This was all it took, Ellie ran out of the door terrified. She was red in the face and panting when she opened the taxi door

“Drive” she said dramatically “get me out of here.”

The driver smirked as if to say I told you so and set off as Ellie turned round panicked to find out if they were being followed. The last thing she saw was the big man standing in the door of the burger bar watching them drive off. Sonya had not come outside the burger bar.

The driver took Ellie to the Peachtree Center. She paid him and then walked into Nieman Marcus. Normally she would be thinking how expensive it was, but today it felt luxurious and comforting. She had lunch alone in a café and hailed another taxi to take her to the university to listen to Kevin and John’s research presentation. As she sat in the auditorium dread filled her body. She was terrified she was going to have an anxiety attack. She knew she had worsened the situation by being daft enough to go to the burger bar. What on earth was she thinking of going there? What a fool she had been. It was obvious the woman was lying through her teeth and Ellie felt she had been paid to keep her mouth shut. But she had known that all along. What had she achieved? All she had done was stir things up. This was something she would not be sharing with Kevin.

She would not give up though – she had to find a different way to help Barry Watkins............

Chapter 15

Big Daddy's Burger Bar
Atlanta

The Wednesday following Ellie's visit, Big Daddy's burger bar had been very busy during the lunch time rush hour. The burger bar was housed in a shop front in South Atlanta. There was seating for about ten people on stools at a bar and four additional tables. The décor was faded and looked tired. The kitchen was open to the main room, and this is where Eric Senser's partner, Sonya in the absence of Eric, was working as a short order cook flipping burgers. The stove was ancient, and they needed to order a new one soon. A big expense that they really could not afford. The burger bar was being run by Sonya since the attack in the alley. Eric was still in hospital with extensive injuries but was making a very good recovery.

Sonya hoisted her ample frame onto a bar stool and started to eat her own lunch while contemplating her recent visit to Eric. Over the last couple of weeks seeing him lying there in the hospital bed wired up to various equipment was upsetting, he looked so old and vulnerable. It was good that he was now off the equipment and was starting to walk again with the help of hospital staff. Deep down she still loved him, although that had proved harder to do as the years went by. They had been together for 20 years now and he had never once offered to marry her. They had had such big plans for the burger bar. Sonya looked around and sighed, what a dump it was. They barely made a living out of it. In fact, they had to work very long hours to just breakeven, never mind make a profit. It really needed a renovation, but that needed money. It was only by employing workers without papers who Eric paid less than minimum wage that they managed to squeeze a profit out of the business. They had always done this, but when Sonya first worked in the burger bar there was maybe one illegal worker and the rest of the workers were American. As the years went by it became harder and harder to manage and this is when they switched to employing all illegal immigrants. These workers were always paid cash, no questions asked. Over the years they had employed a variety of nationalities. The Chinese girl had been the most trouble, though, that was without a doubt. Now that she was gone, Sonya was employing three Mexican workers.

It had been quite shocking the previous Friday when that large, strange woman had come into the Burger Bar. Sonya had panicked when this woman had started talking about Song as if she knew her and what had happened the night of the attack. Who the hell was she? Sonya mused. However, she knew one thing for sure, she could make something out of her visit.

On Saturday when she went to the hospital, Eric had been sitting in a chair next to his bed. Sonya told Eric that Sun Le would be joining them. Sun Le was a Chinese man and private investigator who Sonya had got to know quite well since the attack. He had arranged for Eric's hospital bills to be paid, when he found out that Eric's health insurance had lapsed. He had talked to Sonya the day after the attack and instructed her on what she remembered from the night before. He set it out, so it was easy for her – there had been an unprovoked attack by Barry Watkins. There had never been a Chinese woman who worked in the burger bar. Sun Le had emphasised how much trouble they could be in for employing her if the Immigration Authorities found out. He reminded her that she could go to prison for employing illegal immigrants and also would have to pay a fine. Sonya was so grateful that she had done everything he had asked. She could not believe their good luck in this generous man taking away some of their financial worries. If it meant selling a man (even if he was a customer) down the river, then she could live with that.

Sonya sat in a chair next to Eric and she could see his face was pale and drawn and he seemed to be wheezing as he breathed. He was a long way away from making a good recovery. Sun Le arrived a few minutes after Sonya. He sat in the third chair in the room and put his briefcase on the table.

Sonya had begun by setting out what she believed: "I believe that a trial date will be set soon for Barry Watkins. I had a phone call on Friday from Gavin Gates, who is the public defender who will be representing Barry I will be asked to give evidence in the trial."

She remembered that Sun Le had sat up straight and started to really pay attention when she mentioned the public defender.

She had gone on "Also last Friday there was a very worrying incident. Just before lunch a woman came into the burger bar. I had never seen her before. She was a big woman with an English accent. She asked about Eric and if he was making a recovery and then she asked about Song, the Chinese girl." Here Sonya paused for effect, and looked at Sun Le to see how he was reacting. Sun Le looked back at her inscrutable.

"This person seems to think that the Chinese girl, Song, was in the burger bar and in the alley on the night of the attack. She knows Song"

Sun Le had said "But that is not true, is it Sonya?"

"That is just the problem" said Sonya "that evening was so traumatic for me that I had blanked it out in my memory. But it seems that" Sonya paused and then carried on "as time goes by and having visitors like this woman..............." Her voice trailed off.

"What do you mean, Sonya?" said Sun Le "you know there was no Chinese woman there that night. If you tell the court that she was working in the burger bar then you know that will mean a big fine and possibly a prison sentence for you and Eric for employing her when she didn't have papers."

Sonya, looking into space and twisting her hands together, continued "The big problem is that I was so traumatised by what happened in that alley that I lost my memory. Seeing my beloved Eric lying there bleeding and that big bastard kicking the shit out of him will never leave me till the day I die. But you know what.." she paused here for emphasis and looked around "gradually it is starting to come back. Now I am not sure that there was just Eric and Watkins in the alley... there might have been a Chinese woman ..."

Eric joined in then "But there was no Chinese woman in the burger bar. We do not employ illegal immigrants. Of course Sonya is not going to say that in Court."

Sonya said "It was not in the burger bar that I remember her – but I might remember something about someone being the alley......"

There was silence for a moment. Then Sonya said "this is very painful for me, but I do feel I am recovering my memory...."

Sun Le was now furious and he jumped up and interrupted her. "How much do you want Sonya?" he said

Sonya looked at him innocently "I hadn't even begun to think about money. However, we are in a bad way at the burger bar with Eric off sick now and I don't know how we are going to go on."

"I will forward your message and get back to you." Said Sun Le "in the meantime I would recommend you keep your mouth shut."

On Monday as she was opening the burger bar Sun Le arrived and sat on a bar stool. He pushed a brown envelope across the counter at her. "You may want to open this" he said.

Sonya took the envelope and went in the small back room. Opening it she counted out $10,000 in cash. She put the money back into the envelope and put it into the safe. She then returned to the front of the burger bar and spoke to Sun Le.

"You were right" she said "I have remembered now when I went into the alley that night there was Barry Watkins giving Eric a good kicking. He ran off when he saw me. There was no one else there."

"Very good" said Sun Le "I am pleased you are getting your memory of the night back, Sonya. That will be helpful to you when giving evidence in the trial."

Sun Le left the burger bar without eating soon after.

After Sun Le left, Sonya couldn't wait for the lunch crowd to die down so that she could rush round to her own bank to deposit the money. For the first time in years, the business account looked healthy.

Today Sonya smiled to herself at the memory of that meeting. She checked the clock on the wall. She had a visitor due any minute now. Bob Rowlands of Rowlands Contractors was due to pay her a visit to discuss the cost of renovating the burger bar so that it looked fresh, new and inviting. He was willing to do the job at a discount as she did not require credit. The door opened and in walked Bob, looking around as he walked towards her.

“Hi, you must be Bob” she said “come and sit down and we can discuss the work I want.”....

Chapter 16

Jinni
Life goes on…

"Perhaps someday I'll crawl back home, beaten, defeated.
But not so long as I can make stories out of my heartbreak, beauty out of sorrow."
(Sylvia Plath)

During March I was still heartbroken, but I was determined not to be beaten. I knew that Song's lawyers would make sure that I was not investigated for employing an illegal immigrant. I made a promise to myself to never do it again. In addition, I had tried to make amends with my extended family for the hurt I may have caused them.

Although he Purple Orchid salon was still successful business had not been as good since the Immigration raid in January. I decided that people have short memories, and nothing was proved at that visit, so business would pick up again. I decided to go ahead with leasing a second premises in the regeneration section of the City. I had been to look at a property which I thought would be perfect. I had discussed the expansion with my close friends and one friend, Noi had suggested something different. Noi had been to visit relatives in the north and there she had visited a nail salon that shared the premises with a coffee shop. She said that you entered the building into an espresso bar with stools at the bar and a seating area. An arch led through to a reception and nail salon. You could order a free coffee with your nail appointment and sip the coffee while you had your nails done, or you could just pop in for a coffee.

I agreed that this would be a great idea for the Purple Orchid to expand. I also had the well-being products that I was selling and there was room there to display them. The Purple Orchid could become a stop-off place to just enjoy a coffee, browse the products and/or have a manicure/pedicure. I felt excited as I imagined the Purple Orchid becoming a hub for chat and well-being near to the downtown in the new regeneration area.

I spoke to my lawyer and my financial adviser about this expansion, and we started to move ahead with the new lease.

So, it was exciting times though tinged with sadness. My thoughts still often returned to Song and wondering what she was doing. I wondered if she had been able to resume classes at Highbridge College. When I looked up the College on the internet it seemed that it was much bigger than Song had implied. The original premises were in Reseda, in the San Fernando Valley outside of Los Angeles. However, in recent years the college had expanded and was now housed in a large campus near to Thousand Oaks, north of Los Angeles, in Ventura County. Pictures of the campus showed beautiful buildings and a palm tree lined campus. Song had told me her degree was in Business Studies. I read information on the degree and students studied a wide variety of subjects including sustainability and finance. I knew it would all be very difficult for Song if she had returned to class. I wondered if she ever thought of me and the time we spent together?

I remembered her stroking my hair, giving me a massage and kissing me. I loved everything about her and my memories of her were still wonderful. She was the most wonderful lover, and she had made me feel alive and loved. I missed her so much.

In the salon I remained bright and smiling. There was much discussion in the salon about the running race on Sunday 2 April. Janine and her granny and her granny's friend, Amy were entered in the race and would be running the 5k. Apparently the Brothers of Swing were going to be singing at a "key" (according to Lila) point along the route of the run. I planned to go along and watch the runners myself. It would be a nice break from work and Janine's granny and her friend had my vote running in their 70s. I hoped I could do something like that when I was older.

I also kept checking social media, and (fingers crossed) there were no posts this week about illegal immigrants so I hoped that whoever was doing that had decided they were getting nowhere and had given up.

So as March progressed, I was starting to get my life back together and business was getting better and I felt I could put the past with Song behind me…………

Chapter 17

Lila

Meets the jazz band

Ronnie and the boys were practising and finalising the set list for the day of the run. They had been downtown to see where they would be playing and spoken to a representative from the mayor's office who told them a stage would be built for them.

Lila continued to clean the classrooms on the top floor at the Institute for the Blind and Visually Impaired on Tuesday afternoons so heard the jazz band practising. This week as she was leaving, Bruce, the man conducting the jazz band came out of classroom number 5 and headed towards the elevator. Lila held the door for him.

"Hi Bruce" she said "I must say I have been enjoying hearing the band play. How long have you been playing together?"

Bruce smiled and said that he had joined the Institute as a music teacher in January 2023 and had offered to put together a jazz band as an extra-curricular activity for the students. He said he was very impressed with the level of ability of the students.

"We have a pianist, percussion, brass and a saxophone soloist who are learning to play together."

"How can they learn the music when they are blind?" Lila wanted to know.

"Some are totally blind and some are visually impaired. There is a variety of ages in the band between ages of 11 and 18. They learn through braille, using their i-pads and memorisation. There is a lot of memorisation and they practice a lot! They keep playing a tune until they have memorised it. They are awesome" he said.

Lila enquired who was playing the piano – this student sounded to be extremely talented.

Bruce nodded "the pianist is Alex" and he indicated that Alex, although not sighted, was working towards applying to the Juilliard School in New York.

Lila asked if the band had ever played together before an audience. Bruce said not yet, but they were working towards that.

An idea started to form. When she got home, she mentioned this to Ronnie "why not ask some of these young musicians to back you up for part of your singing gig at the running race?"

At first, Ronnie acted like he thought this was a particularly odd idea and dismissed it.

Then last Thursday he said he had been thinking about the idea of the blind students backing up the Brothers and he thought it was actually a brilliant idea.

"They could not back us up for all of our songs. Playing for three hours would be way too much for them." He said "but if we asked them to do a few songs with us at the beginning of the race when most of the runners are passing us, it would be really good publicity, both for us and them. I don't know what the rules are about students under eighteen performing in public, but we could find out."

When Lila went to the Institute on Thursday afternoon, she asked Bella, the receptionist, if Bruce was on campus and if she could speak to him. Bella said she would get the message to him. Lila was in classroom two when he caught up with her. She explained about the running race and the Brothers of Swing and she asked if the band would be willing to back up the Brothers on a few tracks at the start of their set? At first, Bruce seemed taken aback, and then he gave a huge smile "Was this your idea, Lila?" he said "what an excellent idea. I will need to look into the logistics and legalities and also what songs the Brothers would want back up for, but it seems like it would be marvellous exposure for our new jazz band."

True to his word, Bruce followed up on the event with the Mayor's office and it seemed it would be fine for the jazz band to perform in the open air on a Sunday morning.

Ronnie, Niall and Pete met with Bruce and they went through the playlist and how many songs the Institute jazz band could help out with. It was agreed to do four songs at the peak of the race as most of the runners ran past. After this the Brothers would carry on singing but with their backing track. The Brothers would practice with the jazz band on Saturday mornings and several early evenings before the race.

The students were excited about playing in public and to such a big audience. Apparently 10,000 people had signed up for the various races and would be running past – and then there were also the spectators.

Lila wrote on a large banner which was intended to put on the stage above the Brothers and the students saying "The Brothers of Swing and Institute for the Blind and Visually Impaired student jazz band".

They also had posters printed which were intended to be given out at the concert at the end of the race. Lila had checked with the mayor's office who were very nice and accommodating.

These were exciting times and Lila knew that the event was going to be a big success for the Brothers. She couldn't wait for them to perform in front of a larger audience............

Chapter 18
Ellie
Makes a plea for help...

On Saturday, the day after the disastrous trip to Atlanta, Kevin put the television on in the kitchen as they sat eating breakfast. Ellie had managed to stay quiet and had not said a word to him about going to the burger bar. First and foremost she was embarrassed she had made such a mess of things and had not been able to do anything to help.

Fox news was on the TV, and a picture flashed up of a famous actor. The anchor said, "We should say thanks today to Cliff Hardy who has come to the aid of a Texas family who have lost their business to a fire". A clip was shown of a couple and their two children Apparently the family owned a coffee shop which had burned down the week before. The couple did not have fully comprehensive insurance and they could not afford to replace everything. Cliff Hardy had come to their aid with a large sum of money.

An idea began to form in Ellie's head. She had always been a very persistent person and she did not want to give up on Barry Watkins.

When Kevin left to go the gym, she opened up the laptop and went onto the internet. She was looking for black celebrities in Atlanta who may be able to afford to pay Barry Watkins legal bills for an attorney who would have time to represent him rather than use the public defender. She was still furious that lies had been told and a man framed and could potentially go to prison for a long time when others got away with illegal activities with no consequences. Searching through she found five potential people. The next step was to go to their social media and sign up to say she was following them. She then wrote a message and sent an individual DM to each of them. The DM read as follows:

> *"A brother needs your help. He has been framed and set up as a scapegoat for a crime in South Atlanta. On 23 February, Eric Senser the owner of Big Daddy's Burger Bar attacked and attempted to rape a Chinese woman who worked for him and who was in the US illegally. Barry Watkins came to her defence and beat Eric Senser. He has been charged with aggravated assault and battery. The Chinese woman's family*

have employed expensive lawyers to remove any trace of her from the scene and to put all the blame on Watkins. He is accused of aggravated assault and battery. He cannot afford private representative and has taken the hit for this crime. Please help him, he is now in Fulton County jail waiting for a trial date to be set."

Finally she posted this and waited for a response. In her heart Ellie felt sure at least one of the five would get back to her or at least a PA would. But she waited and waited, and no response came.

By now Ellie felt like a complete fool. What was she doing writing to celebrities? Even worse, what if Kevin found out she had been writing to celebrities? Kevin thinks only "brain-dead" women write to celebrities. Ellie felt slightly panicked, he might even divorce me, she thought. "Why do I keep interfering and doing things that I seem to get wrong?" she said out loud. A terrible feeling of homesickness came over her and she longed to be back in Birmingham, England. She remembered with affection the office she shared with three other lecturers at the college. They ate biscuits and took it in turns to get the coffee. There was always some harmless gossip about the management or events from the news. Today, she felt really lost and alone.

Ellie decided to be stern with herself and told herself to stop being so stupid. It was pathetic and she was lucky wasn't she? She had a nice home, a husband, she was pregnant, and now had a better teaching contract thanks to the Union, and a mother-in-law who cared and looked after her. She felt sorrow for Barry Watkins but she had tried hadn't she to help him? She had now run out of ideas and was going to have to let it drop. She told herself that the old saying "you reap what you sow" is true and something would happen to Song's father and his expensive lawyer and private detective even if she did not interfere. Song might even run away again when she couldn't do the academic work at the college.

Ellie was determined to think about other things and to be positive...

Chapter 19
Buckhead, Atlanta
A large mansion

Matt Carey, woke up in his own bed for the first time in three months. He had just returned from a world tour with his band. The tour had been very lucrative, but he had missed home. He looked around the beautiful room and thought how lucky he was to live here. He was 42 years old and a multi-millionaire. He believed if you have it, flaunt it. He had treated himself to a new Lamborghini at the end of the tour and he was looking forward to a drive later that day.

He reached over to the side table to get his cell phone. He checked his messages. There was a message from his agent about meeting tonight to discuss his new recording contract. Also a message from his ex-wife about seeing little Georgie, his daughter and the love of his life.

He then went into Instagram and looked at his posts. There were over 200,000 likes on his latest post. Not bad, he thought, he was getting older, but he still had his fans. He then flipped onto his DMs. He never responded to these, but they were a laugh. As usual, there were women offering him sex. He read them smiling but wondered what possessed them to think he would respond. Then there were the begging messages. People wanting to sing in his band or write songs for him. People wanting him to pay their hospital bills. He was getting bored now. He was about to flip off the messages when he saw it. It was very long for a DM and written in what seemed to him to be funny language.

> *"A brother needs your help. He has been framed and set up as a scapegoat for a crime in South Atlanta. On 23 February, Eric Senser the owner of Big Daddy's Burger Bar attacked and attempted to rape a Chinese woman who worked for him and who was in the US illegally. Barry Watkins came to her defence and beat Eric Senser. He has been charged with aggravated assault and battery. The Chinese woman's family have employed expensive lawyers to remove any trace of her from the scene and to put all the blame on Watkins. He is accused of aggravated assault and battery. He cannot afford private representative and has taken the hit for this crime.*

Please help him, he is now in Fulton County jail waiting for a trial date to be set."

Three words jumped out though:

Big Daddy's Burger Bar. Eric Senser. Rape.

Matt felt sick to the pit of his stomach. He read the message again. "OMG" he said aloud "who wrote this?"

Memories, long buried, flooded back. He was no longer in the luxurious mansion in Buckhead, he was in Big Daddy's Burger Bar plating up burgers. He was 26 years old and trying to make it on the music scene. So far, he had been spectacularly unsuccessful. He lived in a shit hole on a major throughfare and worked in the burger bar to make ends meet.

Fat Sonya was the short order cook flipping burgers and passing them to him to put together with the bread and pickles. Eric Senser owned the place and took the money. He was also fat and gross. Maria Morales was a beautiful young girl who washed up and cleared the tables. Matt had been in love with her. She was an immigrant from Mexico and spoke mainly Spanish. She had a few words of English but not much. Senser and Sonya took advantage of her. They paid her a pittance and made her work long hours.

Matt got out of bed, as he felt sick and made his way to his luxurious bathroom. Surely, he had imagined this DM? He returned to the bedroom and picked up his cell – no, the message was still there.

It was so long since he had thought about that evening at the burger bar. He had been helping Sonya tidy up and took some trash out to the back alley. He saw Senser pressing Maria up against the dumpster his hands all over her grunting. Maria could see Matt, but Senser had his back to him. Matt remembered wanting to beat Senser, but Maria shaking her head and waving her hand indicating that Matt should leave.

Later as they were leaving to go home, he asked Maria about the incident in the alley. She struggled to speak English and she was in tears. The message that she managed to get through though was she needed a job and did not have papers, if she reported Eric she would be deported or worse. If she did not say anything Eric let her keep her job and additional perks. It seemed he gave her a few extra dollars without Sonya knowing.

Matt had only felt disgust. He wanted to tell her to get out of there and develop some self-respect, but wondered if that were even possible. She was in the USA without working papers and had no rights. Senser was taking advantage of this fact. The sight of Senser made him want to throw up. The man was scum of this earth.

He read the DM again. It was still going on, all these years later. Except it seemed Barry Watkins was more of a man than him. He had interfered and beaten the pig. If anyone deserved it, Senser did. But how could the Chinese woman have an expensive lawyer? That bit did not make sense.

Matt got dressed and went downstairs. After breakfast he asked Ron his driver to take him out. He decided not to take the lambo, and instead they went in the Cadillac Escalade. If Ron was surprised with the address Matt gave him, he did not show it.

The Cadillac pulled up outside Big Daddy's Burger Bar.. It was just as filthy and rundown as Matt remembered. As he sat looking at it, a woman showed up with a key. It was fat Sonya, waddling along and wheezing as she struggled to breathe. She was just as bad as Senser. She knew what he did and condoned his behaviour.

Matt fought the nausea back as he looked at her. Then he got out his cell and put a call in to his attorney. "I want to instruct you on a criminal case I need help with" ....

Chapter 20

Lila

Practising with the Institute jazz band...

In the couple of weeks before the running race the Brothers met with Bruce and the students to practice the numbers they would play together. Four Motown classics were chosen for them to perform together. Pete was a runner (he had run a marathon!) and said these were perfect for running – he often played them himself through his ear pods.

These were the songs:

"You can't hurry love" by the Supremes

"Uptight" by Stevie Wonder

"How sweet it is (to be loved by you)" Jr Walker and the All Stars

"Stop her on sight SOS" Edwin Starr

Bruce had put together arrangements that the students could play to back the Brothers and which were in the right speed for a running event.

The week before the concert they practised on three nights. It was a very different performance to their usual act – but Lila had every confidence that it was much better.

There were 6 students who would back the Brothers on the day. Alex would play the piano. She was accompanied by trumpets, a saxophonist, a drummer, and Shelia who was only 11 and would play the cymbals.

Although no-one knew this the Jazz band had practised many more times without the Brothers. They had memorised the music and played until they were perfect. They were so excited about performing in public.

Lila couldn't wait for Sunday for the running race and the concert. The day before she asked Jinni if we could play Motown over the Purple Orchid sound system. Jinni didn't know what Motown was, but she allowed Lila to line up some tracks.

Soon the whole salon came alive to the classic music of Diana Ross, the Four Tops, Junior Walker and the All Stars, Jimmy Ruffin and Stevie Wonder.

"Come along to the running race tomorrow" Lila said to customers "You can hear this music live. The Brothers of Swing are singing together with the students from the Institute for the Blind and Visually Impaired jazz band."

No-one knew what Jinni really thought of this – but she did not interfere and smiled and said she liked the music. Lila saw her eyes glaze over with tears when The Marvelettes sang "When you're young and in love". She must have a secret love in her past, Lila thought. Maybe that is what is making her unhappy? Yet she is no longer young, more middle aged.

After that track had finished Jinni got up and changed the music to the usual "cool vibes" tracks. Lila had really enjoyed the Motown session though, and from the upbeat atmosphere it seemed the customers had too! Tomorrow was going to be a big day for the Brothers of Swing playing at the running race and Lila couldn't wait....

Chapter 21

The Running Race

Sunday April 2 dawned bright and clear. 10,000 people woke up and got into their running gear and made their way to Gent Town Park. The Park had never seen such crowds. There was a stage set up and KAVC98 radio had a presenter sitting on the stage playing sounds while the crowds came into the park. There were tents around the park for the various sponsors and charities. The race was being sponsored by Alex Gold, CPAs. The charities were such as: Guide Dogs of America, Oxfam America and a local charity "Farmers without pesticides". There were also places to eat and of course, the Runners Registration HQ where runners got their numbers and registered for the race.

Among the crowds of runners were Janine and her granny and Amy. Janine's husband Gene had gone along with them to support them and also the firm he was a partner in, Alex Gold, were sponsoring the race. Granny and Amy were both in their early 70s and had gone from sitting in front of the television inactive a few months ago to being able to take part in a 5k run. They were nervous before the race and just wanted it to start.

Jinni had also gone along to watch the running with her friend Noi. The park was very near to the new premises she intended to lease, and she could see how the whole area could be regenerated to be beautiful again. It was still run down but other businesses were starting to move in, and of course, there was the Institute for the Blind and Visually Impaired already in the area.

Jenni and Ellie and her husband Kevin were there to support the Brothers of Swing. Ellie still worried about the Park after she had been mugged and robbed there. They did not go into the Park but stood next to the stage the Brothers were playing on which was on the road the runners were going along.

Edgar Dumont, the mayor, was on stage to wish the runners luck and at 5 minutes to 11 am they were told to go to the pens for the start. Jerry Levens from the radio station did the count down and at 11 am the horn sounded, and the race started.

Along the route were marshals and water bottles for the runners. Additionally, there were two stages with musicians at different points in the race. The first stage was where the Brothers of Swing and the Jazz Band were. At this point the route divided and the half-marathon runners went one way on a longer route, and the 5k and 10k runners went another way. There was quite a crowd cheering on the runners at this point.

By the time the runners approached the first music stage the field had begun to spread out. Towards the back of the runners were Janine and granny and Amy. As they approached the Brothers were singing "Uptight" by Stevie Wonder. It was very different, but Janine loved it and also the cheering from the crowd. The cheering was the very best, it made her want to run faster and forever.

The first runners came back in with amazing times. 35 minutes for the 10k and one and a half hours for the half marathon.

Janine kept with her granny and Amy, and they made the 5k in 45 minutes. A reporter from the Pinnacle took their pictures as they crossed the finishing line. They weren't the oldest runners but they had made such progress in such a short time.

After all the runners were back, Edgar Dumont presented the prizes and then there was a concert in the park. A local band played to much applause. Lila had to admit they were good, but there had been a lot of comments on the Run's website about the Brothers act.

"Amazing performances from blind children"

"The blind children were the best"

"Love the blind children – wow they were amazing."

"The old classics are the best"

"Prefer Eye of the Tiger for running music. But this was different."

"Love the Brothers when can we see them again?"

She was happy and Ronnie was happy too with how the event had gone. There had been one or two problems with the music, but it seemed no-one had noticed or if they had it didn't matter.

The Brothers were moving forward and expanding their range. Lila saw great things in their future.

Jinni and Noi had enjoyed the day. It was only when they were on the train going back home that thing took a turn for the worse when Jinni's cell rang....

Chapter 22

Jinni

An alcoholic bender

I had had a good day out at the run in the park. Noi is a good friend, and it was good to see customers taking part in the race. I enjoyed the music and had eaten from a Mexican food stall. On the train home I was feeling happy and relaxed when my cell vibrated. I picked it up, I couldn't believe who was calling. It was Barb – my brother Somchai's ex-wife.

"Hi Barb" I said, "Is everything okay?" I knew full well it wasn't, or she wouldn't be ringing me.

"I am at St Joseph's Hospital." She announced, "I am with Somchai and you need to come as soon as possible as he asking for you."

I felt sick when she mentioned Somchai "Oh no. What is wrong with him" I asked.

"He turned up at my house today after lunch. He had been on a bender. That bitch Randi had been on his case all week. She knew he was broke when she agreed to move in with him. Now she expects to live the millionaire lifestyle. What a bitch!!"

"He'd been on a bender?" I queried.

"I have never seen him in such a state" Barb said "he looked like shit! He came staggering up the drive and collapsed on the doorstep. I managed to get him inside. He got to the bathroom just in time and was violently sick. He then lay on the sofa and passed out. At first I thought he was just tired. I've seen him drunk so many times. But he didn't come round after an hour so I went over and noticed his breathing was shallow and irregular. Jinni, he nearly died. How that bitch could let him get into such a state! Of course, he wanted me when he was ill. He knows who cares for him and loves him."

She broke down crying and became incoherent.

From what I could gather she had rung for a doctor who came and said that Somchai had to be taken to hospital where he could be put on an IV and given oxygen.

"He fucking nearly died" Barb was shouting now.

"I will come now" I said. "I am on the train but will be with you as soon as I can"

I rang for an Uber at the next station and, saying goodbye to Noi, got off the train and went to the hospital.

Somchai was lying in bed hooked up to an IV and there was an oxygen tube clipped to his nose. He looked dreadful. Barb was by the bed, very much in charge as the concerned wife.

"They pumped his stomach" she said "He's been to hell and back. How that bitch could let him get into this state!"

I sat down in the other chair and took hold of his hand and squeezed it. He seemed unresponsive and limp. Somchai had been on benders before, but this one seemed really bad.

A few minutes later a doctor came into the room to speak to us.

"Which of you is his wife who brought him in?" asked the doctor

"I am his wife," said Barb

"He is lucky to be alive." Said the doctor "This is a very extreme case of alcohol poisoning." Referring to notes the doctor told us how low his vital signs were when he was brought in. "We need to do tests for liver damage and any brain damage from his loss of consciousness"

He paused and then said "Can you give me a bit more background on his drinking at the moment? How much per day? What prompted the excessive drinking today?"

Barb didn't know of course, so she started making things up. "He doesn't drink regularly" she said "He had been to a family celebration and just got carried away this weekend."

The doctor looked none too convinced by Barb's explanations. "We will talk to him tomorrow when he is able. He is scheduled for tests on Tuesday. In the meantime, please let him rest and you can come back tomorrow and be with him. He is off the danger list now that we have stabilised him, so you can go home without worrying."

As we walked to the elevator, I felt close to tears. Somchai was a hopeless alcoholic. He had been a heavy drinker for years, and we had all kept quiet as his drinking had tipped over into alcoholism. Barb was tired of his drinking, and it had been the cause of many arguments. Then he left her and of course, he had hooked up with a woman who worked in a bar. We had all ignored the fact that he was going to the Black Cat bar where Randi worked most evenings to be with her. Sitting on a bar stool boozing all evening. Making a bad problem far worse. No-one had intervened. Barb was right, his being with Randi had worsened the situation. Also, there was the issue with his hours being cut recently and him taking the extra shifts at the chicken processing plant. I wondered if that was going badly. He had only been there for about a week but maybe that had driven him over the edge. I realised I had not called to see how he was coping either, I had been busy with the salon and my own thoughts.

I promised Barb that I would return on Monday evening to see Somchai again when the salon closed. Barb was in her car, and she drove me home. It was a difficult drive, there was so much unsaid between us. I thanked her for the ride and said I would see her tomorrow.

I felt uneasy all-day Monday and was glad when it was time to close the salon and I could make my way to the hospital.

Somchai was sitting up in bed. He still looked very ill but was at least conscious and able to talk. Barb was sitting by the bed, holding his hand. It seemed he had had some tests carried out on Monday and there were more planned for tomorrow.

"The results are not good," said Barb

It seemed that Somchai had damaged his liver by his excessive drinking. The message was that he had to stop drinking now to have any hope of a future. This meant stopping completely.

"I will be there to guide him" said Barb "Somchai will be coming home later this week with me and I will make sure that he keeps to all the rules set by the doctors."

Somchai seemed resigned to his fate. He smiled weakly and said he would stop drinking now. "I will never touch another drop." He said "they told me I have not even to have alcohol in cooking."

I wondered if he would be able to keep to this and felt really worried about him.

Where was Randi? I wondered if she had thrown him out and that is why he had been on the bender. I wanted to interfere but knew better.

I sat with them for an hour and then I left promising to return on Tuesday evening.

In the uber going home I wondered if it was a mistake Somchai returning to Barb. But the alternative had been even worse. I felt sorrow overtake me as I sat in the car. Why do we waste this precious life in relationships that are toxic and destroy our bodies with poison? I should have told Somchai to be strong and leave both women and develop some self-respect. I would never do that though; we always maintain face at all costs.

"The ultimate measure of a man is not where he stands in moments of comfort and convenience, but where he stands at times of challenge and controversy".

Martin Luther King Jr.

Chapter 23

Lila

Randi's problems

The day after the run Lila was feeling happy that it had been such a success for the boys. They were mentioned on the Jerry Levens commuter show on the radio and everyone seemed to have enjoyed their music and that of the Jazz Band.

Lila was just getting ready to leave for her cleaning job when her cell phone vibrated. It was Randi. She picked up and said "Hi Randi, how are you?"

Randi was in tears and barely coherent. "It's Somchai." She said "He's in the hospital."

Lila was immediately concerned "What is wrong?" she said.

Randi was barely coherent. Lila immediately said she would call in to see her now.

After the call with Randi ended, Lila called in sick at work and drove to the apartment Randi shares with Somchai. It is in a very bad area. Homeless people live and

congregate opposite under the railway bridge and there is a piece of rough grass in front where people leave trash and old furniture. It was a very depressing place. Lila climbed the stairs in the apartment building and knocked on the door. Randi flung the door open and there she was in an old dressing gown. She looked every year of her age without her make-up and her eyes were puffy and swollen from crying. Her hair was stood on end. Lila reached out and hugged her.

She had calmed enough to talk. "We had the mother of all arguments on Friday night." She said: "Somchai had got this new work at the chicken plant that he was supposed to go to in the evening. He had been on Thursday night, but on Friday night he came into the Black Cat and started drinking heavily. I know I shouldn't have served him. He wouldn't answer about the chicken plant. By the time my shift ended and we were leaving he was very drunk." She paused to take a breath. "I had to support him walking out of the bar or he would have fallen down. We got into the car and I drove. I asked him again why he had not been to the chicken plant. He turned on me and called me a bitch and greedy. I had no idea how difficult it was working at the fucking chicken plant. It stunk and you had to handle slimy raw chicken. You had to stand up all the time. It killed his back. Blah blah blah. I told him to stop being a baby and do some work. By the time we got back to the apartment we were yelling at one another. When the car stopped, he opened the door, got out and disappeared."

"Are you saying he just stomped off and you did not see him all evening?" Lila asked

"All weekend" said Randi "at first, I didn't worry too much. But he didn't come back on Saturday or Sunday. I knew he was out drinking with his friends. He had stayed away overnight before but not for this long. The Sunday evening late about 11 pm I got a call from Barb, his ex-wife. She told me he had turned up at her home on Sunday afternoon very ill from drink. She had taken him to hospital where they were treating him for alcohol poisoning. He very nearly died. She blamed me for letting him get into such a mess."

"How is it your fault?" by now Lila was furious "the man is an alcoholic. He needs to go to AA and get sorted out! So, when is he coming back?"

"That is just it" she said "he isn't. She told me when he is released from hospital he is going to stay with her again. She is going to help him to get off drink and make him happy and well again."

"For goodness' sake!" Lila said "I know this must be heartbreaking, Randi. Can you not talk to him and make him see sense?"

"I don't even know which hospital he is in." she said "Barb didn't tell me and even if I go, he is not answering my messages." She showed me the text messages she had sent, which to a casual observer would seem like the actions of a crazy, deranged woman. Randi needed to calm down and keep her self-respect. But that was easier said than done.

“It may be that he hasn’t answered your messages as he is too ill – passed out or having tests at the hospital.” Lila said “why don’t you give him a little time. Wait for a day or two to contact him again. At least you know where he is. Just hold back. That is my advice.”

Randi sat with her head in her hands. She was wretched.

They sat for a long while, and Lila made her tea and toast. As the morning progressed Lila found it hard to talk to her and say anything that would make her feel better. Eventually Randi went and showered and got dressed. Lila drove her over to the Black Cat bar for her shift realising that it was now quite late in the day. As she got out of the car she turned to Lila and said “You are right Lila, I will wait to speak to him. When he is feeling better I am sure he will see sense and want to come back to me.”

Lila was furious, she would have liked to have driven to the hospital and punch Somchai. She thought, how dare he treat my sister like this? But deep down she knew he was an alcoholic who was really struggling. She just hoped that she had the strength to keep away from him and that she would not welcome him back if he decided he wanted to come back to her.

Chapter 24

Lila

The Brothers of Swing

When Lila got home after her day with Randi, she was ready to talk about the reactions of the public to the Brothers set at the Running Race yesterday. It seemed that the Brothers got a lot of reaction to their set with the Blind school jazz band on their social media. Comments were overwhelmingly positive – most people loved the young people in the jazz band and were surprised by the change of music by the Brothers, but had enjoyed it.

On Tuesday evening, the Brothers met at Ronnie and Lila's house to discuss Sunday. They had been singing sets that were completely different from anything they had ever done before, and also singing with a live backup band. Lila started by saying she felt that day had been a huge success for the boys and it was great to see them extending their range.

Niall wanted to know where they were going with it? "I realise we had got a bit complacent with our act, but will this change mean we appeal to a larger audience or just to a different audience?"

Lila said she felt that singing with the blind jazz band would really extend their appeal to a wider audience.

Ronnie said "yes, but is Motown the right choice for us? We have always been more into the big band era and swing music"

Pete seemed to imply that he felt they should do another set with the blind jazz band. However, he was wondering if Nat King Cole would be more appropriate.

Finally, they agreed to meet with Bruce to discuss doing another set and where that would be. Also, what his thoughts would be on the choice of music.

As it turned out before they had a chance to meet with Bruce, Niall received a call on his cell from the mayor's office asking if the Brothers and the Blind jazz band would do a set at a convention the Mayor was hosting in the City Hall. It would be on a Saturday afternoon, and there were 1,000 guests expected. They would play in a break from the proceedings while the guests were drinking tea or coffee.

The Brothers were delighted by this chance to play in front of a convention. When they met with Bruce they asked him what he thought. He said he was happy for the jazz band to also join them. At the meeting, they sat trying to decide on the choice of music for the afternoon. It was decided to structure their performance around some classic swing jazz songs. They would be playing three songs during the break. Bruce would work on the arrangements for these songs. These were the songs:

"Mack the Knife" - this would give Billy who played the trumpet a chance to play a solo

"Pennies from Heaven" - a real favourite of the Brothers.

"Autumn Leaves" – with a back up for the piano, Alex and guitar – which would be played by Bruce.

It was planned to do rehearsals together with the jazz band again.

In the meantime, the Brothers of Swing continued to do their original act at a wedding, a 50th wedding anniversary and a bar mitzvah. At the wedding, later in the evening, there were requests for the Brothers to perform some Motown songs. A guest said she had heard them singing as she had run past in the 10k and had "loved it" and now wanted to dance!

Lila couldn't wait for the Brothers to play again with the jazz band.

Of course, she talked about this upcoming performance to customers at the Purple Orchid when she was working on reception the following Friday and Saturday. Jinni seemed distracted and not very happy, but did not caution Lila against saying anything, so Lila figured perhaps she had it right this time. Lila wondered if she should confide in Jinni about Randi and Somchai's troubles. She decided that this might be the right thing to do, so she asked Jinni if she knew how Somchai was.

Jinni said that he was making a recovery and had been released from hospital.

She was very stiff and awkward, and her body language gave off the impression she was not keen to confide in Lila. She started moving away and looking around. Lila immediately felt embarrassed she had said anything. In her mind she was asking herself:

"Why would she not want to talk to me? It was her brother and my sister we were talking about. I don't understand why she wouldn't want to discuss this with me. It was painful for Randi too. Randi had been Somchai's partner. They had lived together. Perhaps Jinni saw her as a marriage-breaker."

Lila took away the impression that Jinni was looking down her nose on her and her family, and she didn't like it.

Chapter 25

Ellie

Moving on...

Kevin and Ellie had joined Jenni to watch the running race on Sunday. Of course, they wanted to hear the Brothers of Swing singing with the Blind Institute jazz band, so they went out to where they were playing and stood near to the stage. Lila was also there watching.

Ellie had got talking to one of the women also standing near the stage. She said her name was Adrienne and she was the mother of Alex who played the piano with the blind jazz band. She was a middle-aged woman with an English accent. Ellie guessed her to be from Lancashire and she confirmed she had grown up in Rochdale and moved to the US when she was 20 years old. Her husband was an engineer and he had got a position here. It was nice to speak to someone English and Ellie liked her instantly. Her daughter, Alex, had been blind since birth but was a very talented musician. However, Ellie felt all the jazz band were brilliant. They may have put a few wrong notes in here and there, but overall they played exceptionally well. Also, the Brothers were moving into a new area singing Motown numbers. Ellie genuinely liked their new act, and she knew Lila had had a big influence on them widening their range.

On the Tuesday after the run Kevin and Ellie were commuting to the State University and had the Jerry Levens show on the local radio station. Jerry started to talk about illegal immigrants. He introduced his guest, attorney Kate Perkins, who had a practice in the City where she specialised in immigration law. They chatted about how the law had changed over the recent years to become really tough on people employing illegal immigrants. Kate said that in this state there was a fine to be paid and a prison sentence of up to 10 years if an employer was caught employing people without the proper paperwork. Apparently, the owner of a chicken processing plant outside of the City had been caught and was facing prison and a big fine.

After the interview Kevin turned the radio off.

"Jinni was really putting her business on the line employing Song. Without Song's father and his attorney Jinni might be facing prison. I had no idea the penalties were so severe, and I wonder if Jinni knew? At least that is all over now."

Ellie agreed and thought perhaps it is best to let sleeping dogs lie. Then a thought occurred to her – she wondered if she had stirred something up writing to the celebrities? She had told them about Barry Watkins case and how he needed legal representation. But she decided to put this out of her mind as she had had no response so it was unlikely they would do anything. Perhaps they didn't read their DMs and spent their time living the high life …

Chapter 26

Atlanta

An attorney visits Bary Watkins in Fulton County Jail

When Barry Watkins, who was in prison waiting for a trial date to be set, was told that there was an attorney here to meet with him, he assumed it was Gavin Gates, the public defender who had been appointed to his case. The trial date must have been set. Barry was less than impressed with Gavin Gates, who had shown little, if any, interest in his case up to now. Barry remembered the words of his late mother who had said "you get what you pay for." Well, Barry couldn't afford to pay for a lawyer, so Gavin Gates was what you got when you had to rely on the system.

He picked up the phone to take part in the visitor video conferencing system and saw a black man wearing an expensive suit and a Rolex watch on the video. The man introduced himself as Derek Lynes, Attorney at law. He explained that he had been asked to visit with Barry to find out more about the night of the attack and what happened in the run up to the trial.

Barry's first thought was why? He felt this will be a waste of time. He stared at the expensive looking man. Why on earth is this person visiting me? However, he had nothing better to do so he decided to go over everything again.

Barry told Derek that he was protecting Song when he attacked Eric Senser. Derek asked if he knew Song before that night.

"Yes, she lived in the same apartment block as me" said Barry "in fact she lived next door. There were I don't know how many of them living in one apartment. I think at least six. They were all Chinese. They weren't loud or anything, but they used to cook and made disgusting smells. I think they used the bed in shifts. Song had started to live there recently. They all looked the same to me, until she showed up. I certainly noticed her. She was a beautiful woman."

Barry confirmed he had chatted with Song and she told him she was working at Big Daddy's Burger Bar. In fact, he had gone to the burger bar that evening specifically to see her. He loved looking at her. She was out front, serving customers and had stopped by to say “hi” when she saw him sitting at the counter.

“I knew all about that place” Barry said. “Eric Senser is a mean motherfucker.”

When asked to elaborate Barry merely said that there were rumours about girls who had been raped by Eric and had been frightened to say anything as they were in the States illegally.

Derek asked if he went to the burger bar that evening to protect Song. Barry shook his head “no, I was hungry and just wanted to see her. But when I saw her taking the trash out, and Eric followed I was scared for her.”

Derek asked if Barry followed them. “Yes when she didn’t come back after a few minutes I went to see what was happening. That fucker was trying to rape her.”

It was a bad memory for Barry and he became angry at the thought of that evening.

“Were there any other witnesses to what happened in the alley?” asked Derek

“You bet your ass there were” said Barry “but none of those motherfuckers would say a word to help me.”

Derek took out a pen. “Names?” he said.

Barry said a couple of names and then he mentioned Sonya. “Sonya is Eric’s partner. She is a mean bitch and will cover up for him and defend him. I know she knows what went on in that alley and she has never said a word!”

Derek said: “From what you have told me there is a good chance we can fight the charge against you. If we can prove that you acted to defend the woman, then you can have the charge reduced to a misdemeanour or dismissed. Would you be happy for me to represent you?”

Barry stared at Derek and then laughed out loud “Hey brother, is this a joke? I have no money.” He said “I can’t pay you.”

Derek flapped his hand “It is all taken care of, brother. You don’t have to pay.”

Barry thought his eyes were going to pop out of his head. What on earth was going on? But of course, he gave his permission for Derek to represent him. What did he have to lose? Perhaps the prayers he had said lying in his bunk in the prison had been answered and all was going to be okay after all.

Chapter 27

Atlanta

A private investigator follows up...

Kathy Becker, was Derek Lynes favourite private investigator. Kathy had worked for him for 6 years now and had a reputation for being able to ferret out the truth. She never stopped until she had results to take back.

Kathy was intrigued by the latest case that she had been handed. It seemed that there may have been several cover-ups to protect a Chinese student named Song. Kathy had not been able to afford to go full-time to university. She had worked several low paid jobs to put herself through college, attending night classes and summer schools. She wondered why someone whose parents were paying for them to attend a private university would run away and end up working illegally in Big Daddy's Burger Bar in South Atlanta. This was going to be very interesting.

Kathy knew the area where Big Daddy's was situated. It was run-down and dangerous. She knew that the District Attorney was aggressively prosecuting crimes in the area, in an attempt to turn it around and make it more desirable. Pulling into the street, the first thing she noticed was that Big Daddy's looked clean and had new paint. It was wedged between a Barbers shop and "Sure Bail Bonds". Across the street was a convenience store with a small parking lot. Kathy looked around to check if there was CCTV in the area. It was very possible the convenience store had CCTV or the Bail Bonds. She walked along the street and talking a right went into the alley that ran along the back of the barbers, burger bar and bail bonds. It was narrow with dumpsters along the back-side and smelled of trash and drains.

A man was standing in the alley smoking. Kathy guessed he worked at the barbers. He eyed her up and down as she walked into the alley. Kathy said she was a PI looking into the attack in the alley the month before.

"I think you got here a bit late, lady" said the man "the fight was a couple of weeks ago and big Barry is in prison. Senser must have got a pay-out as they have just had the burger bar refurbed. Major overall, new kitchen and furniture, the lot."

Kathy nodded as if she knew that and said, "I know Barry Watkins is in prison and Eric Senser has just got out of hospital, but wasn't there a young Chinese woman working at the burger bar at the time of the attack?"

The man smirked "you bet there was. She was a looker. She used to walk past every day, and I would see her and try to make eye contact. Old Eric soon moved her out from the kitchens into serving customers. People would come in for a hair cut talking about her. I think she was only there about a month at the most – she left after the attack. But everyone knew her."

"Did she talk to you?" Kathy got out her phone.

"Not much. I wish" he laughed out loud

"Did people call her Song?" asked Kathy.

The man nodded, "yes that was her name. Why are you interested in her?"

"I guess you were not in the alley when the fight took place. And don't know what the fight was about?"

The man was staring now "jeez" he said "I can really believe it was about Song. Watkins started to hang around when she was there." He shook his head.

"Would you be willing to make a statement to say you saw her in the burger bar serving customers?" Kathy said.

"Where did you say you were from lady?" he said wary now.

"Don't worry I don't work for the Immigration Authorities" Kathy said "this is only about the fight."

The man seemed very wary, and Kathy knew it would be difficult to get him to agree. He stubbed out his cigarette and left without agreeing.

Kathy had recorded him on her phone but knew this was not good evidence. She would return again and try to get him to talk on the record.

She knew she had to get pictures of Song going into and leaving the burger bar to help build the case.

Kathy went next to the Bail Bonds. After she had introduced herself as a PI she was allowed into the premises where Nadine, the supervisor, took her into the office. Kathy explained what she was investigating and asked if they had CCTV she could view.

Nadine was very reluctant "We were not asked for our CCTV at the time of the attack" she said "we do not have CCTV that shows the alley where the attack took place. We have CCTV of the inside of our premises and of our own front door. Even if we showed it to you, I don't believe it would help."

Kathy left and went across the street to the convenience store. Mr Lim, the owner, was happy to speak to her. He was an older man, slightly built with a worried expression on his face. He told her that as far as he knew the trial had taken place regarding the attack at the rear of the burger bar. So in his view all that was finished. He hoped that there would be no more violence.

"What is the world coming to when you can't even take the trash out at the end of the day without being jumped and beaten. He didn't even have any money on him. He must have got a payout though. They have just spent thousands on the burger bar, I hope they now have CCTV in the alley."

Kathy nodded to show she understood.

Kathy asked if he remembered Song who worked in the burger bar. He smiled "of course, I do" and he looked at her closely "you know Song?"

"I do know her and she is now in Los Angeles." She said and then asked if he had remembered seeing Song working in the burger bar.

"Yes, she worked there for a short time. She was a classy lady. I said she should find a nice Chinese restaurant in downtown Atlanta, somewhere classy, but she said she was happy at the burger bar."

It seemed she would call in his store on her way to her shifts at the burger bar and they had got chatting.

Mr Lim was a believer in CCTV. Kathy could see the cameras in the shop. She then asked if he had CCTV of the day of the attack.

Mr Lim did have CCTV, but he indicated that this would only show the front of the burger bar and not the alley. Kathy asked if she could see the CCTV. He was a bit reluctant but finally agreed, telling her to come back later when he had a chance to look through his CCTV. He usually kept it for 90 days so there should be footage dating back to the day of the attack. Kathy had suspected there may have been several robberies at the shop, so he kept CCTV on all the time, and kept the footage.

When she returned, Kathy saw Song for the first time. Mr Lim had queued up the CCTV from the day of the attack. On the CCTV it was late afternoon and still light. The CCTV showed the front of the shop and the parking lot with the street beyond. Smaller and very grainy across the road was the row of shops including the burger bar.

Looking at the film he showed her, Kathy saw a woman with long black hair came out of the convenience store. At first, she had her back to the camera and then she turned to look back at the store and smiled and waved to someone she knew.

“Freeze that” she said “Can we take a pic of that frame?”

Mr Lim nodded and also, he enlarged the frame so they could see a grainy larger view of her face. Even on the CCTV Kathy could see that Song was a beautiful young woman. The tape continued and Song walked through the parking lot, crossed the road and although it was more difficult to see, they could see footage of her going into the burger bar. Mr Lim made pictures from the CCTV for Kathy of her walk to the burger bar and her entering the burger bar.

Kathy was very pleased with this evidence, but it didn’t prove she worked there. However, it showed she was there on the day of the attack even if it was much earlier in the evening.

As soon as she got back into her car, Kathy sent over the pics to Derek who rang immediately. “This is Song?” he said.

“Yes and we have her going into the burger bar on the day of the attack. We now need someone to confirm that they saw her working there and that is going to be difficult. I am going to show these pictures to a man I met today who works in the Barbers shop to try to get him to talk.”

Derek agreed. "There were a couple of witnesses who saw Senser leave the burger bar and Watkins follow who are named in the police report, but I can't see they were ever interviewed. It is also possible they gave false names. I'll send the names over to you. Thanks again for the pictures - they are very valuable."

Kathy thanked him and crossing the road went into the barbers shop. The man she spoke to earlier was alone in the shop and cutting a customer's hair. Kathy took a seat and waited for him to finish.

He came over when the customer left. "I told you I don't have anything to say" he said

Kathy reached into her purse and showed him the pictures of Song. "This is the Chinese woman, isn't it?"

He quickly looked at the pictures "Yes that is her. But why are you bringing this up now? She is long gone. Can't you let it drop."

"Is it fair that Watkins will be sentenced for fighting and possibly go to prison for protecting this woman from being raped?" She asked "If no-one speaks up we can't help him."

The man became very agitated. "I don't know nothing about any rape." He said

"Senser liked the young girls, didn't he?" Kathy continued, "he had a really bad rep for that. Sonya always kept her mouth shut and the girls couldn't complain as they didn't even have papers to be in the US. Come on, you know this is true."

"Senser is a low life bastard" he said "but I don't know what happened that night. I had left and closed my shop earlier. That is the truth."

"Okay I know you were not a witness to what happened in the alley. Would you be willing to say you saw Song working in the burger bar. That you had been in there for food and she served you?"

The man was very agitated "If I do as you say I will sell Senser to the Immigration Authorities. Are you from Immigration?"

Kathy assured him she wasn't, she was just interested in the fight in the alley and the cause of the fight.

"Okay, okay" he said "I will sign something. I don't use wetbacks in here. Senser is scum of this earth. Where do I sign?"

His name was Eric Brand and Kathy got out a form which she filled in for Eric, saying he had seen Song working in the burger bar. He signed and dated it. Kathy immediately sent it to Derek.

Getting in her car she drove home. Her first thought on arriving home was to pour herself a glass of pinot noir and to ring her mom for a quick chat

"Sometimes my job just makes me think how lucky I am" she said "to live in this beautiful condo and to be able to enjoy a glass of pinot noir. Mom, if you only knew what some women go through it would break your heart. Especially women who are in this country without papers."

Kathy's mom was not so empathetic and felt these people should not be in the US in the first place and should return to their own country. They chatted for a while and then Kathy hung up and popped a lasagne in the oven for her meal. Tomorrow would be another day; she had made good progress today.

Chapter 28

Jinni

Family comes first...

The week after Somchai went on a bender and ended up in hospital passed quickly. I had become an expert at putting a brave face on in the salon. No-one would suspect anything was wrong. The salon was still not full, but I felt that people may be starting to come back. I even spoke to my financial adviser about the planned expansion to the new salon in the regeneration area.

Somchai stayed in hospital that week on a detox. I knew the staff were experts and would be able to monitor him, but I also knew it was horrendous for him. He had told Barb that he had experienced anxiety, shaking and rapid heartbeat that suggested Delerium Tremens (DTs) on the Monday after his bender. He had also been hallucinating and imagining he was back in Thailand. The staff had been able to help with medication. Barb said he vowed never to touch a drop of alcohol again.

After he had been allowed home, I took an uber to Barb's house in the Southern Hills to visit with him. As the uber rounded the winding roads leading up to the house, I could see the vista of the City below and the beautiful homes lining the road peeking out from the trees. Barb's house was stunning. It had the most spectacular views of the city. The pool shimmered in the fading evening light. It was the American dream come to life.

Barb came to the door wearing a tight-fitting dress, with her hair hanging loose. She seemed happy as she ushered me into the hallway. Somchai came out to greet me. He seemed fragile and had aged about 20 years in my view.

"Come through to the kitchen. Somchai has been making a green curry. I know it is your favourite. No alcohol tonight – or ever." She said brightly.

I sat up to the island unit and sipped a lemonade they gave me. Somchai was a fabulous cook and I know cooking relaxed him. Barb joined me on the bar stools.

"He will never drink again" Barb said and added, smiling. "Not now he is back home."

We ate the curry, which was delicious. Somchai then told me he was worried about his "stuff" as he called it. It turned out he had a massive row with Randi and she had thrown him out of the apartment. He had gone off in a temper and starting drinking. This had gone on for a couple of days until he had shown up at Barb's on Sunday. He had not heard a word from Randi all the time he was in hospital. He had tried ringing and texting but no answer. He had gone to the apartment yesterday and found the locks had been changed.

"She can't do that" he whined "my name is on the rental agreement. I have to have my stuff."

Oh goodness me. Another mess!! If his name was on the rental agreement his credit would be ruined if Barb did not pay the rent. Also, he had nothing, only the clothes he was stood up in. I knew he had no savings either. How could a man let himself get into this sort of mess, where he was entirely dependent on women?

I also wondered what had happened to his job at the chicken processing plant. He must have only worked there a few days when he went on the bender and ended up in hospital. I presumed he must have lost that job now, and he had his hours cut at his other job. He was in a mess.

Of course, I agreed to help him. So it was the next evening after I closed the salon I went to the Black Cat bar. There are dives and then there is the Black Cat bar, the biggest dive of them all. The smell hit me as I opened the door and walked in. An aged white man with skin like leather and a huge belly was sitting on a bar stool near the door. "Hey babe" he slurred "there is a free seat here". He indicated the stool next to him. He leered at me. I did my best to ignore him. "Hey are you Chinese? I love Asian babes." I turned and looked at him "Get lost creep" I said. This was worse than I could have imagined. Randi was behind the bar and came over when she heard the conversation. "Leave her alone Earl." She said "do you want another?" she indicated his empty glass. He was laughing "I like a woman with spirit." he said but pushed his glass forward for another drink.

Randi indicated that I go to the other end of the bar to talk to her. I went quickly and found a stool. Thankfully the drunks down this end of the bar seemed to ignore me. One was a woman with large floppy breasts, drinking what looked like Jack on the rocks. She turned her back on me as she chatted to the man next to her.

I told Randi that Somchai had been in hospital with alcohol poisoning and had had a detox.

Randi leaned over the bar "No fucking wonder he had alcohol poisoning" she said "he drinks like a fish. Okay he may have cut back a little bit when we were first together, but that didn't last long. He lied about the drinking. He used to buy vodka and decant it into a coke can and tell me he was drinking coke."

"Somchai is an alcoholic, Randi. But he loved you and rented an apartment with you. He says you won't speak to him."

Randi bristled at this, but left for a moment to pour another drink for someone down the bar. She returned and said "I have sent countless messages. All of which he has ignored. Plus, he has been lying to me for weeks, Jinni. He hasn't paid his part of the rent money. I guess that went on booze. I have been paying all the rent and I don't earn much. We have been really struggling and he just shut me out. Last Friday, I lost it with him"

I didn't doubt for even a moment that any of this was not true.

"Do you want to meet with him?" I asked

"Oh fuck off Jinni" she said "I know he is back with his rich wife. She is a complete idiot who will always have him back. He will love it playing the big man living in the Southern Hills again. He left her because she didn't like sex, but after a few months living the wrong side of the tracks I guess he can find a way to get over that." I had never heard such bitterness.

"Okay, Randi, are you going to take over the rental then? Can we arrange a time for me to collect his things if you don't want to see him?"

Randi looked at me as if I was completely stupid "And how am I going to qualify to take over the rental of the apartment on what I earn? I will have to move out. We can give notice to the landlord but tell Somchai that I am not paying the final month's rent. He can do that.

You can come over and get his things. He doesn't have much, and I want it gone."

I explained that I would be busy in the salon during the week and I knew she worked in the bar in the evening. Could I come over on Sunday morning or Saturday when I had closed the salon at 4 pm? We agreed I could over on Sunday.

One of the issues at this time was that Lila was working as a receptionist at the Purple Orchid. I managed to avoid any personal conversation with her on Friday, but on Saturday she brought up the situation with Somchai and Randi. I wished I had never employed her, I do not want to discuss this with her. It is a private family matter and also, I feel Randi has acted badly. Her language is offensive and Somchai's drinking worsened going to the bar with her every evening. Surely Lila could see from the way I reacted that I did not want to discuss the situation? But she kept getting closer and not respecting the social distance between us. I can't stand overbearing, interfering women.

On Sunday I got a lift over to the apartment with my friend Noi. Somchai had confirmed that the landlord had rung him to agree that they were giving notice. According to Somchai, he was off sick but had health insurance and sick pay. I really doubted this, but I saw that he had agreed to pay the final month's rent. As we pulled up to the apartment, I was struck again on how poor the neighbourhood was. The number of homeless sleeping in their cars under the metro arches seemed to have grown in size and there was graffiti everywhere. Randi was in the apartment and let us in. She pointed to three garbage bags in the living room. "That's his stuff" she said. I knew there was more. I looked at the 42" TV. "Somchai tells me he bought the TV" I said "We are going to take that too." Randi folded her arms and looked very combative. "I don't think so" she said. At that moment, the door opened and a white man came in. He was a very big man, and looked intimidating. "Everything okay, Randi" he said. "Yes, they were just leaving" she said. I took the coward's way out and Noi and I left with the trash bags only.

Later when we delivered them to Barb's house, Barb was none too happy. "This is it" she said rummaging through the bags and throwing things out. "What happened to his clothes? This looks like the clothes a homeless man would wear. Yuck"

Somchai hovered looking anxious “Its okay Barb” he said “I can buy more.”

We were all dreading when she would ask where the TV was. Noi and I quickly made our excuses and left. We went to a Thai restaurant in the Southern Hills and sat silently for a while contemplating the day. My biggest fear was that Somchai would not stay sober and he would lapse back into the drinking again. I had to keep going and fight these fears Whatever, I would always be there for my brother……

Chapter 29

Lila

Adrienne and Lila's sister Randi...

Lila was busy with work and the Brothers of Swing and had put her sister, Randi, and her troubles out of her mind. The Brothers and the jazz band were rehearsing together the swing set in advance of the convention. Lila got an invite to the event as one of their "roadies". Alex's mother was also there - Adrienne. Alex is the pianist with the orchestra and is very talented.

The Brothers and the jazz band playing at a break went down well with the people at the convention. The Brothers had put up a banner on the stage so that people could see their names. They had been asked if the local radio station could record their act. This was then played on the radio, the following week during a late-night show.

After the convention, the Brothers and the jazz band were asked to play at a bigger convention in New Orleans. This was really impressive and it seemed having a live backup band was really helping the Brothers to expand their range.

One evening Ronnie came home after a rehearsal with the Jazz Band and dropped a bombshell. He told Lila that Alex wanted her mother to get up on stage and sing a song with the orchestra. "Apparently she loves to sing jazz and soul classics" Ronnie said.

"Hold on a minute" Lila said, "isn't she that English lady with the funny accent? It is hard to understand what she says."

"Yes, that is her but she is going to sing for us at rehearsal next week. Alex was very insistent, and Bruce is very anxious to keep her happy as she is brilliant on the piano."

Lila was very sceptical about this and felt she had to see this for herself. Adrienne was a short skinny woman with red hair. She did not give the impression that she would be able to sing – in fact, to an American audience her voice was very annoying. She did not have an upper class English accent. It was very definitely lower class and it was very pronounced plus it was difficult to understand her.

However, she was going to sing at the rehearsal and Lila was curious to hear her. Adrienne was already there when Ronnie and Lila arrived. She was wearing a dress that looked like a pair of drapes to Lila. She was a very small, plain woman. After a few minutes, Adrienne got up on the stage. She spoke to Bruce, who instructed the jazz band. She then sang “Misty,” the old Ella Fitzgerald standard, accompanied by the orchestra.

It should have been horrible; however, everyone had to admit she was good.

Not just good, but brilliant.

How could such a little white woman have a voice like that? It was magic.

When she finished, the Brothers got up on stage to congratulate her.

Lila stood watching in the wings felt a pang of jealousy. She didn’t like the way Ronnie looked at Adrienne. Lila told herself she was being stupid.

“I can’t sing or play an instrument so perhaps that was what was wrong. Adrienne would make a good addition to their act. It would be another way to expand their range”.

At this same time Lila’s sister Randi had been in touch again. It seemed that there was no chance of Somchai coming back. He was now living with Barb again in her big house. She was looking after him, and Randi was totally excluded. Randi called round to see Lila one evening when the Brothers were rehearsing and she was in the house on her own.

“I can’t pay the rent on my own now Somchai has left” she confided nervously. “I have given notice on the apartment and one of the customers at the Black Cat bar is looking for a roommate so I am going to move in with her.”

It seemed sad that a woman her age was looking for a roommate. Out loud Lila said:

“When will you move and where to?”

"The flat is in Gent Town on Bradley Place." She said "I'm moving at the end of the month. I've paid up to the end of the month. I fucking hate men."

"Stay away from men, Randi. This time – learn your lesson and just stay away. You are better off without an asshole like Somchai. He drank and was a womaniser."

Randi changed from nervous to angry

"Don't you dare lecture me, maybe your life is not so perfect after all. How do you know Ronnie isn't out fooling around? He is always out at rehearsals. How do you know that is where he really is?"

Now they were both furious

"Ronnie would never fool around on me."

Nothing more was said but it was obvious Lila wanted Randi to leave. In Lila's view she would never change...

Chapter 30

The beginning of April at The Purple Orchid

March had not been the best month for the Purple Orchid. There were still empty seats even at busy times. Jinni had worked hard on social media campaigns where she offered discount prices. As the month drew to a close it seemed to be getting better. Maybe people, who have notoriously short memories, had started to forget about the visit by the Immigration Authorities.

Jinni was always there making sure that everything ran smoothly and also servicing her own customers.

As the weeks passed she started to put Song out of her head. She had so much to concentrate on with her existing business and the new premises she was going to lease in the regeneration area. Thoughts close to home also filled her mind, with Somchai and his recent problems with excessive drinking.

Ellie was still checking her social media to see if any of the celebrities she had sent DMs to in Atlanta about Song had responded. However, as the weeks went past this seemed less and less likely. Ellie began to also put Song and Barry Watkins out of her mind. It was unfair but there seemed little she could do about it, she had to move on.

Lila was on reception, and she was only interested, it seemed, in promoting the Brothers of Swing. Something so far she had been very good at, even though she was now experiencing some jealousy. She had not worked at the salon in the fall when Song was there and so she did not even know who Song was.

Meanwhile in Los Angeles....

Highbridge College, Los Angeles

Office of the International Dean

Kirsty Wareham, International Dean at Highbridge College opened up her laptop and signed in to Zoom. She was due to speak to Song's father, Professor Xingping Zhang. Professor Xingping Zhang was Dean of International Students at his university in Ghangzhou, China. After a few seconds Professor Xingping Zhang's face appeared on the screen, and after initial pleasantries, they began a conversation.

"I am happy to say that we have signed up 25 potential students to come over next term. My assistant will forward their files for you to review, but I am sure you will find all is in order."

Kirsty smiled "That is brilliant news. I will look out for the files and we can process them quickly."

Professor Xingping Zhang was smiling widely and looking direct at the camera.

"As you know, we must have assurance that attendance will be required, for these students."

Kirsty also looked directly at the camera, but her expression and tone was that of someone who was very sincere and serious

"As you know, we have had a total overhaul of our regulations since the incident last term. Each international student now has their own personal tutor. The student must have a face-to-face meeting with the tutor every week now. Registers are taken at the beginning of every class. Any student who misses class more than once and/or does not meet with their tutor will be followed up on. We have really tightened up on our regulations and believe me there will be no unexplained absences in future."

Professor Xingping smiled to show he was happy with her comments. He then said in a more conversational tone

"How is Song settling in this time?"

"She is settling in very well. She has been meeting with her personal tutor and she has 100% attendance."

"That is very pleasing news, we will make an academic of her yet."

After the Zoom session ended, Kirsty let out a sigh of relief. Kirsty had let the member of staff go who had not monitored Song last term and led to the embarrassment of her disappearance for months! When Professor Xingping had queried where his daughter was, and the mess had come to light she had been incandescent with rage. It was all sorted now though. Song was back in class. The college had been able to sign the forms saying that her absence was due to sickness, and this seemed to keep the Immigration Authorities happy. They could finally move on, and there were more students coming in the pipeline. She dreaded to think what would have happened to her if the university had lost the business with China. She was well aware of the massive loans that the university had to pay for the expansion projects in recent years. They needed all the students they could get. She knew if the Chinese students kept coming, her job was safe.

Professor Xingping, sitting in his office in China, also let out a sigh of relief. Business with the USA was resumed, and Song was back in class. He could now finally move on.

And finally April begins in

Atlanta, Georgia

So, it seemed that Song was back in College and settling in. The Immigration Authorities had accepted the forms stating that her absence related to an illness. Song's presence in the Purple Orchid was being forgotten and people were moving on... If only they could have seen beyond the close confines of their own worlds to what was happening in Atlanta. Song certainly had not been forgotten. It would not be long before her name was on everyone's lips. But what would that mean for Highbridge College? And for the Purple Orchid?

Chapter 31

Atlanta

Kathy interviews witnesses...

Kathy Becker, the Private Investigator, had established that Song was in the area and had CCTV pictures. Her next task was to talk to people who had come forward to say they were in the Burger Bar on the night of the attack. She had contact details for two people Barry had provided to Derek. There were also two people named in the police report, who as far as she could see, had never been contacted for their stories.

Kathy first contacted the two people Barry had provided. It turned out Tomas was Barry's roommate and she arranged to go over to visit with him the following day. It was more difficult to get in touch with Gayle, who was the other person but she kept trying. Meanwhile she spent the day trying to track down the contact details for the two people in the police report. She used public records to help her with her search. Nevertheless, it was slow and painstaking. After a few hours she had contact details for one of the people and she attempted to make contact. This person, Maria, agreed to talk to her also on the following day. She carried on trying to find the other person.

The next day she drove over to the apartment block where Barry had lived with Tomas as his roommate. It was in an area not far from the Burger Bar. Although it faced a green area with some trees, the apartment block had seen better days and looked tired and rundown. It looked like it had been built in the 1960s. Each apartment had a large window overlooking a parking lot. The stairs were around the back of the block and were outside. There were outside walkways to reach each apartment and Barry's apartment was on the third floor. Kathy walked up the steps and arrived at the door slightly breathless.

Tomas was a very small, thin man in his early thirties. He invited Kathy in and the first thing she noticed was how tiny the apartment was. The door opened directly into the kitchen, which was only an efficiency, and this was open to the living space. Kathy noticed a woman sitting on the sofa in the living area. Tomas introduced her as Leticia his new roommate. "I had to get a new roommate with Barry gone for so long." He said.

Kathy had told him briefly that she was a private investigator looking into the attack when she spoke to him the day before. She now went into more detail, and brought out the picture of Song.

Tomas whistled looking at the picture

"That is Song. There are about 15 Chinese living next door. It's a two bed place and how they fit in is anybody's guess. We think they take the bed in shifts. She lived there and worked at Big Daddy's."

He took out his phone and showed Kathy a picture of what looked like a party. Barry was in the picture as was Tomas and they were surrounded by Chinese women, one of whom she recognised as Song. It seemed Song was sitting on Barry's knee. She had a drink in her hand and was smiling.

"Barry was crazy about her he would have done anything for her."

"Were you in Big Daddy's on the night of the attack?"

Tomas had to admit he wasn't there so could not come forward as a witness. He went on to say that he knew about Senser's rep with women.

"He liked them young and without papers. Has Song now been deported?"

"No, she has left Atlanta but is still in the USA so far as we know"

Kathy asked if he would be willing to go on the record saying that Song lived next door to him and that he had been in the Burger Bar and seen her working there. Tomas agreed and they filled out the form which he signed. Kathy then asked if he would send her a copy of the picture on his phone, which he did. She thanked him for his help and told him she would keep him informed.

Kathy was pleased with how this meeting went and as she left she asked Tomas which was the apartment the Chinese lived in. He indicated to the right of his.

Turning right Kathy knocked on the door. Nothing happened, so she knocked again. The door was opened by a young Chinese woman.

Kathy asked if she could ask her a few questions. The woman looked terrified and said "no speak English". She tried to shut the door but Kathy put her foot in the door. The woman then became agitated speaking loudly in a language Kathy didn't understand.

A Chinese man then came to the door and pushing the woman aside screamed:

"Go away"

When she did not, he opened the door and pushed Kathy so hard she fell backwards on to the floor. He then slammed the door shut.

At the sound of the commotion other doors started to open and people looked around the doors to see what was going on. No-one came to Kathy's aid and when she banged on the door again no-one opened it. Finally, she had to admit defeat and left.

Arriving back at her car she quickly sent the picture to Derek, the attorney and then she drove to meet her second contact, Maria.

Maria had agreed to meet her in a coffee bar near to Big Daddy's. The coffee shop seemed clean but was not very busy. A woman she assumed was Maria was sitting nursing a cup of coffee by the window. She smiled and waved when Kathy arrived. Maria was an older lady in her 50's who was massively overweight. Kathy asked if she would like another coffee. Maria indicated she would and a donut.

When Kathy had made the order, she came to sit opposite Maria. She explained why she wanted to speak to her, saying that she had got her name from the police report from the night of the attack.

Maria confirmed she had been there on the night of the attack, but she had not been contacted by anyone for her version of what happened, although the police had taken her details. She had been to see a movie and had called for a burger on her way home. She often went to Big Daddy's. The burgers were good and cheap. Kathy showed her the picture of Song from the CCTV and asked if this person was in the burger bar. Maria studied the picture. "Yes, I ordered my burger and fries and went to sit down and she brought my order over. I was surprised she could speak English. Eric always employs foreigners, but usually Mexicans, she was different. Where is she from now?"

"China"

"She's a long way from home." Said Maria "What's she doing here? We need to stop this immigration now! This country is overrun with foreigners."

Kathy let her have her rant and then she asked if she had seen Song going out of the burger bar into the alley. If she had, Maria was not going to admit to it. After a few minutes Kathy asked if she would be willing to sign a form to say that Song had waited on her in the Burger Bar on the night of the attack. She seemed very hesitant about this.

"Will she be deported?"

"If we can prove she was working in the Burger Bar when she did not have papers."

Finally, Maria agreed to sign the form to say she had seen Song there and Song had waited on her. There was precious little concern for Barry Watkins who was in prison. In fact, she did not once ask about him.

Kathy thought about this for the rest of the day. That evening, her cell pinged with a message from Tomas. "Chinese gone" it said. Kathy immediately rang to find out that after her visit the Chinese had apparently packed up and left in a hurry. She wondered if they thought she was an Immigration official.

What Tomas did not tell Kathy though was after her visit, Leticia had stubbed out her cigarette and getting up to leave had said "Who employed that PI?" Tomas shook his head, and said it was beyond him.

"Well someone has put her up to it. A total stranger helping Barry, and you, his best friend, have done fuck all."

This stung as Tomas knew she was right, he had done nothing to help Barry. He decided he would help. He also saw his chance for 5 minutes of fame on social media. He took the picture of Song at the party and edited and trimmed it to cut other people out and so that it showed only Song. She looked beautiful and would he felt attract attention. He then posted it on all his social media channels with this caption.

DO YOU KNOW THIS CHINESE WOMAN?

Innocent black man to stand trial accused of aggravated assault and battery after trying to save this Chinese woman from rape in S Atlanta. She has left Atlanta and will not provide a defence for this brave brother. She is in USA illegally. Please share so we can find this woman."

Tomas was always posting on social media so had many contacts. However, there was something about this picture and message that just caught people's attention. Who was this beautiful woman? What happened? Why was someone in prison? It was a mystery people wanted to know more about. Within an hour of posting there were over 200 comments and 400 shares. There were sightings across the country including Alaska and Hawaii, and people wanted to know more about what had happened. No-one could accuse Tomas of not helping now.

Chapter 32

Ellie

FREE BARRY WATKINS!

Although this was now repetitious, Ellie had decided to put Song and the attack in the Burger Bar out of her mind. Her pregnancy seemed to be progressing normally and she was busy at work. She was rather annoyed that she had received no replies to her DMs to celebrities She thought to herself "I really do feel celebrities should answer their DMs. They are messages from their fans and where are these people without their fans?" But then she decided it was not her call.

On Saturday she went to the Purple Orchid for her manicure. Sitting at the next station was a black lady who she had seen at the salon previously but did not know very well. She was called Sheri. She was asking the manicurist questions.

"Didn't there used to be a Chinese girl work here? Real cute?"

The manicurist continued filing her nails

"I have only been here a couple of months so I wouldn't know, but it is possible as Jinni is from Thailand."

Sheri wasn't to be put off

"Wasn't this place raided by the Immigration Services in January? It was a bit of a scandal at the time."

The manicurist thought for a moment

"It was but they certainly didn't find anything. Why are you asking?"

Sheri asked the manicurist to stop for a moment and then showed her something on her phone. "My friend Lissy sent me this. She works in Atlanta as an actress."

The manicurist was staring at the phone with her eyes popping out of her head.

Ellie's curiosity go the better of her and she couldn't help but intervene.

"Sorry to eavesdrop on your conversation but there was a Chinese girl used to work here in the fall. Is this a picture of her?"

Sheri turned to look at Ellie

"I thought so."

She showed Ellie her phone. It was a post on Instagram showing a picture of Song and saying

DO YOU KNOW THIS CHINESE WOMAN?

Innocent black man to send trial for aggravated assault and battery after trying to save this Chinese woman from rape in S Atlanta. She has left Atlanta and will not provide a defence for this brave brother. She is in USA illegally. Please share so we can find this woman."

It seemed to have been forwarded from someone called Tomas.

Jinni was at the other end of the salon giving a customer a pedicure and out of hearing distance.

After studying the post Ellie spoke

"That sounds like a bad situation. But that wasn't the Chinese woman who worked here. I think that woman left to go back to China. I wouldn't worry Jinni about it. The Chinese woman upped and went on short notice and left Jinni in a bad place. It is best to let sleeping dogs lie."

Sheri eyed Ellie up and down

"Are you English?"

Ellie indicated she was.

"I thought so. Here in the States we are too soft on illegal immigrants like this Chinese woman. Why the hell has she not been deported? Why are places employing people like her when there are Americans looking for jobs? A man is in prison now it says."

She could see Ellie looked horrified, so she nodded to acknowledge what she had said.

"Okay I will not say anything in the salon. I am sure this woman has nothing to do with the Purple Orchid. But it is time that somebody stood up and spoke out to get these people deported."

Nothing else was said and Ellie left the salon after her appointment and went home. Sheri was right though; somebody should speak up. A man was in prison and Song (apparently) was back in university after violating all the immigration regulations.

In the fall Ellie had made several YouTube videos speaking about issues she felt strongly about. These included issues such as fat shaming, Prince Harry and Meghan Markle leaving the UK to live in the USA. In particular, the video about Prince Harry and Meghan Markle had attracted controversy and this had led to arguments with people who accused Ellie of racism.

Kevin had been furious. He felt that behaviour like this online was not becoming for someone who taught at a university. In fact, he felt that Ellie did not get selected for an interview for some teaching because of this behaviour. As a result, Ellie had vowed not to make any more YouTube videos.

Yet she couldn't get the man in prison out of my head. The whole thing was so unfair. He was part of a cover-up for a young girl who had run away from college. It seemed if he was found guilty he could get ten years in prison for someone who had not spoken one word in his defence. Too busy covering her own ass. The more she thought about it the more angry she got.

Her thought process then became: "If I made a YouTube video it would be relatively anonymous in this City, yet it might prompt people to do something to help Barry Watkins. Surely it would do more good than harm?" She talked to myself like this all day.

By that evening when Kevin had left to go to the gym Ellie had talked herself into doing another video. First, she went through the information she had put together before ringing the Public Defender. Doing this exercise she was stunned by how little information there was. It seemed the bare minimum had been done. If she had been angry before it was nothing on how she felt now. It had been dismissed as an example of casual violence.

The District Attorney was working to stamp out instances of casual violence was the message and Barry Watkins was being made an example of.

In addition it seemed to Ellie that the Chinese woman was being allowed to get away with this without any consequence. Of course, this was only because her father was an influential man who could afford an expensive lawyer. Ellie thought to herself "It was wrong, wrong, wrong in my book!! I had to speak up for what I believed."

She set herself up to film and then started the filming process by stating the facts of the case as it had been reported. She then said that Barry Watkins was defending a Chinese woman. Then she showed Song's picture which she had tracked down on the internet after her earlier conversation at the Purple Orchid. She was worried about being sued so did not say her name. For this reason, she implied that Song may have been working at the burger bar illegally and for this reason her presence was covered up. It was believed that Song had fled the city but it seemed had not been deported.

Turning to the camera Ellie then made an earnest plea

"We must find this woman and ask her to speak up for Barry Watkins. He was defending her when he attacked Senser in the alley. He should not be standing trial for this crime."

She then put up a banner with these words on it:

FREE BARRY WATKINS

There were over 100 views to the YouTube video in the first day. It may not seem much in the grand scheme of things but it was a start. It seemed suddenly people were beginning to care about Barry Watkins. People wrote comments saying that the Chinese woman had to be found and asked to give her side of the story. Somebody said they had seen her in Seattle and somebody else said they had seen her in Tuscon and so on.

To be fair to Ellie when she posted this video, she never thought for one minute that this might affect Jinni and her business the Purple Orchid. This might sound naïve, but all she cared about was getting justice for a man who had been wronged. Of course, she knew Song had worked illegally at the Purple Orchid, but she conveniently forgot that as she tried to help. In fact her biggest concern was keeping the YouTube video a secret from Kevin, who she knew would be unhappy with her for sharing her opinions on the internet.

Chapter 33
Atlanta
Harry Zine threatens...

Harry Zine sat in his office with the social media post about Song blown up on the screen of his computer. He had had an assistant trace it back to its original source and to count the number of shares. There was also an analysis of where the post had appeared – Facebook, Instagram, X, etc.

At the time of the trial no one had been very interested in a sleazy burger bar in South Atlanta and a fight in an alley. It had all been so very easy to cover up. Harry had to get to the bottom of the sudden interest.

The original source was a "Tomas J". This turned out to be the former roommate of Barry Watkins. Why had he suddenly done this? He had made no attempt to come forward at the time of the arraignment.

Harry had asked his Private Investigator Robert, to use his contacts at the prison to find out if Barry Watkins had had visitors. It turned out he had been visited by Derek Lynes and they had discussed the trial. Now that was interesting. Derek was an attorney who Harry was sure Barry Watkins could not afford. He usually represented celebrities and millionaires. Who had put him up to visiting Barry Watkins?

Harry sat deep in thought. The more he thought the less it made sense. He didn't know Derek very well, but he knew Katy Jones, another attorney in the same firm. He decided to ring her and ask her to find out if he was representing Barry Watkins.

What he found out shocked him. It turned out a client of Derek's was footing the bill. This person had insisted on anonymity so no one knew who it was. However, it went without saying that it was a very rich person. Why on earth should that person pay to try to defend Barry at his trial – it didn't make sense. How could a multi-millionaire know a low life like Barry? What if this person was a celebrity and they were doing it to "up" their profile and show how a brother had been treated unfairly? How would this make Harry and his firm look if the cover-up around Song came out? He had to act quickly.

Harry called his PI Robert into the room. He instructed him to visit Tomas, Barry's roommate. He should tell him that the woman in the picture he had posted on social media had not given her permission. The woman has a reasonable expectation of privacy. If he does not remove the picture and the comments, then she will bring a lawsuit against him. The picture should be taken down and a statement made retracting the comments. This should be done immediately. This might be enough to get Tomas to retract the posts. If not, he would up the pressure.

There was a knock on the door. It was one of his assistants. "I have something to show you." She said "do you have a minute?"

Harry told her to come in and she set her laptop down on his desk. She pressed play on the video. It was a YouTube video "FREE BARRY WATKINS" narrated by a large blonde lady with enormous breasts barely contained by a white lowcut top from which they were threatening to escape. She had an annoying accent. British, he thought. He hated the British accent. She sounded so patronising. Who the hell was she? Why would she care about Barry Watkins? Perhaps she liked big black men, he thought smirking. He could just imagine her poncy little English husband. He probably couldn't satisfy her! He could just imagine her rolling around naked with big Barry and crying out in that ridiculous accent. He smirked. But as he listened to the video, he realised with horror the problem was that she seemed to know what had really happened in the alley behind the burger bar. He felt sweaty under his arms and his shirt threatened to stick to him despite the air conditioning. This was not good.

He thanked his assistant. "Do you know who this person is?" he said.

"She is an English woman – real name Ellie Watson. Other than that, not much."

"Track her down" he said "we need to get Robert to pay her a visit and outline the consequences of making videos using pictures of people who have not given their consent."

"I'll get on it" she said and left the room.

Harry needed to speak to Professor Xingping Zhang to inform him of the developments in the case. It now seemed there may be a defence put forward by Barry Watkins. There may be the need to interview potential witnesses. This could include Song if they could track her down. He would require another retainer before he could proceed further. He did a quick calculation on the amount. He checked his watch to work out the time difference in China, and then picked the phone up to ring Professor Xingping.

Chapter 34

Los Angeles

Song is on social media...

Flipping through her social media, Candy Boval saw a face she despised. She zoomed in. Surely it couldn't be her. Song, a Chinese student who had got her fired from her position at Highbridge College, meaning that she was now unemployed and struggling to manage financially. Candy had had a full-time position at the college teaching business classes and acting as personal tutor to a number of first year students. Nobody had told her that Song was the daughter of an important professor in China. Her father was Professor Xingping Zhang who was in charge of sending Chinese students to Highbridge College.

Candy read the post carefully. It had been shared numerous times and it seemed that Song was wanted in Atlanta. The post did not name Song – but it was her without a doubt. The post had been shared numerous times. Many people had written comments claiming to have seen the Chinese woman at places all across the USA.

Candy remembered the first time she met Song. It was February 2022 and term had just started. The girl had been uncommunicative and had sat in her office staring into space. Candy had told Song that they should have regular meetings as she was her personal tutor. Candy did not know if this had registered or not. If it had there was no response. Song was also a student in her Business Studies class. Song had been there for the first couple of weeks. She would have her head down appearing to concentrate on something so that she did not have to answer questions. When Candy had specifically asked her something, Song had refused to answer. After a couple of weeks Song started to go absent. This was the case with a few of the Chinese students, and Candy and some of the other lecturers were tired of it. Candy sent an email reminding them that they should be in class. She got no response. Song also missed her personal tutor meeting. Again, no response to an email.

Song appeared after a couple of weeks to take the first test of the term. When Candy marked it, her work was appalling. She should not be in a university, Candy thought as she failed her. Why is she here? What a waste of time. She had asked Song to see her in her office. Song had turned up and sat sulking while Candy went over the test with her. Candy's memory was that Song had no interest whatsoever in the subject and also her knowledge of the English language was insufficient. She wondered in retrospect if she had been too hard on Song. Certainly, she had told her that she had to pull her socks up if she was to be successful in the course. Song was sulky and uncommunicative. That had decided Candy's feelings towards her at the time. When Song missed class Candy did not try to follow up on where she was. The truth was that Candy thought she was a waste of space who should not have been allowed into the college.

Song had attended sporadically during the spring semester, but it was during the fall semester that she had been totally absent from class and had not turned in any work for marking.

It was not until January when the proverbial hit the fan. It turned out Song had not been in touch with her family over the holidays, and her family turned out to be Professor Xingping Zhang and his wife. Suddenly everyone wanted to know where Song was and how long it was since she had been to class. Had she taken end of term tests in December? The answer was no, she hadn't done anything. Various tutors were called out, but the one who had to take the can was Candy, her personal tutor, who had not followed up when she did not come to meetings and was skipping class.

Through the grapevine she had heard that Song was back and had been reinstated. Song's father's lawyer had helped get the paperwork sorted out the Immigration Authorities. However, up to reading this post all Candy had cared about was her own situation. She was out of work and bitter due to this person.

Candy read the post about an attempted rape in Atlanta and a man in prison. Suddenly she wanted to be involved and she had information about where Song is. Also, she believed the post as she could well imagine Song running away when things got difficult. She typed into the comments "I know this woman and I know where she is. She is at a university on a student visa. Contact me for more information."

Chapter 35

Atlanta

Kathy Becker makes progress…

Kathy had spent the last few days trying to track people down from the police report of the attack at the burger bar, which had proved very difficult. One person had given a false name and that had proved to be a dead end. Kathy had tracked the other person, a person called John Dane, and was due to meet him the following day. She was now at home relaxing. She was watching Netflix with a glass of wine when her cell vibrated. Kathy did not immediately recognise the number, and was surprised to find it was Tomas, Barry Watkins, former roommate. He seemed upset.

"Is everything okay, Tomas?"

He blurted out "No, it is not. I have had a lawyer here today threatening me."

Kathy was immediately interested. "Threatening? What do you mean?"

Tomas explained about the social media post using Song's picture.

"Send it to me." Kathy said. He did and a few seconds later she was looking at the post.

"He said that the woman had not given her permission for her picture to be used. She would bring a lawsuit against me if I don't take it down. He said it would cost me everything."

"Don't panic, Tomas". Kathy said "Take it down but I doubt if she will sue you. She would have to come out of hiding to do that and she certainly won't want to do that!"

Kathy looked at the number of shares and comments. "Has anyone identified her? Or said where she might be?"

Tomas said there had been a lot of comments. He could pass all the comments from the various social media sites over if it would help.

Of course, it would help, Kathy thought, why on earth had he not told me about this earlier! Out loud she said:

"Please pass over what you have, and I will look through it. And don't worry too much, I doubt if there will be a lawsuit. But you certainly have them scared! We may be coming close to exposing where Song is!"

These comments on social media might be just what she needed.

Kathy switched the TV off and started to look through the comments. There were so many, it was difficult to see which were relevant. There were sightings across the country and people saying that she was working at various places. These included a massage parlour, an ice-cream parlour, IHOP and McDonalds. Kathy knew these were unlikely as she believed Songs father's lawyers were trying to have her education visa reinstated.

After a few hours Kathy felt like giving up – there was just so much information. Then she saw a comment from a woman in Los Angeles. "I know this woman and I know where she is. She is at a university on a student visa. Contact me for more information."

Kathy started to type a response through messenger. "I am a PI interested to find this woman. Please DM me if you have information."

A couple of minutes later her message was accepted and she received a message back.

"The woman is named Song. She is at a private university in Los Angeles. I will talk to you if you want to arrange a meeting."

Kathy replied "Are you in LA? I am in Atlanta. Do you want to talk on Zoom?"

A meeting was arranged and a few minutes later Kathy saw Candy Boval on Zoom. Candy was in her mid 30s with short curly hair and what seemed like a friendly manner. After introductions Kathy asked how she knew the woman in the picture.

"The woman is named Song. I taught at Highbridge College, which is a private university in Thousand Oaks, north of Los Angeles. Highbridge used to be in the San Fernando Valley and had been in business for about 20 years. Just before lockdown they decided to expand to a new campus in Thousand Oaks, north of the valley, which is very beautiful. There is a big campus with new buildings and sports facilities. The downside was they got into a lot of debt."

Kathy was listening politely but wondered where on earth this was going.

Candy went on "They had always accepted Chinese students at master's level, but when they got into debt during lockdown they decided to expand their Chinese provision. They badly needed money and the Chinese paid full tuition fees plus other costs such as English classes etc. They got into an arrangement with a university in Guangzhou in China. Professor Xingping Zhang was their contact. He arranged to send students, for back handers no doubt."

Kathy wished she would get to the point…

Candy continued "Highbridge had no idea how to deal with these students. Some couldn't speak or write English well enough to do the work in the undergraduate degree classes. They had no idea what was going on. They were supposed to be studying Business but could barely string a sentence together in English."

Kathy decided to interrupt her at this point "And Song was one of these students?"

Candy smirked "She sure was or should I say is. She is Professor Xingping Zhang's only daughter. I guess you know about the one child policy in China which stopped in 2015."

OMG things were starting to make sense now, Kathy thought.

Candy was still talking "Song was about the worst student ever. She had a bad attitude and couldn't understand anything we were doing in the class. I was her personal tutor and was supposed to see her outside of class. These meetings were a disaster. She was uncommunicative and not interested in anything I had to say. Sadly, they did not tell me she was Zhang's daughter. I did not follow up when she started missing classes and she disappeared for over four months."

Kathy was really interested now. "Has she been reinstated now?" she said

Candy shrugged "As you might have guessed I am no longer employed there. She cost me my job, but from what I have heard through the grapevine it seems she is back. For what purpose I don't know. She has no idea what she is doing."

Kathy was beginning to understand the cover-up a lot better now. A pushy father and a daughter who was not academic. It was a recipe for disaster.

Candy liked to talk and she was on her favourite subject. "Highbridge is a private college so they can accept who they like. These Chinese students shouldn't be in a university. The whole thing is a scam. They will go back to China and say they have an American degree, but what will they know?"

Kathy was only interested in one of the students "Do you know anyone who you could ask to confirm that Song is actually at Highbridge now?"

Candy indicated that she did and she could get the information confirmed, although she was 99.9% sure she was back there.

Kathy thanked her for her information, which had been very helpful.

The next day she met with John Danes; the witness who had not been interviewed at the time of the attack. They met at a coffee shop near to Big Daddy's Burger Bar.

Before Kathy had a chance to introduce herself, John rushed in "Look Lady nobody asked me about this at the time, are you following up because of the post about that Chinese girl on Instagram?"

Kathy said that it was felt that not all evidence had been gathered and Barry Watkins now had a lawyer who was going to help him at the trial.

"There is no doubt that motherfucker beat the shit out of Senser that night." Said John "But Senser was all over that Chinese girl, and it was driving Watkins mad. Watkins was cussing and ranting on before he went out to the alley. Senser had a reputation for messing with young girls. She was hot man and Senser couldn't keep his hands to his self."

"Was the Chinese girl working in the burger bar?"

"Yes, she was out front tidying the tables and bringing the food over."

Kathy took her phone out and showed him the photo of Song. "Is that her?" she asked. John nodded.

"Why did no-one take a statement from you at the time?"

"Why do you think lady? They wanted to set Barry up. It looked good for the DA if he could say that he was fighting crime in S Atlanta. Also, no-one wants to admit that Atlanta is being overrun with illegal immigrants. Best to cover it up. Barry has no money for a fancy lawyer. He was easy to set up. So who the hell are you? How is he paying you?"

"I can't reveal that" Kathy said "But if I can get you to sign a form I feel we have enough now to file a motion for an appeal."

John agreed to sign. It was a pivotal point in the case.

After she left John Danes, she had a conversation with Derek Lynes. He thanked her for her work and said the evidence from these people was very valuable. Once Song's location was confirmed they could serve a subpoena on her to come to the trial. A trial date was due to be set for the end of April.

Chapter 36

Lila

The New Orleans convention...

The convention in New Orleans was on a Saturday and the Brothers and the Jazz Band were scheduled to play for four numbers. They would hardly breakeven after paying the costs of the travel, but it was widening their appeal again. This time Alex was insistent that her mother, Adrienne, be able to sing with the Brothers. They decided to do the same set they did at the Mayor's convention plus Adrienne singing "Misty". This involved a lot of rehearsal and Lila went along to all of the rehearsals and was so very impressed with their singing.

Randi had moved in now with a roommate and let the apartment she shared with Somchai go. There did not seem much chance he would return to her. He was back with his rich wife in the Southern Hills mansion. Lila tried to keep in touch with her, but it was difficult with their different working schedules and she knew she should make more effort. The truth was she was just so tied up with the Brothers and trying to promote them.

Also, at the Purple Orchid last Saturday something strange happened. Sheri, one of the customers, was leaving and she came over to reception to pay for some well-being goods she had bought. She chatted for a minute or two and then she got her phone out.

"Do you recognise this woman?" She enquired. She showed Lila a social media post of a Chinese woman who seemed to have been involved in an attempted rape in Atlanta. Someone was now in prison for trying to protect her.

"Should I?" Lila wasn't immediately interested

"I think she used to work here." Sheri said "Ellie has just denied it. But I used to come in the fall and I am sure she did my nails. Very beautiful and a bit shy. I got the impression Jinni and her had a thing, you know."

Lila thought her eyes were going pop out of her head. "I only started work recently. So I don't know all the people who worked here. But can you send me that post?"

They exchanged numbers so Sheri could send her the post.

"I might be wrong" said Sheri "But I am sure I know her. She certainly got in the shit after she left here if it is her."

When Lila got home she showed Ronnie the post. "Lila, this has nothing to do with you." Ronnie said "if it is true she worked at the Purple Orchid then Jinni must have employed an illegal immigrant. If they were involved, she may still be hurt Jinni has left and won't appreciate you interfering."

He was right, but Lila's interest had been piqued and she wanted to know. That week when she went to Janine's house to clean, she decided to show Janine the picture. Lila knew Janine was a long standing customer of the Purple Orchid. Janine recognised the picture immediately exclaiming

"That is Song"

Then she read the comments. "Oh my goodness" she said "She worked as a manicurist at the Purple Orchid and left, I think, at the end of last year. Noone knew where she went. It was never discussed."

"It seems she got in a real mess in Atlanta, was she an illegal immigrant?"

Janine looked troubled.
"I doubt that, or Jinni would not have employed her. Have you told Jinni about these posts? They are very damaging for Jinni and her business! She may be able to do something to stop people sharing these posts, by proving Song is not in the USA illegally."

Lila indicated that she had not shown Jinni the posts.

"I am going to my nail appointment tomorrow so I will tell her." said Janine. "Can you forward the post to me."

Lila was suddenly worried about her job.

.
"Please don't tell Jinni that you got the posts from me." Lila said

Janine looked at Lila quizzically
"If that is what you want. Of course, I won't. But we are trying to help her. The Purple Orchid is an upscale salon. I can't imagine

that it is involved in employing illegal immigrants or with criminals. We need to help Jinni keep her reputation."

Janine had to dash off then. It was only after she had left that Lila wondered if she should have kept her mouth shut. She thought: "Am I getting involved in something that was way above my head?"

Chapter 37

Fulton County Prison

A visitor for Barry...

Barry Watkins had a visitor today. The visitor had been approved by his attorney Derek Lynes. Barry had no idea who this person was. Her name was Dr Abeba Majola PhD. What did he need with a doctor, he thought, he was not sick, but he had nothing better to do so he had agreed that he would see her.

As he sat in front of the video conferencing system he waited for his guest to arrive. His life had gone to shit, he thought, sitting here desperate to talk to anyone on the outside. Who the heck was this person. As if on cue, a woman picked up the phone and appeared on the screen. OMG he thought she is butt ugly! She had hair so short it looked like it had been razor cut, and a big, fat face. Zero makeup. She was about 50 he guessed. She was wearing what looked like a shapeless top, he guessed, as she probably had no shape.

"Hello Barry" the woman said "I am Doctor Majola. I am a professor of Women's, Gender and Sexuality Studies at Georgia State University. I am very interested in your case. How are you today?"

Barry said "Good" but was completely at a loss what a professor would want with him. As if she had read his thoughts, Dr Majola went on to say:

"I have been studying immigrant women to the USA. Those that arrive undocumented are often victims of sexual violence as they do not have a voice. These women are marginalised in society. They suffer psychological distress yet have no-one to turn to."

Barry was at a complete loss what to say.

It seemed she liked the sound of her own voice as she went on "I have been studying Mexican women and have been to the border to interview women. Some feel that rape is their rite of passage to the USA. I am interested in what happened to the Chinese woman in the alley. You were her saviour. It is not often that anyone stands up for these women and I want to know more about what you did."

Barry stared at her, at a loss for words. Here he was incarcerated and then he had been visited by an attorney who was going to represent him at his trial, and now a professor from the university who was "interested" in what he had to say.

"Can you give me a bit of background leading up to the night of the attempted rape?" she said

She knew all about Song – how could she know. As if awakening from a dream, he said "Hold on a minute lady. How do you know about my case?"

"Good question" Dr Majola said "let me explain a little bit of the background." She got her phone out and showed him Tomas' post on social media. Barry who was not allowed access to social media or the internet gaped when he saw it and what it said. Tomas hadn't abandoned him like he thought.

Dr Majola went on "I saw this post and got in touch with Tomas, your roommate. He filled me in on the background. I immediately wanted to come and see you. You approved the visit but it had to be run by your attorney. He was keen that I come to see you and get your side of what happened."

Barry brightened up "Can you get me out of here?" he asked.

"Well, I am not an attorney but I can speak up for your case." She said "if you can tell me more about, Song, wasn't it?"

Barry looked at her through the video screen "Do you know Song?" he asked.

"No, I need you to tell me about her. Where was she from in China?"

Barry was finding this woman difficult. He couldn't answer her questions. How should he know? "I don't know, she was just from China. We didn't talk about it." He said feeling stupid.

"Okay, do you know why she was in America?"

"I think she came to go to school ma'am." He said

Dr Majola nodded, this was very interesting. This was a very different case to the women she normally interviewed. "Just tell me what you know." She said

"She lived next door. There were about 20 Chinese living in a 2 bedroom apartment, I think. They lived there in shifts. They all looked the same. I mean, they were quiet but man their cooking stunk. I didn't talk to them until Song turned up. She was beautiful. She could speak English and I saw her in the hall and also she went to Lim's convenience store. We got chatting. She wanted to be an actress like one of the Kardashians. Her father had made her go to school to be an accountant. She hated it! She would have been wasted as a bean counter. She liked our TV shows. She would come round and we would drink and have fun. She liked to drink beer and eat with us. She worked at Big Daddy's Burger Bar. That was where there was trouble."

Dr Majola agreed. "You mention her father, was he in the USA?"

"No" said Barry "He was in China, he had sent her to the USA to school."

Dr Majola was intrigued now as there were Chinese students at Georgia State. Yet she couldn't imagine any of them working at Big Daddy's. They were usually hard working serious students carrying out research for advanced degrees.

She probed a bit further "Do you know what school she came to the USA to attend?"

Barry looked lost "No ma'am" he said.

"Okay then Barry can you tell me a bit about the night of the attack?"

Barry went through it with her, as he had gone through it so many times before. The difference was she seemed to care and be really listening to him.

"Can you get me out?" he pleaded "I fucking hate it in here. Where is Song? Why does no-one know where she is? She would tell them I was trying to help her. I loved her."

Dr Majola said she would do all she could to help his case, but she was not an attorney.

"I believe a trial date has been set now. If we can find Song then she can testify on your behalf and that will be very important."

She tried to get more details out of Barry, but it was very difficult. The meeting ended soon and Dr Majola promised to keep in touch.

After she left Barry was escorted back to his cell. He didn't want to get too excited about this visit. It would probably all come to nothing. It was great to think Tomas had put that post on social media though.

What Barry did not know, and Derek Lynes, his attorney did know, was that Dr Majola had been invited to speak on her research on the local TV news. She would talk about undocumented women being raped and having no voice. She had been invited as this was a very controversial area as these women should not be in the USA. However, once people knew how they had suffered it may encourage them to feel some empathy and the fact that Barry had stood up for someone with no voice might be viewed positively. Rather than be viewed as a thug who had attacked a business man in an alley..

Chapter 38

Jinni

A secret may be revealed...

My lease of the property in the regeneration area was finalised this week. I was given the keys to my new property. There was a lot of work to do to refurb the premises, but I could see the big picture and was excited. My friend Noi went with me to visit and we talked about the layout of the new salon and coffee shop. I had invited along an interior designer who shared our vision and we spent an hour there talking about the new business.

Somchai was still living with Barb and seemed to be making a recovery from the alcohol poisoning. He swore that he was now sober. He had lost his job at the chicken plant, and he needed to find more work. He was actively looking at the moment. Barb had her lodger to help with finances and Somchai was back now working part-time at the DIY store (after having his hours cut).

On Thursday the salon was busy as usual and I saw that Janine had booked in for a manicure. She is one of my favourite customers. During the manicure Janine said "After we finish is it possible that I could have a word with you in private?" I thought this sounded ominous, but I agreed and said I have a few minutes before my next appointment.

We went into the back room after her appointment where we could speak in privacy. Janine seemed embarrassed. She had her phone in her hand.

"Jinni, I am concerned about you. I wondered if you had seen this post on Instagram?"

She showed me a post with a picture of Song and text underneath saying

> **DO YOU KNOW THIS CHINESE WOMAN?**
>
> **Innocent black man to be tried for aggravated assault and battery after trying to save this Chinese woman from rape in S Atlanta. She has left Atlanta and will not provide a**

defence for this brave brother. She is in USA illegally. Please share so we can find this woman."

I felt sick. Who on earth had posted this? This was far worse than the texts re illegal immigrants. This was specifically about Song.

I stood there staring at it.

"It's Song isn't it?" said Janine "I know she left here suddenly, but it seems she went to Atlanta and got herself into a lot of trouble."

I continued to stand there staring at the phone.

Janine started babbling "It is Song, isn't it? It has to be her. It looks just like her. I didn't know you employed her when she didn't have papers. I don't want this to come back on you."

I still had not spoken. I suppose I should have guessed that the secret would come out. But now it had it felt scary and threatening.

Janine was still going on "It is Song, isn't it?" she said again

"I don't think it is her" I said "Song went back to China." I was lying and this felt terrible.

"Are you sure?" Janine said; "Look again, it looks just like her."

I physically stiffened and I looked her direct in her eyes "It is not Song." I said "She is back in China and has never been anywhere near Atlanta. Now if you will excuse me, I have to get back to my customers. If you go to reception, Lila will arrange your next appointment."

Janine was looking at me strangely and I could sense she didn't believe a word I had said. But I wasn't about to confide in her.

What did the social media post mean? When I got home that evening, I searched for the person who had posted it "Tomasj". I then requested to follow him, and was immediately accepted. I then started flipping through, but I couldn't find the post. He had several posts on Instagram but it was very strange the one about the Chinese woman seemed to have disappeared into thin air. How weird! I had looked at the post long enough to remember who had posted the original. I had definitely keyed it in correctly. Perhaps if it had disappeared I could forget about it?

Later that evening as I was getting ready for bed my phone pinged. It was a message from Janine with a link to a YouTube video. I clicked on the video but there was nothing there. I sent a text to Janine to ask her to send it again. A few minutes later she wrote and said "The video has been deleted. Forget I sent it." I knew the video was about Song without having to ask her. It seemed that Harry Zine had not done such a good job at covering things up as he had indicated. I thought about Barry Watkins in prison waiting for a trial for defending Song. He had been seen by Harry Zine as dispensable, a scapegoat. It seemed he had friends who were standing up for him. The social media posts must be from his friends – who was this "Tomasj"? For the first time, I was really worried, this was turning out badly. I slept very badly that night and got up the next day to go to the salon tired and worried …

Chapter 39

Ellie

A frightening visitor…

The spring semester was passing by quickly, and Ellie's pregnancy was progressing without problem. All was well or seemed to be.

On Thursdays Kevin and Ellie both taught at the State University. They carpool and, on the way, back, Ellie usually dropped Kevin off at the gym. Ellie then went to the grocery store to shop for food and then she picked Kevin up from the gym and they went home and cooked.

This Thursday was no different. Ellie had dropped Kevin off and was wandering around the store picking up bread, milk, cheese, meat etc. She had a funny feeling that a man was following her but tried to shrug it off as silly paranoid feelings. She kept seeing him as she went up and down the aisles, but she told herself that he was just shopping like her.

When Ellie came out of the store, she noticed that the man left at the same time.

As she pushed her trolley over to the car, he came over to her. He was an ordinary looking man in his 40s dressed casually. Not really threatening. But Ellie didn't know him. He then spoke

"Eleanor Watson?"

"Who wants to know?" Ellie said rudely. Who the heck was this?

"I am Robert Pearlman and I act on behalf of Harry Zine, the attorney of Song Zhang, a Chinese woman I believe you know of"

He paused and, reaching into his pocket, brought out his card

"I am a Private Investigator and this is my license. Can we go somewhere to talk?"

Ellie nodded as it was ridiculous talking in the parking lot of the grocery store. She loaded up the car and followed him over to a coffee shop next to the grocery store. She let him buy her a coffee and they sat by the window.

"You recently made a YouTube video about my client, Song. I do not believe you have her permission to make that video."

Ellie stared at him and started spluttering

"the whole point of that video was that Song is missing and she needs to come forward and speak up for the poor man who tried to defend her and is waiting for a trial date. He will be sent to prison for aggravated assault and battery unless she speaks out!"

"So are you saying you did not have her permission? She is entitled to a reasonable amount of privacy especially if her picture is used online."

"I was trying to help find her." Ellie blustered on "Where is she? Can I meet her and ask her permission?"

Robert smiled and wagged his finger at Ellie

"She does not give her permission. In fact, if you don't take that YouTube video down now, she will consider bringing a lawsuit against you for invasion of privacy."

Ellie continued blustering

"She can't sue me. I know my rights. This is the USA and there is freedom of speech in this country. I was only expressing my opinions."

Robert shook his head

"But you used her picture, and she did not give you permission to use her picture. That is the issue. She can sue in civil court for damages. I hope that you have deep pockets."

Although there was a possibility that he was bluffing, Ellie was worried. She knew Harry Zine was Song's father's attorney as Jinni had mentioned his name. This man said he was his PI. If she was to be sued for one of her YouTube videos, Kevin would go mad. She could just hear him shouting "we can't afford it!" All these thoughts swirled through Ellie's mind.

Finally Ellie stood up

"I will take the video down but please give Harry Zine and his client Song a message from me. Song should do the right thing and speak up for Barry Watkins. He tried to protect her, and she has done nothing in return. I don't know how she sleeps at night. Free Barry Watkins!"

Robert also stood up and held his hand out to shake her hand, which was declined.

"That is the right decision. You are a very sensible and clever woman. It is nice to have met you."

Ellie left the coffee shop in a hurry and dashed over to her car. It was not until she was sitting in the car she realised she was shaking. She was upset, angry and impotent. She felt she had handled the PI so wrongly. She had given in so easily. But sometimes Ellie felt so foreign living in America and didn't know how to react. Also, this was something she knew for certain she couldn't mention to Kevin as she had promised him that she wouldn't make any more YouTube videos after the fiasco last December.

Finally she managed to pull herself together and set off for the gym to pick Kevin up. When she got there he was waiting outside.

"Where the hell have you been." He said "I've been waiting ages and you were not answering your phone. What have you been doing?"

He was looking at her strangely. She felt hot and bothered and her face was bright red.

"Shopping, Kevin and there was a long queue at the checkout and it took ages. I'm sorry if I'm a bit late."

She hated lying to Kevin but there was no way she could share this with him. When they got home they both worked together to get the meal ready and then they sat eating it. This was followed by a time watching TV and then they went to bed. Ellie meant to delete the video but as Kevin was with her all the time she put it off until later.

So it wasn't until later that night when Kevin was asleep, that she slipped out of bed and went to the study and got my laptop out and deleted the YouTube video. It had attracted over 1,000 comments. She was sorry to delete it, but she had decided she couldn't risk leaving it up.

As Ellie went about her work the following day, she decided that this was the end of trying to help Barry Watkins. She had deleted the video and none of the celebrities she had written to had responded to her DMs. She had to move on and forget the incident.

Chapter 40

Atlanta

The morning show...

Dr Abeba Majola PhD, appeared on early morning TV in Atlanta to talk about her research into the sexual exploitation of women with no voice. Dr Majola was talking about women who are in the US without paperwork and have no one to speak up for them. There was a lively discussion with Arnie Mann, the anchor man, saying that these women should not be in this country without paperwork. The country was being overrun by illegal immigrants. At some point during the discussion Dr Majola mentioned that much of her research had been with women from Mexico, however, she had recently encountered an interesting case where there had allegedly been an attempted rape of a Chinese woman in S Atlanta.

"This case is very controversial as the woman has disappeared and no-one knows where she is. However, a man who is incarcerated in Fulton County Jail awaiting a trial for aggravated assault and battery alleges he was defending her from a rapist when he beat another man. The problem with all these cases is that the women are frightened to come forward and speak up. She fears that she may be deported, and she has no one to take her side. She is probably poor and can't afford a lawyer."

Arnie Mann was very interested to hear about the case

"Can you tell us more about this attempted rape, such as where did it take place?"

"I believe in an alley behind a burger bar in South Atlanta. It was late in the evening, about closing time. The Chinese woman was working illegally in the burger bar. She was asked to take the trash out and encountered the owner in the alley behind the burger bar. When she did not return after a few minutes, another man went to look for and found the owner trying to rape her. He beat the owner to stop the attempted rape, I believe. As I said, he is now facing trial for aggravated assault and battery. The woman has not come forward and the police believe it was a motiveless attack."

"But surely there must have been witnesses to this attack? Somebody else who was eating in the burger bar or just in the area?"

"There were no witnesses who came forward, so far as I am aware."

Arnie seemed unconvinced but he asked

"So you are saying this woman disappeared because she is poor and here illegally."

Dr Majola looked at Arnie and spoke sincerely

"She is most certainly terrified, and probably poor. She would not feel she could speak to the police or anyone official."

She turned to the camera and carried on

"If you are that woman or know who she is, please come forward, tell her she would be dealt with fairly and the authorities might be able to help with her immigration status. If this woman doesn't speak up and say it was not a motiveless attack, a man will be incarcerated for many years for defending her."

Arnie agreed with her

"I can see that this woman may be in a quandary. Terrified to speak up, yet knowing that this man is in prison for her. She has no voice."

Dr Majola went on. "Don't forget traumatised by the attempted rape as well. Having to run away from her job and may now even be homeless."

Arnie made his concluding remarks

"That is all we have time for today. But if you know this woman please encourage her to come forward to the authorities."

Across town in an expensive downtown office Harry Zine had the early morning news on in his office. He had turned the sound up when he realised what Dr Majola was discussing. He let out a loud shout "Oh fuck off lady" as he gesticulated at the TV screen, causing his PA to come running into the office to see what was going on.

"Are you okay?" she asked. He was red in the face and looked like he was about to have a heart attack.

"Get me Robert" he said angrily.

A couple of minutes later he was speaking to Robert, his PI

"Who the fuck is this woman Majola? Where did she come from?"

Robert had his cell phone out madly googling while talking to Harry "It seems she is a professor at Georgia State University. She is a feminist and researches women's rights. At the moment she is interested in illegal immigrants. She thinks she is standing up for Song."

"She might think that but she sounds like she is blowing hot air out of her ass!" Harry said "I'll have to think this one over. I'll be in touch."

He was furious, this one was going to be more difficult to shut up. This was really going to cost Xingping Zhang. He went into client accounts on his computer and keyed in a few figures. This helped calm him as he thought around how to deal with Dr Majola.

Chapter 42

Jinni

When a secret is threatened to be exposed...

When I went to the salon on Friday I was nervous and frightened about what might happen. I carried out my duties professionally so that none of the customers would realise how I felt.

During my lunch break I went into the back room and closed the door. I have a small TV on the wall in this room and I switched it on while I ate my lunch. There was a news item on our local news. The news anchor explained that this had been a discussion on the news in Atlanta this morning. A black lady appeared on the screen. I saw her name was Dr Abeba Majola PhD. I knew she was discussing women's rights. I know my rights and I didn't need her to tell me! I was only half listening at first until she started talking about illegal immigrants and an attempted rape of a Chinese woman in S Atlanta. I turned the volume up and my heart starting beating very quickly. OMG how could she possibly know? Had this Watkins man put her up to it? She was encouraging Song to come forward and speak up. This was getting really frightening. I really did not know what to do. I sat with my head in my hands.

I decided to ring Harry Zine and ask his advice. His PA picked up the phone. "Mr Zine is in court today" she said "Can I get him to ring you back?"

I gave a number and went back to the main room, numb and scared. I welcomed my next appointment and started work on her nails. Out of the corner of my eye I could see Lila looking at me. I decided to ignore her and chat to my customer.

After the appointment ended Lila came over and spoke to me. "Is everything okay, Jinni?" she asked

"Yes of course" I said "why would you ask?"

"You seem upset" she said "I say this with concern for you."

“I am perfectly fine” I told her. I wasn’t about to discuss any of this with her. I could see her looking at me with a very concerned expression on her face. I wished she would go away and leave me alone.

The afternoon seemed to drag by and finally it was closing time. I tidied up and went to catch the train home. As I sat on the train my cell vibrated. It was Harry Zine.

“Hi Jinni. How can I help you?” he said.

“I am very concerned that the truth about the attack in the alley is going to come out and Song is going to be very exposed.” I said.

“Where are you Jinni?” Harry asked “Are you in a private place?”

I looked around and there were only a few people on the train and none close to me. I decided I could speak frankly.

“I am on the train going home” I said “but there is no one near to me who can overhear our conversation.”

“All the same I think you should ring me back when you get home and are in a private room away from prying ears.” Said Harry.

I thought he was fussing, but I expect he was right. When I got home, I kicked my shoes off and sat down and rang him straight back.

“Hey Harry” I said “I am home now and it is private here. There is just me here.”

“Hey Jinni. Okay I heard what you said on the train. Why on earth would you say that?” said Harry

I explained about the social media posts, YouTube video and Dr Majola’s appearance on Atlanta TV.

“Have you actually seen these posts on social media, Jinni?” said Harry “and can you send them to me?”

“I’ve seen them and they seemed to have attracted a lot of attention. But I can’t send them to you as they have been deleted.”

“How about the YouTube video? What is that about? Can you send it?”

“I have never seen the video, it has also been deleted, but I just know it is about Song.”

Harry sighed “Look Jinni, I know this has been very upsetting for you. But think this through. You saw some posts on social media that have now been removed. There is supposedly a YouTube video which has also been taken down, but you don’t really know if it is about Song. Then Dr Majola was on daytime TV in Atlanta. If you lived in Atlanta you would know about her, she is well known here. The woman is a crackpot, Jinni. She is an academic with extreme left leaning views. Nobody in Atlanta takes her seriously. If she is the one who spoke up, I doubt anybody would have listened to her.”

“So you think I am panicking? Over worrying?” I said

“I think you need to relax and stop worrying. Everything is fine.” Said Harry

We rang off then, but he had not convinced me. I made some food and after I had eaten, I rang Kevin, Ellie’s husband.

“Hi Jinni.” Said Kevin “What a nice surprise. How are you?”

“A bit worried” I said “I am frightened for Song.”

“Let me put you on speaker.” Said Kevin “Why are you frightened? I thought Song was back at Highbridge College and the past had been smoothed over by her father’s lawyer.”

“So did I” I said “Until this week.” I explained about the social media posts and YouTube video. Then I mentioned Dr Abeba Majola PhD speaking on the TV this morning.

“I have heard of her” said Kevin “she is a feminist who has been an outspoken advocate of women’s rights. She is a professor at Georgia State. I believe at the moment she is looking into the sexual exploitation of women who are illegal immigrants.”

“Yes, that is what she was talking about on TV this morning. She specifically mentioned Song’s case without mentioning her name. How would she know about that case?”

"Interesting" said Kevin "she may have picked up something from these social media posts you mentioned. But certainly a case like this would be very interesting to her. Very different from the usual cases she encountered. Many of these women are very poor and have no-one to defend them. But Song is different, she has a wealthy, influential father who can intervene on her behalf."

Suddenly another voice spoke. I have to admit I had completely forgotten Kevin had put the call on speaker and Ellie was there.

"But even if she is from a rich family, she ran away and put herself into jeopardy. To be attacked and have a man try to rape you in an alley would be traumatic for any woman. But like these poor illegal immigrants Song cannot get any help as her father's lawyer is covering up the attack to keep her visa. How must she feel? How would any woman feel if she had been attacked? How would you feel Jinni if you were her? Put yourself into her shoes.

Yet Song is supposed to go back to university and act as if nothing has happened. I guess she wouldn't be able to discuss it with anyone at the university in case her cover was blown.

And don't get me started on that poor man who rescued her!! No-one cares about him. He has been used as a scapegoat. Unless he can prove he was helping Song he will be locked up in prison. All he was doing was trying to help her for goodness' sake. But of course, no one will believe him. There are no witnesses as Song's attorney has covered everything up."

A thought flashed across my mind about the YouTube video and who might have made it, but I decided not to follow up on my thought. I was ashamed that I had not thought more about Song and how she might feel. My thoughts had been entirely selfish. I had loved her and she had left me. I had thought about myself and how hurt I had felt.

Out loud I said "Yes, running away ended very badly for Song. I can't bear to think of how she must be suffering now."

"I do believe if she spoke up, the Immigration Authorities might be lenient on her." said Kevin "she was in an unbearable situation in Atlanta and did as her father asked her. I also feel that a man might have to serve a long prison sentence because of her failure to speak up and that is not fair."

"I feel I must go to her and try to help her." I said "My gut instinct tells me that it is only a matter of time before she is exposed. I am not sure Harry Zine can protect her."

"Not if BLM decide to take it up." Said Ellie

"BLM?" I said

"Black Lives Matter" said Ellie

"I'm not sure what they can do." Said Kevin "But Dr Majola is a respected academic and if she takes up the case she can make waves, believe me."

"I think BLM could do plenty!" said Ellie

"Thanks for talking to me." I said "I'm not going to abandon her. I will try to help her. What would the college do, Kevin, if this all came out?"

"I should imagine they would be appalled" said Kevin "The best damage limitation would be to ask her father to take her back to China. This might save the link with the Chinese university. But it would be very bad publicity for the university. The fees are high there, and they don't rank among the top universities in the US, so I am not sure they could take publicity like that. They could also try to get her moved to another American university. However, given her academic track record it is doubtful if anywhere would take her!."

The discussion with Ellie and Kevin had made me determined to try to help Song. What a mess! I knew that I should just forget her and get on with my business. But I was in love and there was no way I could abandon her. If I could get to her I could provide comfort for her and get her any help she needed.

I was sure I could help. There were so many secrets and it was time they were out into the open. I decided that this weekend I would fly to Los Angeles on Sunday evening and then go to Highbridge College first thing on Monday morning to look for Song. I could leave my senior manicurist Julie in charge of the salon for Monday.

Song needed my help and I knew it was time I went to her. However, this was before I received some very bad news on Saturday morning that upset me more than ever...

Chapter 43

Lila

Adrienne sings with the Brothers and a very sad day...

When Lila returned home from the Purple Orchid that Friday, she was emotional and tired. She could not stand Jinni's attitude towards her. In Lila's view she had been ignored all day and Jinni would not speak to her even to say how she was feeling. Lila had initially been worried about her. In Lila's view she treated her as if she was dirt beneath her shoes, and Lila would not stand for that. Lila had also figured a few things out. It was obvious now that the Chinese woman had been Jinni's lover and had left Jinni to go to Atlanta, where she got herself into some bad shit. Even if Jinni was upset about this, she should show some consideration for her staff. Although Lila needed the money, she figured she could find work elsewhere. Perhaps this would be somewhere with a more caring and kind manager.

While Lila sat musing about Jinni, Ronnie had got ready to leave for the evening's show. He told her to get changed quickly as the Brothers were playing that evening at Harry's bar which was a bar in the next city and a long drive away. On the drive over Ronnie seemed in a good mood and confided that the Brothers were going to give Adrienne a try out tonight in advance of the Las Vegas convention.

"I thought it was her daughter Alex who was insisting that her mom sang?"

"Yes that was true initially. But when we heard her sing, man the woman is brilliant! We felt that she should sing with us even if the school jazz band is not playing with us."

Lila reluctantly had to agree that she was a brilliant singer – but still this was a surprise. This was not the way she had seen the Brothers developing.

When they arrived at Harry's Bar, Adrienne was already there, having gotten a lift with Pete. The boys set up their backup tape and then Niall turned up with Jenni.

The bar had a small stage at the front for acts to perform on. The audience sat below the stage at tables for four.

Jennie and Lila got a table near to the stage. The bar was full that evening. The Brothers set out with some of their old standards "Fly me to the Moon", "New York, New York". Then Niall took centre stage and said:

"We have a special treat for y'all tonight. We have a guest vocalist who I am sure you are going to love. Let me introduce Adrienne."

The boys had been stood together and they parted so that Adrienne could walk between them and take centre stage.

Adrienne came onto the stage looking very small and shy. She was wearing a blue dress that seemed to be too big for her, and her shoes were ballet flats. This seemed a strange choice for a short person – heels would have helped to elevate her. Her hair was piled up on the top of her head in a strange style with wisps hanging each side of her face.

She walked up to the mic and looked around. By the expression on her face, it looked like she was terrified. Lila sitting watching genuinely felt for her and wondered if she was going to freeze in front of an audience. She was such a little, inconsequential thing.

Then she seemed to pull herself together and she said "I'm going to do a Whitney Houston tribute tonight" in her funny northern English accent. She then went straight into "Greatest Love of All". When she began singing it was amazing, what a voice! It was hard to believe it was coming from such a small, inconsequential looking white woman. When she sang, it was like she was a different person. She had "it", whatever it is, meaning star quality. That special something. When she sang it was not like when the Brothers sang. Yes, people enjoyed their singing but this was entirely different. People were mesmerized. They never wanted the song to finish!

When the song did finish the crowd were on their feet, cheering and clapping, while she stood in the spotlight looking like a deer trapped in headlights. She did not smile or say anything.

She then went on with her tribute by singing "I will always love you" from the film "The Bodyguard". She was amazing. It seemed that the boys were right to include her in their act, but for some reason Lila felt uneasy. She was smart enough to know if the Brothers were ever to achieve fame, then having Adrienne sing with them would be their key to success. Lila should be happy, she was brilliant, but why did she feel uneasy?

She stayed on the stage and sang another couple of songs. All met by rapturous applause. And then she finished and she was gone from the stage. The Brothers came back on and did their Motown tribute. By this time the crowd were up dancing. It was a great evening.

Ronnie said as much as we drove back home. "I think we are destined for great things with Adrienne on board." He said "Who would have thunk it? What a pair of lungs that woman has on her."

Lila had a funny feeling which she couldn't explain as she knew he was right but something deep down said this woman spells trouble. Yet she was a plain, little woman with a funny accent who was painfully shy. She was the mother to a blind girl, who was also extremely musically talented. So far as Lila knew happily married to a man who was an engineer at the aerospace factory outside the city. Why she felt like this was hard to say, but in the past she had found that her gut instinct was seldom wrong.

As she sat musing over these things, her cell phone vibrated and from then on things only got worse.

Lila did not recognise the number but she decided to pick up "Hey"

"Is this Lila?" a woman's voice said

"Who wants to know?"

"This is Paula, your sister Randi's roommate. I know you don't know me but I thought I had better ring you. Randi is in St Joseph's

Hospital ER" she said, Lila knew something was horribly wrong. She felt sick inside "Yes I am Lila, What is wrong?"

"Randi was admitted earlier this evening after taking an overdose of prescription meds. I went with her to the hospital and they have pumped her stomach and stabilised her."

Lila felt like she was going to be sick. Surely this couldn't be true. She knew Randi had been going through a rough time recently but this was way over the top.

"Can I see her?"

"Yes, she is resting now and very tired."

"I will be right there." Lila rang off without thanking Paula for taking Randi to the hospital.

Sitting in the car Lila was shaking and very near to tears.

"How much must Randi have been suffering to do something like that?"

Worse deep-down, Lila knew she hadn't been there for her. She had been too busy with my own world. OMG what if she had died?

Ronnie could see Lila was very upset and he was immediately concerned and said he would drive to St Josephs as fast as possible immediately.

"She must have been heartbroken over Somchai" Lila sobbed "That scum. He treated her like shit."

In Lila's mind the drive seemed to take forever, but in fact, they arrived at St Joseph's in about 20 minutes and she dashed in while Ronnie parked the car.

Randi was in a room on the 5th floor. Lila went straight there without waiting for Ronnie. Randi was lying in bed, with her eyes closed. She was as white as a sheet and looked so frail and ill Lila started to cry. Lila took hold of her hand and sat at the side of the bed. Randi may or may not have been conscious and it was not obvious if she could hear Lila speaking, but Lila went ahead anyway.

"Randi, it's Lila."

"I'm here for you now darling".

Inside Lila was heartbroken - she knew this was too little, too late. But at least she was there for her now. Sitting by the bed, she felt a hand on her shoulder, and turning she saw Ronnie had come into the room. He squeezed her shoulder.

After a few minutes a nurse came into the room. "She is being kept in overnight." She said "She is sleeping now. I would recommend you go home now. Come back tomorrow. The doctor will see her in the morning."

They left soon after this and walking along the long, quiet corridor with Ronnie's arm around her, Lila continued sobbing. "Oh, Randi, I have let you down so badly." She said out loud. That evening and in that corridor, she was determined to look out for her in the future.

Chapter 44

Jinni

Randi and Lila

Oh no. Could things get any worse? Song was threatened to be exposed. Then I got the call from Lila. I was on the train on my way into the salon on Saturday morning when my cell vibrated. I saw it was Lila and I picked up "Hi Lila, I hope all is well." I said

"Actually, things are not okay" Lila said "Its Randi. She tried to kill herself last night. She took an overdose but her roommate was able to get her to the hospital in time and they pumped her stomach."

I felt sick. I had had no concern at all for Randi. Somchai had been drinking excessively and had left her. All my concern had been for him.

"Is she going to be okay?" I asked

"I guess" said Lila "I am on my way now to the hospital and will not be in the salon today."

"Take all the time you need" I said "I will ring you again when you arrive at the hospital to find out how she is."

We agreed to speak again and then Lila rang off.

I sat on the train and thought about Randi for the first time in weeks. I had always seen her as a hard faced white woman, who was little better than a slut. She tended bar at the Black Cat bar which was a place frequented by lowlife drunks in my opinion. Somchai had left his wife for her and his drinking had worsened during their affair. When he was admitted to hospital with alcohol poisoning I blamed his relationship with Randi. He had spent evenings sitting at the bar in the Black Cat boozing while Randi worked her shifts. When his hours were cut he would not have been able to afford the rent on their apartment and I knew they were struggling. I felt that giving him money had absolved me of any responsibility. I knew Randi had to move out of the apartment after Somchai moved back with Barb, his wife. However, I had never once asked where she was going or how she was.

To me, she had been irrelevant and a marriage wrecker. I saw her as an older woman in her early 50s who broke up my brother's marriage. Perhaps karma had intervened as she was now alone in the world with only her sister to care for her. The big issue in my mind was that she did not have the capacity to earn a good salary and she had no financial assets. She was poor but for goodness sake, it had not needed to be so. Why had she not developed some business skills and why had she not invested in property?

I judged her as a woman who drank too much and relied on a man to take care of her. Not just a man – any man, including a married man who was an alcoholic. I guessed that she had a string of disastrous relationships in her past just like the relationship with Somchai. I realised that I always passed judgement on women like Randi and, yes, I admit it, I felt superior to her. I was a successful businesswoman who had no need to rely on anyone. To me women like her were not worthy of my time and care.

As these thoughts passed through my mind, I realised how cruel I was. What right did I have to judge Randi, or indeed anyone? Randi must have been heart broken when Somchai left. Yet I felt she was not worthy of my compassion.

Also, I had previously felt that there was no need for anyone to take care of me – I had my own business and looked after myself. Then Song came into my life and, for the first time in my life, I fell head over heels in love. Suddenly I didn't care about money any more. Song was what was important to me. I knew I shouldn't have continued to employ her in the salon when I found out she was working illegally. But I did! I couldn't bear to let her go. When she left me and ran away to Atlanta, I felt my life was over. It was as if my heart had been broken in two.

What right did I have to judge Randi because she had fallen in love with a married man? If Song had been married I would still have loved her with every fibre of my being.

What right did I have to judge Randi for anything she did or was?

I could see now how cruel I had been to her. She must have been dying inside and yet I did nothing to help her or even show her any compassion. What type of person was I?

I rang Somchai. He was still sleeping and seemed surprised to hear from me.

“Somchai, I have some bad news.” I said “Its about Randi.”

He was instantly awake “Randi?” he said “Is she okay?”

“Not really.” I said “she took an overdose last night and is in hospital.”

“Oh no” Somchai said “she can’t have done! She was living with Paula and I thought she was doing okay. Where is she?” he wailed

“So far as I know she is in hospital, but Lila is with her, so she may go to Lila’s house.”

“I’m going to her now” Somchai raised his voice and rung off.

What on earth would Barb think if he suddenly ran off after Randi? I was sick with worry. I somehow got through my first two manicures and then I rang Lila. She didn’t pick up at first. Then she send me a text and said Randi had been discharged and they were going to Lila’s house.

I also thought about the way I had treated Lila. She was Randi’s sister. Yet I had never once asked her how Randi was. In fact, I had never once asked how Lila was. I had taken Lila on as an employee as a favour to Somchai when he was in a relationship with Randi. I had never taken to her from day one. I saw her as loud, overbearing and lacking in basic manners. Again, I felt superior to her. I didn't see her as worthy of my time.

As I sat working, polishing nails and smiling and chatting no one would have known how I felt inside. What a mean, uncaring person I was. I sat in judgement of people and lacked humility and kindness.

I couldn't wait until 4 pm to close the salon. I then booked an uber to take me to Lila's house. I took with me a huge bunch of flowers for Randi.

Lila lived out in the northern suburbs not far from my own home, it turned out. I had not known this previously which shows how little interest I had in Lila.

I knocked on the door and Lila let me in. To say she seemed surprised to see me would be to put it mildly! Randi was lying on the sofa. She looked pale and tired.

Everyone looked at me expectantly as if waiting for me to speak. It was a very difficult moment.

"It was a great shock to hear what had happened, Randi" I said and realised I was speaking in a very formal way. "You still have so much life to live. I feel so badly that you did not feel that you could talk to any of us. But in my case, I suppose I never gave you any encouragement at all to believe you would have been listened to."

Noone spoke. They were both looking at me.

"I want you to know Randi that there are people who care about you and were heartbroken to hear what had happened. Lila loves you and Somchai wanted to come straight over to be with you as soon as he heard. I have thought about you all day today. I may not have been the easiest person to talk to, but I want you to know that I am there for you. I will always be there for you."

Randi struggled to sit up and she held her arms out. I gave the flowers to Lila and went over and we hugged. We were both in tears.

“There have been times” Randi said “when I felt no one cared about me. No-one wanted to listen to me. Some days the only time someone spoke to me was to order another beer! I felt I was practically invisible. I loved Somchai but he had gone. Somchai had gone back to his wife. Lila was too busy with her new marriage and work. I have no children and when times got hard, it seemed like I had no real friends.”

I hugged her tighter “We are all alone, dear” I said “I too have no husband or children. The woman I loved left me. Life is so hard. But we don’t have to live life with no one to talk to. This is where we go wrong. We believe no one wants to hear us.”

Lila spoke up then “We get busy. We work more than one job and we dash around. We mean to visit or ring but we put it off as we are always busy. We forget that there are others who might be suffering and want to hear from us.”

“I wanted Somchai back so much when he left. Yet at the same time I was furious he had left me in such a financial mess. He never got in touch with me. He sent you to get his stuff” Randi said indicating me. “Today he showed up crying but unable to help me in any way.”

“I should have talked to you. I should have tried to help you.” I said “But I didn’t. Somchai is my brother and I will always love him whatever he does. I should have cared more. I am sorry.”

Sorry was all I could say. I had been unkind and deaf to the needs of others.

Lila was watching me and I felt that her gaze on me was critical. I knew I deserved this as I had shown very little, if any, interest in her or her family. But this is the way I had been with everyone. It had all been me, me, me. My salon, my hurt feelings, my money and so on. I realised that I had not shown others love and respect. I was not a kind person. I was not a humble person. All around me people were suffering and I never heard their voices. All I thought about was me. This had been a wake up call.

Lila did not offer me a drink so it was a short visit. In my mind it was a new beginning where I would be a much more caring person. It was hard to imagine what Randi had gone through and I felt the future would be tough for her. However, I was determined to be there for Randi, and Lila, in future. This was not about money, this was about friendship and providing a shoulder to cry on.

As the uber made its way to my apartment, I knew that I could help Song in the same way and I was determined that is what I was going to do…

Chapter 45

Lila

Makes amends...

Saturday went by so quickly. Randi was discharged during the morning and Lila came to the hospital and brought her back to her house. She seemed pale and very frail. She laid on the sofa and Ronnie and Lila brought her drinks and snacks. She didn't seem to want to talk so they didn't push her to say anything.

She did, however, get a call from Somchai who was in tears and asked if he could come over to see her. She remained strong and refused to see him. Lila didn't say anything but inside she felt so proud of Randi for distancing herself from him.

Lila was very surprised when Jinni came by on Saturday afternoon and apologized.

"There was me thinking she did not care anything about anyone and it seems she has a heart after all."

Randi agreed and was very impressed by Jinni taking the time to visit and bring flowers.

After Jinni's visit she sat up and started to go through what had happened. Ronnie and Lila both sat with her listening.

"It was fucking Janet Girling that did it." She said, lighting up a cigarette. Lila looked at this disapprovingly. Normally she didn't let anyone smoke in the house, but this time she decided to let her get away with it.

"I don't think I know her, Randi."

"She has the biggest mouth in the southern states. I was on the early shift when she came in for a drink. She was sat up at the bar chatting and called me over.

"Hey Randi" she said "It was the TV awards last night for our local station. I was serving there when I saw your ex."

I really didn't want to have this conversation so I went away to serve someone else down the bar. I kept trying to avoid her, but had to go back to serve her.

She was smoking and really enjoying herself I could tell. "Is that his wife he is back with now? She must be rich. She had on a beautiful dress and when she put her hand out for the drink I saw a big diamond on her ring finger. Is she rich, Randi?"

"She's a looker too." Said old Denny "She came in here once with her daughter. Added a real touch of class to the place."

"Janice who was on drinks service with me told me that she owns a big mansion in the Southern Hills. Once Janice went up there to cater a party she held. Wow he has really landed on his feet getting back with her. I must say he looked very handsome in his tux. Dark and mysterious looking."

She waited a moment and then said "Just wondered, have you heard anything from him?"

I know I should have ignored all this bullshit and just gone about my job. She was enjoying winding me up. But I didn't I went for it.

"No I haven't heard anything from the bastard." I said "he is a lying, drunken asshole and she is welcome to him."

"Well, they certainly seemed very happy together" she said "such a shame. Still I'm sure you will meet someone else soon."

Lila could see how this conversation would have upset Randi

"People will always behave like that Randi, She is a nasty, jealous woman. You have to ignore it. She is not worth it."

Randi inhaled deeply from her cigarette and then said looking around

"I was furious and upset. I managed to get through my shift somehow, but inside I felt what was the point of life? I am 52 years old, I work in a bar serving people I don't like most of whom are drunks. Instead of serving them I should be taking them to AA. I earn so little that I have no savings and live pay check to pay check. I also live from one toxic relationship to the next.

None of my relationships have ever worked out. I have no husband or family. Somchai had left me to go back to his wife and his daughter.

Things had gotten so bad that I now had to live with a roommate. I did not even earn enough to rent an apartment on my own.

I felt invisible, unloved and my whole life was a waste of time.

I called at the store and bought a bottle of bourbon. When I got into the house, I went into my room and washed down all the prescription drugs I could find with the booze. I was passed out on the floor when my roommate Paula got home and it was she who rang for the paramedics who took me to hospital.

I guess she saved my life but today before I could thank her she texted me and said she can't handle the drama of having me live in her spare room."

Lila found it difficult to know how to speak to Randi to make her feel better. It couldn't get much worse for her. What on earth could Lila say to make her feel better? Lila had tried to talk to her before about the men she dated and she always ignored her. Same about her job. The Black Cat bar is known as one of the worse dives in town yet she still worked there. The customers are drunks and whores.

They lapsed into silence. It was Ronnie who spoke to her.

"Randi" he said "the Lord loves you. The Lord will always love you unconditionally. If you give your heart and soul to the Lord and stop worrying your life will turn around."

He quoted to her from Jeremiah 29:11 "For I know I have plans for you declares the Lord, plans to prosper you and not to harm you, plans to give you hope and a future."

Randi seemed skeptical sitting there twisting her hair with her finger and smoking. She had no idea that Ronnie and Lila were committed Christians who go to church every Sunday. This was a first for her.

"Come with us to church tomorrow." Said Ronnie "The Lord will help you to heal."

She agreed to go to church but Lila was not sure if that was just because she was now homeless and felt she had to rely on them, or if she really wanted to find out more. Lila guessed she was planning to ask for an upgrade to her depression meds after this weekend and could not see how the love of the Lord could sustain her. Lila reached over and took her hand. She realised that her faith had let her down too as she had neglected her own sister in favour of ambition and pursuing her dreams for Ronnie's band.

Tomorrow would be another day and they would all go to church and pray for a brighter future...

Chapter 46

Ellie

Dr Abebe Majola...

After the PI had warned Ellie to take her YouTube video down she had decided to remain silent. Yet she knew after the conversation with Jinni about Song that the situation was not going to go away. Too many people knew that Song had been in Atlanta for it be completely covered up. Ellie was a sensitive person and she felt empathy for Song. It was hard to imagine what she had suffered there. To be attacked in an alley by your boss must have been terrifying. As a lecturer who was around students, it would set her apart from her peers, and Ellie doubted if she could have settled back into university and forgotten the incident.

On Monday Kevin and Ellie went to the State University to teach their classes as normal. The day passed uneventfully and Ellie was ready to leave at 5 pm and waiting for Kevin in the main lobby of the business school. She couldn't understand why he was late as usually Kevin was a very punctual person. When he did not arrive she decided to go and meet him. So she took the elevator up to his office on the 10th floor.

Kevin was a professor and had a very nice office. This consisted of a space which you entered through a door from the corridor. This space had a sofa for students to sit on while they waited to see him. There was then an inner door to his main office where Kevin had a desk and book cases. Ellie opened the door from the corridor and saw there were no students on the sofa waiting to see him.

His office door was ajar. It soon became apparent he was on a Zoom call as the booming voice of his research partner from Georgia State University, Dr John Strickland could be heard, and this was accompanied by loud laughter. Ellie hesitated for a moment and was absolutely shocked at what she overheard. She had never heard such filth. Two respected academics talking on a university

Zoom call and it was disgusting what they were saying. It was obvious they were talking about Dr Abebe Majola due to the references to her research.

"She is investigating immigrant women who have been sexual victims and have no voice." Said Dr John "hahaha I'll bet she hasn't been a victim herself."

Kevin, to Ellie's horror joined in laughing

"Well she is not easy on the eye is she?"

And then the conversation degenerated into pure filth.

John Strickland made a filthy comment "If I fucked that mine would drop off!" and they guffawed.

Just as Kevin was in the midst of roaring with laughter and responding "I wouldn't fuck her with yours!!" Ellie walked in and stood there with her arms folded.

When he saw her his face went bright red and he shut up for a moment and then said.

"What a nice surprise, Ellie" and to the laptop screen "my wife has just arrived John. She must have finished her teaching."

John went very quiet and there was a fair amount of coughing and clearing of throats.

"Do you want to wait outside, Ellie?" Kevin said "John and I were just discussing our research."

Ellie stood there with my arms folded and smirked

"Sure you were. No darling. I think I will wait for you right here."

And with that she sat down in the chair across from Kevin, and kept her arms folded.

The conversation ended very quickly after that.

"Ellie, I really am going to have to ask you to knock when you come to my office." Kevin said imperiously.

"Ellie I am going to have to ask you to knock??" she repeated "no wonder you want me to knock. I had no idea you talked such filth, Kevin. How disgusting you and that Strickland guy are. Also, the arrogance of your comments. What on earth makes you think that Dr Abebe would be interested in either of you?"

"It was just a little joke, Ellie. Can you not take a joke? It was just harmless male humour. You have to roll with the punches if you are going to work with guys."

"Bloody Hell." Ellie said "A joke? Talking in a disgusting way at the expense of another academic just because she is a woman. And…don't give me the old excuse you have to roll with the punches. Be one of the guys. You wouldn't talk like that about another man. What a load of bullshit."

Kevin was still red in the face and shuffling papers and his laptop around on his desk.

"What would happen if it got out what you two talk about in your research calls? You would both lose your jobs."

"It was a private conversation" Kevin said indignantly "You came barging in during the middle of it."

"It wasn't private. If you were at our house, okay it was private. How can it be private while you are on university premises." Ellie decided to keep the upper hand while she had it for once. "I am concerned about you Kevin. I am thinking of course of Dr Stacey Peterson, who is in charge of Diversity, Equity and Inclusive Education."

Kevin blanched at the mention of her name

"For goodness sake Ellie" he spluttered "stop being so ridiculous"

“Mmmm. I am thinking of gender equality, racism.....It certainly wasn’t unconscious bias. It was blatant.”

Kevin puffed his chest out and said in an imperious voice

“Ellie stop exaggerating. John and I would never say anything racist. You know that. You always go too far.”

“Oh I see” Ellie stood up tall and then leaned over the desk “So its just women in general you put down and body shame is it? Doesn’t matter if they are white, black or sky blue pink with yellow dots on if they are a woman they are fair game to you and Dr John.”

Kevin glared at her across his desk “What do you want Ellie?” he said “I am tired of this conversation now.”

“Get your buddy Dr John Strickland to introduce me to Dr Abebe Majola. I would love to talk to her. It seems he knows her, correct?”

“If that is what you want Ellie” Kevin said “ and it will shut you up I can arrange it for you. She is even more of a rabble rouser than you though so I am not sure I like the idea of the pair of you together.”

Ellie gave him a foul look and he nodded and started packing his things up.

Ellie found it hard not to laugh out loud. She thought, what a first this was – the first time she had ever seen Kevin at a loss for words. A victory for her. All his rhetoric training had let him down. The man who never lost a debate during his undergraduate degree. She smiled inwardly.

She was really looking forward to meeting Dr Abebe Majola and asking what she could do to help her.

Chapter 47

Highbridge College, Los Angeles

A whistleblower....

On Fridays Monroe Stevens taught a course in the Business School called "Do the right thing – how to deal with Fraud and Ethics" to a group of first year undergraduates at Highbridge College. She ran four seminars each week which were designed to be very interactive. Today Monroe had put the students into groups and they were supposed to report on the FTX Cryptocurrency case. FTX was a cryptocurrency trading company with a turnover in the billions of dollars. It crashed in November 2022 due to mismanagement of funds. Within a few days a class action lawsuit was filed in a Florida court alleging that FTX was a fraudulent cryptocurrency scheme which was designed to take advantage of unsophisticated investors across the USA (source: Investopedia).

The case had been in the news recently and there had been much talk about Sam Bankman-Fried, the CEO. He was one of the youngest billionaires in the USA before the fraud was uncovered. He had been very good at getting influencers and celebrities to publicise the company. (source: Investopedia)

Monroe had been fascinated by the case and hoped the students would enjoy researching it themselves and reporting back to the class.

The first two seminars went well. The students had researched what had gone wrong at the company and who had been involved. The classes were interesting and engaging.

In the third seminar, she had a large group of international students. These students were often shy at participating, and it could be difficult to get a discussion going. Monroe wondered how they would react at having to present to the rest of the class.

The first group gave a short talk with some insights into FTX.

There was a pause after this group finished before the second group got up to present. There were four students, one of whom was Song. Monroe's heart sunk at the sight of her. Song was a difficult student who, in Monroe's view, should not be in an American university. She would not answer questions in class and her written work was very poor. Monroe also knew that Song had caused a lot of trouble in the fall semester by being absent. Monroe believed she had not attended any classes in October, November or December and by some fluke this had got past the wellbeing staff. There had been a huge bust up about it and now her professor father had had her reinstated.

The group stood at the front of the seminar room. Three students talked about the fall of FTX and cryptocurrency. Then it was Song's turn. Song looked sulky and uninterested standing at the front of the class.

Song looked around the class and then looked down at the notes in her hand "FTX spent a lot of money that was not theirs. This money was spent on" she stopped here and continued with a tick list

"an expensive apartment in the Bahamas. This was a penthouse apartment.

A private jet

and other property for his parents and other people. This was all a fraud."

The class were listening to Song, but there she stopped. It seemed she did not have anything else to say.

Monroe said "Can you tell us more about the expensive real estate and private jet? Were these paid out of company funds?"

Song looked at her and for a long time said nothing and then she said "I expect it was. It was a fraud."

Monroe went on "Can you elaborate on why it was wrong to spend money on these items?"

She sighed inwardly – goodness me, it was like pulling teeth! But also so obvious to anyone that Song had no comprehension of a fraud case. She didn't understand what had happened and at the end of the day had absolutely no interest. Why was she here?

When she got no answer from Song, Monroe then opened the questions up to the class. No-one had any questions for Song or her group. Song went and sat down again at the back of the classroom and did not speak again for the rest of the session.

After all the seminars were ended, Monroe went for a coffee. She was deep in thought about Song. She knew about the social media posts about Song. It seemed Song had been involved in a scandal in Atlanta. She also knew that Professor Xingping Zhang was her father and he was responsible for sending Chinese students to Highbridge. Without these students there were rumours that Highbridge would not be able to continue as the College would not have enough students to pay their bills.

Monroe felt that the fact that Song had a very influential father had been the reason no-one had spoken up about the events in Atlanta and the social media posts. Candy Boval had sent her a text about it the other day. Poor Candy had lost her job over this. Candy told her she had spoken to a PI in Atlanta, and there was a lawyer looking for Song. At this point, and given this reflection, Monroe decided she had had enough and she was going to speak up.

Monroe went over to the Executive Offices and made an appointment with Dr Jerry Brill, the Dean of the Business School. The following week on Tuesday, Jerry met with Monroe in his office. He was a middle-aged balding white man, who looked well-fed.

"Sit down. Sit down." He said indicating a chair that was lower than his. He sat opposite her with his legs spread and a false smile on his face. He didn't recognise her. His PA had told him her name. He was thinking: what does she teach? He tried not to get too involved with the "coal face" as he called it. He hadn't been in a classroom in years.. Out loud he said: "So, how can I help?"

Monroe tried to avoid looking at his crotch. She knew tactics like this and mustn't allow him to make her feel like a 3-year-old child. He was an oleaginous creep in her view but she must be brave and speak out.

“I need to speak to you about events that might bring the university into disrepute.” Said Monroe

“I see.” He said still with the big smile on his face, “Go ahead, I am listening.”

Monroe told him about the social media posts about Song that had been circulating implying she had been involved in an attempted rape in South Atlanta. A man was now in prison waiting to be tried for aggravated assault and battery. He had tried to defend her against an attack by a man in an alley behind a burger bar. However, Song had run away and would not speak up for him. Her father’s lawyer had covered it up.

“You should know, people are looking for her. There has also been a YouTube video and an academic from a university in Georgia was talking about the case on television.” She then paused as he seemed to be looking around the room, rather than at her.

Dr Brill made a waving motion with his hands and said, “Go on, I am listening.”

“In fact, a PI acting for a lawyer in Atlanta called a former staff member to ask if Song was here. I believe there is going to be a trial soon for the man who is accused of aggravated assault and battery.”

“If what you say is true then if there is a trial Song’s testimony would be important. Yes, I can see that.” He said, the smile had gone now. He looked serious now and was stroking his chin.

“Well, thank you Monroe for telling me this information. Do you know the name of the lawyer who may be representing the man accused of aggravated assault and battery?”

“No I don’t” Monroe said “I don’t have that information.”

“I will think about the best way for us as an Institution to follow up on your information.” Said Dr Brill.

He stood up, his knees creaking and as Monroe stood, he shook her hand.

After she left, he sent a quick email to the Executive Team requesting a meeting as soon as possible.

Chapter 48

Jinni

Visits Highbridge College....

I caught a very early flight to Los Angeles on Monday morning. I had left the salon in the safe hands of Julie, my senior manicurist. It was about 10 a.m. when I arrived on the campus of Highbridge University.

Highbridge was not what I expected. The campus was stunningly beautiful with palm trees and flowers. The buildings were new but had been built in the style of the old Californian missions. White low-level buildings with arched openings at the windows and entries. The roofs were of red tile and the doors had carved wooden features. I could see there was a sports centre with swimming pool and basketball court. The drive around the campus was lined with swaying palm trees. Why would anyone want to run away from this beautiful place, I asked myself? Then I pulled myself up, it was a place of learning and Song had struggled with the learning.

Students were already on the campus walking between classrooms. They were chatting and laughing as if they did not have a care in the world.

I followed the signs to the main reception. This was a beautiful area with dual height ceilings exposing the rafters above. I walked over to the counter and spoke to "Becky" who was on the desk.

I explained I was looking for Song Zhang, a student who was a friend of mine. I asked "could you let her know I am here looking for her or let me know which class she is in so I can go and meet her?"

Becky looked at me strangely "And who are you ma'am?"

"I am a friend"

"We are not allowed to give out personal details of any of our students. That is against regulations. If you are her friend do you not have her cell?"

It became obvious quickly I was going to get nowhere going through official channels. I thanked her (for nothing!) and walking out of main reception saw that there was a student café in the next building. This café had tables and chairs on a terrace outside. I went over to the café and ordering a coffee I saw that there were several Chinese students sitting at a table on the terrace talking in a language I didn't understand.

With my coffee in hand I went over to them, and stood at the table. They stopped talking and looked at me. I had my cell in my hand. "Hi" I said "I am looking for a friend of mine who is a student here and I wondered if you might know her." I then showed them a picture of Song. It was a favourite of mine taken at my apartment last December. She was happy and smiling on the picture.

The students passed it around the table and all looked at it while commenting in their own language.

"We have seen this student on campus, but we are not friends with her" said the person nearest to me.

"Do you know what classes she takes?" I asked

"I think she is a business student" said another person "the business school is over there" he indicated with his hand.

I didn't get much more information from them. Thanking them for the information, I made my way over to the Business School. Going into the lobby I saw notices pinned up of events this week. The building was quiet and I realised that classes were in session. Looking at my watch, it was 10.25. I guessed the changeover time for classes would be 11 a.m. I decided to sit in the lobby and drink my coffee and wait to see if Song passed through there on her way to and from classes.

At 11 the lobby became very busy with students going to and from classes. No sign of Song. At 12 same thing. By now I was getting bored, but I decided this was the best thing to do. If I stayed still in the place where she took class surely I would see her eventually?

My thought process paid off as at 1 pm I finally saw her as she was coming into the lobby. She looked even more beautiful than ever. She had her hair tied back in a ponytail and was wearing a white blouse and shorts. Her legs were toned and fit and seemed to go on forever. She carried her books in her arms.

I stood up and pushing through the crowd I called her name "Song" I said

She seemed to look in my direction and then turned and left the building. It took me a couple of minutes to get through the crowd to follow her. When I got outside I did not immediately see her. I could see other students walking across the campus going from one building to another.

I did not know which way to turn. I started running towards the main building. I saw a person with a ponytail and white shorts moving ahead of me. When I caught up with this person, I touched them on the shoulder and the person turned, and it wasn't Song. It was a stranger who wanted to know why I had touched them.

It was an absolute nightmare. I was running round the campus, growing increasingly desperate. I saw a second student that I thought looked like her and running over touched her arm. She turned annoyed and again it was not Song. This time though I felt someone touch my arm. I turned around and stared at a very tall man wearing a black uniform and reflector sunglasses. He must have been about 6 foot 4 inches tall. He towered over me. He was wearing a body camera and had his cell in his hand.

"Can I ask what you are doing on campus, ma'am?"

Of course, it was obvious that this was a member of the campus security police.

"Yes, I am here looking for my friend." I said "Perhaps you can help me with that."

"Do you have a pass to be on campus?" he enquired. "Please show it to me."

I did not have a pass, and if Becky on reception had been supposed to give me one, then she never mentioned it or offered me one.

"I can go to reception to get a pass"

"I don't think so, ma'am. You have been observed running around shouting and touching students. I think you need to come with me."

I was adamant "I'm not going anywhere. I am here looking for my friend."

A crowd had started to gather, with students stopping to stare. I was aware that some were laughing and making comments. Someone had their cell pointed at me filming what was going on. I felt deeply humiliated.

The security policeman moved to get hold of my arm and I instinctively jumped away. With that he moved quickly to get hold of me. He then physically manhandled me and and put me into the police vehicle that pulled up alongside us. His partner was driving the car.

What a loss of face. As I was being bundled into the car I was aware that I was centre of attention, with some students taking pictures on their cells.

"Please help me to look for my friend" I said, but realised I sounded strange and that students were filming and nobody was going to help me.

I sat in the back of the vehicle and the security men shut the doors. They drove me off campus.

"Please do not attempt to come back on campus" the security man said "we will leave you at the bus stop and you need to go home. This is private property and you need to have permission to come onto the campus. If we catch you again on the campus without a pass there will be consequences. Think yourself lucky we are going to let you go for now."

With that they stopped the car and left me at the bus stop on the road outside the campus.

I sat down on a bench and put my head in my hands and started to cry. I felt like a stalker! I believe Song did see me but didn't want to acknowledge me. How stupid of me to then run around shouting her name and touching students! Also, why did I not check that visitors to the campus needed a pass. Why was I such a fool coming here? I should be back in the Purple Orchid doing what I always do, waiting on customers. It hurt so much to think Song didn't want me, it was like someone had put a knife into my side and they were twisting it.

Although I loved her with all my heart, I still judged her. Only on Saturday I had vowed to stop judging people but here I was doing it again. Deep down I felt Song was stupid to not accept my help. I could rescue her and help her. Goodness knows what was coming her way. I was old and wise enough to know that her father's lawyer was not going to be able to cover up what had happened in Atlanta for much longer.

I would just have to console myself with the fact I had tried to help her. I had to accept that she had moved on and did not want me in her life no matter how much that hurt. The way she had turned and left that building had proved that she didn't want me as I truly believe she saw me. There were other people in my life who also needed my help and care, and they would not reject my help I believed. I should concentrate on them.

I took out my cell and booked an uber back to the airport. I would go home and tomorrow would be another day in my salon.

Chapter 49

Los Angeles

Highbridge College

Serving a subpoena...

Derek Lynes and his team had prepared a defence for Barry Watkins which relied heavily on Song being able to give her testimony. It was therefore important that his team were able to find Song and serve her with a subpoena.

Kathy Becker his PI had been in touch with Candy Boval again to find out if she had been able to find out an address for Song. Kathy knew that she would not be able to serve Song with the subpoena on campus. It was private property and the campus police could have the service declared invalid.

Candy Boval had messaged her friend Monroe about Song. Monroe agreed to meet her for a coffee off campus.

"How is it going?" Monroe asked "Any luck with your job search?"

"Not really" said Candy "I have just applied for work tutoring for a company that do classes for the Certified Public Accountant (CPA) exam. It's not full time but it will help pay some bills."

"It was so unfair what happened to you." Monroe said "I am sick and tired of having to teach international students who can't even speak English! Then we are told we have to pass them or it will look bad for the university."

"I guess Song is back then?" said Candy "Is she in your class again?"

"You bet your ass she is in my class" said Monroe "Just my luck! She is just as bad as ever. Can't really string a sentence together and seems to have no interest in anything we are teaching."

"I guess it's great to have a father who provides so many Chinese students to the university that they will bend over backwards for her. She will end up graduating and will know nothing. What a joke!" Candy sipped her latte. She looked around the coffee shop. She could not see anyone she knew from the university and there were no students. It was quiet and okay to have this conversation without anyone overhearing. She became more bold and said "Do you know much about her? Is she coming to all her classes now?" and here Candy smiled "does she turn up on time?"

Monroe looked at Candy curiously "Amazingly she is coming to class now. I try to have minimal to do with her. She usually arrives at the last minute or is late. I am pretty sure she lives off campus as last week she came in late and told me there had been an accident and her bus had been held up in traffic."

"Is that your 1 pm class?" asked Candy

"Yes that is the one – I run it twice a week today and Friday at the same time. Song has been attending both classes. Watch this space for how long?"

They chatted for a while longer and then Monroe had to leave to teach her 1 pm class. They arranged to meet up again.

Candy hurried over to the bus stop outside the university. At 12.45 a bus pulled up – Candy could see that it had come from Thousand Oaks and was a local bus mainly for university students. As she stood way back at the bus stop she saw students start to get off the bus. A number filed off and then she saw her – Song. She was carrying her books and had her hair in a pony tail. It was all she could do to stop herself going over and giving her a piece of her mind. Song walked towards the university campus.

Candy checked the schedule for the bus on her cell. It ran every half hour during the day. She made a note of this. She then sent a picture to Kathy Becker the PI for Derek Lynes with the message that she should come out and that she would be able to catch up with Song at the bus stop.

With that Candy drove home happy she had done something to help a PI looking for Song. Perhaps Song would get all she deserved now.

On Wednesday, Kathy Becker caught the plane out to Los Angeles and an uber to Thousand Oaks. They still needed an address for Song to be able to serve the subpoena. She caught the bus that arrived at Highbridge University for the 1 pm class. Sitting at the back she hoped no one would notice her. A couple of stops into the journey in an area of low rise apartment blocks the bus stopped and she saw the person from the pictures get on. It was Song. It was the first time she had seen Song in person. She was a very beautiful woman but was she really worth all the fuss that had been made about her. Song was with another student and they sat chatting while the bus rumbled on its journey to the university.

Kathy also got off at the university but did not go on the campus. She found a coffee shop near to the campus and sat there waiting for a couple of hours. She then returned to the bus stop. Song did not come for the 3 pm bus. Kathy hoped she had not missed her. Song arrived with her friend for the 3.30 pm bus. Kathy also got on this bus. When Song got up to get off, Kathy also stood up and followed her off the bus.

Song seemed to be unaware of Kathy. She walked quickly down the street and turned into an apartment block on the right hand side. The apartment block had a security door and Kathy followed her quickly through the door. “Thanks for holding the door for me.” She said.

Song walked down the corridor on the first floor and Kathy pretended to look for something in her bag so that she did not follow too closely. She then set off down the corridor. She saw that Song went into apartment 6B.

Kathy then turned and left the apartment block quickly messaging Derek Lynes with the address.

She got a thank you back quickly. A process server could now be employed to serve Song with a subpoena to appear in the Barry Watkins trial. It was a good day's work for Kathy.

Chapter 50

Los Angeles

Two Deans meet at Highbridge College

Jerry Brill, Dean of the Business School at Highbridge College had sent an email to Kirsty Wareham, Dean of International Students demanding an urgent meeting and the duo met in his office at 6 pm the same day.

Jerry didn't even bother with pleasantries as he told Kirsty to take a seat in an informal seating arrangement by the window in his office.

"What the hell is going on, Kirsty?" he demanded to know "Is it this student, Song, who is causing all this trouble?"

Kirsty knew he would find out about Song sooner rather than later and the moment she had been dreading was now happening.

"Song is the daughter of Professor Xingping Zhang from Guangzhou." She then added "As you know."

"I know she's Ryan's daughter for goodness sake" blustered Jerry Brill using Xingping Zhang's "English" name. "But I have been told by a member of staff that it is on social media that she has been involved in an attempted rape in Atlanta, of all places. What the hell was she doing in Atlanta?"

"Yes, good question." Agreed Kirsty. "She was absent for most of the fall semester. We believed that she was sick. In fact, she was visiting friends in Atlanta."

"Why was her sick note not checked out properly?" Jerry Brill's already florid complexion was now bright red and the veins on his neck were standing out. "Are you saying this is fucking true? She was in Atlanta?"

Kirsty picked some invisible lint of her blouse before replying.

“yes, it would appear to be true. The bit about Atlanta. Harry Zine, who is Ryan’s attorney, brought her back from Atlanta. I haven’t heard about an attempted rape.”

“Can you imagine what the publicity about this would do to this University?” Jerry spluttered. “A Chinese girl doesn’t attend class for weeks on end and is half way across the country in another state during fucking term time. Meanwhile, our wellbeing and pastoral care miss this completely. What the fuck happened there Kirsty?”

“It was an unfortunate incident.” Kirsty spoke soothingly in an attempt to placate him “I am afraid Song slipped through the net, so to speak. She had a personal tutor who was not up the job. It would have been picked up by a competent tutor.”

“Really?” queried Jerry “It is like a PR nightmare. Heads should be on the line.”

“Oh don’t worry” Kirsty said imperiously “the tutor in question has been dealt with and is no longer with us. There will never be another case like this.”

“My whistleblower also told me that this Song was working in Atlanta at a fucking burger bar.”

Kirsty hated profanity and was finding it hard to listen to Jerry Brill and his swearing which was followed by him gesticulating. He went on “And what has Ryan had to say about this? Its his daughter after all.”

“Ryan has been most understanding.” Said Kirsty “In fact he is going to send us another 25 students for next academic year. Think of the money Jerry. We need that money to keep going. We have had to…..” and here she paused, and cleared her throat “cover up for Song’s indiscretions. I am sure she will not attempt anything else. As you may know as she is a student in the Business School, academics are not her strong point. I think she will be lucky to graduate with a 2.5 GPA.”

"There is a man in prison in Atlanta who supposedly defended her. His people want her to act as a witness at his trial. Can you imagine what will happen if she does?"

Jerry got up from his chair and began to pace back and forth.

"This is an unbelievable disaster. I don't know Ryan and his attorney have enough power or money to shut the internet up. People are out baying for her blood."

Kirsty thought that was a little dramatic, but sadly it may be true. She found it hard to believe that someone hadn't already put on social media that Song was a student here at Highbridge.

"We can't ask Ryan to take his daughter back to China or ask for her to be transferred to another college." Kirsty said out loud.

"You bet we can't" agreed Jerry "Who the heck would take her? I presume you are talking the States? In reality, how many days has she actually attended class? What do we put on the transfer – this girl was sick for 4 ½ months out of the 8 months she had been a student. However she is an exemplary student!!"

They both sat in silence for a few moments that seemed to stretch out for what seemed like an eternity. Then Jerry spoke

"She can't stay here. This is a fucking PR disaster in the making. No American college would have her. But wait, do we know anywhere in Australia?" he went on "Do you think Woomeray Tech would take her?"

"I don't think we can do that Jerry"

"Why the hell not! We have to get that girl out of this university now before our reputation is ruined. Can we not offer her something – I'm thinking a scholarship coupled with an internship to help a Professor at Woomeray Tech with research? You know as well as I do Woomeray are usually very accommodating They do not feature very highly in the Australian rankings and anything international is very tempting to them."

Kirsty had to admit that this was a good idea. Woomeray Tech was in the middle of the Australian outback as far from civilisation as it was possible to get in her view. They may very well help out if Kirsty agreed to a transfer for one of their students to Highbridge on a scholarship.

"I will explore this Jerry. However, the issue is if we can do it in time. Are you saying there is going to be a trial in Atlanta?"

She stopped there as she felt if she went on it was possible that Jerry was going to spontaneously combust in front of her.

"You do that." Said Jerry "I want that girl out of this college ASAP but at the same time I do not want to lose her father's business. You know the state of the finances of this university. ½ billion dollars in loans that have to be paid. This girl could cost us dear." He stopped then and composed his features into a terrifying rictus grin. "You know you can sort it out Kirsty."

Kirsty smiled a fake smile and took her leave as soon as possible. She had a lot to do. Deals to make. She would smooth it over though she was sure of that.

Chapter 50

Highbridge College

Song's story...

It seemed to Song that she didn't sleep any more. When she closed her eyes, her dreams were so vivid that she wakened again quickly and lay there in the dark sweating and crying.

In her heart she longed to be back in the beautiful garden in Guangzhou where her mother grew orchids. The Song plum orchid (after which she was named) and the extremely rare parrot orchid. Even in her memory the sights and smells of these plants was almost overwhelming. The birdsong would fill the air – all varieties of birds including the Great Barbet, Common Tailorbird and Light Vented Bulbul She would return from school and run into the garden looking for her mother. The garden gently sloped down to the banks of the river and there her mother would be tending her plants. They would sip tea together and Song would tell her mother about her day. To think of her mother and being in that garden was so powerful that Song would cry out in longing.

Her eyes would gradually become heavy and tired and she would give in to sleep and then the dreams would start.

There she was on her trek across America after running away from Highbridge. Lily was with her of course. Lily was the person who had got her into this mess, she told herself. Lily, was also a student at Highbridge who she knew from Guangzhou. Lily, who was even less academic than she was. They had sat together when they first arrived at Highbridge and kept their heads down in case they were asked questions in class. The American students were so outgoing and always knew the answers. Song and Lily struggled to understand what the teacher said. They struggled with the homework. They struggled with everything. It was all over their heads and they just wanted to leave the college and get on with their lives.

Song's father had insisted that she go to the American university. He wanted her to have an academic career like him. She was his only child and he saw her following in his footsteps. Song could never follow in his footsteps. She had no interest in academics and only wanted to make herself look pretty, listen to music and gossip with her friends.

Attending the American university was really difficult for Song and Lily. It was not just the academics it was the American students. They seemed so rich. The parking lot was full of BMWs, Teslas and Porsches. They wore clothes that looked comfortable and casual but which were in fact very expensive designer items. Shorts from Dolce and Gabbana and Pucci. Casual pieces from Zimmerman and workout gear from Alala. Gold jewellery including watches from Cartier and Rolex. Lily and Song felt like they did not have enough money to be able to dress in the same style. Plus what was worse was that the Americans were so self-assured. They answered questions in the classroom and they could be seen in the café on campus holding forth about their social lives and vacations.

Song and Lily did not feel able to compete with or to talk to any of these people. They sat quietly in class, hoping not to be noticed.

Then Lily had the bright idea of working as cleaners for wealthy Americans. This would give them money to be able to buy clothes and look like the American students. They went to a Cleaning Agency Lily had found out about. The agency had taken them on for cash to be paid under the table. They had cleaned homes in Hollywood Hills. It had taken hours to get there on the bus from Thousand Oaks. They were missing classes to do the cleaning. Then Lily had suggested they stay in the San Fernando Valley for a couple of days a week to be nearer to their work. She had a friend who had an apartment It turned out there were about eight Chinese sharing a one bedroom apartment on Reseda Boulevard. It was tiny and overcrowded. Then things got worse as Lily had started to steal things from the homes. Little things at first and then they gradually got bigger. Someone had complained a watch had disappeared. Lily swore she had not taken it, but Song wasn't sure. The agency wouldn't turn them in as they shouldn't have employed them in the first place, but they had to leave. Or at least that is what Lily said. The police might catch up with them at Highbridge.

Lily was tuned into an underground network of Chinese in the US who worked and lived illegally. Li was their contact in the network and he helped them find a city to go to where there were jobs and other Chinese people who they could share an apartment with. They never met him this time and he did not take a fee.

There had been moments of kindness and love in that City and Song had loved her job at the Purple Orchid. It was different there. She really felt she belonged. She loved painting nails and talking to the Americans who came into the salon. But it was Jinni, the owner of the salon, who she had grown to love. She had never loved another woman before, but it had felt so right. The first time Jinni had kissed her she had felt like this was something she had wanted to do all her life. She loved lying in Jinni's arms. She felt safe and loved and valued for herself and who she really was.

But then things had gone bad, as a raid on the Purple Orchid salon was threatened by the Immigration Service. Song had to run again. This time Li acted differently. He said he would help with a job and accommodation but it was getting more difficult.

He was quite threatening on the Zoom call

"You girls are causing me a lot of trouble. I can't keep finding you places. You keep attracting attention from the police and the Immigration Service. You are fucking difficult."

He hummed and hawed for a while and then he finally said "I will need a fee for helping."

Lily had then decided to stay in the City and at the last minute told Song she was not coming with her. Song knew now that Lily actually headed back to Highbridge. They took her back, no questions asked. Song had seen her in classes since she returned. But this time Lily was not so friendly and they gave each other a wide berth.

Song remembered the ride on the Greyhound bus headed for Atlanta. She was now alone. Li kept in contact with her on a cell she had bought just for that purpose. He had told her where she should go in Atlanta. An apartment she could rent cheaply in the south of the city. A job at a burger bar. He would meet her when the bus arrived.

As she got off the bus in Atlanta she could see a man waiting at the bus stop and thought with a sinking heart please don't let that man be Li. He was a scruffy, sleazy older man. But of course it was him. He seemed delighted to see her and although all her instincts told her not to get into his car what choice did she have?

"How much have you got sweetheart?" he asked her

"I got 500 dollars." She said. It was a lie but she did not want to give him all her money.

"Its not enough sweetheart. Atlanta is an expensive city." He said "But we can find a way around it."

The apartment block was tired and seedy. The apartment was on the third floor. The stairs were outside at the rear of the building. Entering the apartment through the door into the main living area Song could see that it was very sparsely furnished. There were 2 bedrooms. One bedroom had the door closed, but she could see the other had bunk beds. She knew that there would be many people living there in shifts. It would be overcrowded and she would have to keep her possessions with her at all time.

Li told her that there was a job for her at Big Daddy's Burger Bar. She would receive $12 an hour and out of the $12 she must pay him $4 for his fee.

Song felt dirty and used. He was standing too close to her and he touched her hair. "We go over to Big Daddy's now" he said.

This is when her nightmares really started. Big Daddy's. It was the most sleazy, greasy, disgusting place. The smell of frying and grease overlaid everything. Eric Senser, a white man in his 50's. Fat and gone to seed. Leering at her. It was all so wrong. She wanted to run from day one.

Then there was Eric's partner, Sonya. This woman sat there either at the till taking money or flipping burgers all the time pretending her partner wasn't leering at Song. She was a big, fat woman who would only speak to Song if she was forced to. She swore every other word and shouted. She used American words and also Spanish words such as "puta". She smelled of body odour and stale fat. But she was not as disgusting as Senser.

Sometimes when Song was asleep Senser came to her in her dreams. He had huge, beefy hands and she felt them running all over her. She remembered his onion breath as he came close to her and rubbed against her in the shop. Some days he also smelled of stale body odour.

The comments he made. "You are such a naughty girl. Do you know what you do to me?" He would say. "Stop teasing me."

She should have run from that place on day one. But she had little money, and nowhere to go. She did not want to lose face by admitting she had made a mistake in running away from school. She wanted to be back in Guangzhou with her mother.

There were brighter moments – Barry Watkins, the huge black man who lived next door. He made her laugh and she liked spending time with him.

But those moments were forgotten when the night of the attempted rape came back to her. Song experienced these feelings every day, and particularly at night when she tried to sleep.

She was in the alley taking the trash out as asked to by Sonya. It stunk in the alley and she wanted to make the visit quick. Suddenly she was aware of Senser's presence.

"You really are hot, babe." He said "look at you, taking out trash and you look like a million dollars."

He came nearer so she could smell his onion breath and his hands ran through her hair.

She wriggled to get away from him. He stood in her way. He was blocking her exit from the alley.

She remembered this so many times. Then his hands were on her. He was breathing deeply and groaning as he ran his hands over her breasts and down her body.

Song had struggled to get away, but he was strong.

"Fight me, would you?" he groaned "Come on, babe. You know you want it."

He pressed against her and his hands were now inside her pants pulling them down.

She started to scream but he put his hand over her mouth.

Song would never forget that moment and the smell of him and the touch of his hands.

It was this she dreamed of so many nights. He would have raped her. He was that close. A couple more seconds and it would have happened. He smelled bad and he was groaning and sweating. It was the smell she remembered. The smell of the garbage in the alley. Then there was Senser's filthy, disgusting smell. She would wake crying and shaking and check every door and window in her room. She would never be safe again.

But then a large figure had come up behind Senser and dragged him off her. She was standing there with her pants down shaking while this man beat the shit out of Senser. Senser was lying on the floor bleeding and begging.

A few people had heard the noise and had started to come into the alley.

“For fuck’s sake Bro leave it” someone said “Fat Sonya has called the police.”

Barry had taken her hand and they had run together out of the alley to his car and back to his apartment.

The beating was also something she would never forget. She had never seen violence before. The noises – the crunching, the groaning. Senser pleading. The blood. Sometimes she would be in class and she would hear those noises and tune the teacher out. She would look at her laptop but see only blood and guts.

Barry had washed her in the tub at his apartment, but she would never be clean again. The stink of that evening would be on her for the rest of her life.

When her father and his lawyer had rescued her from the Immigration Detention Centre she had gone back to Highbridge University. But she would never be the same again.

Everyone thought she would carry on as if nothing had happened. But something had happened. She would carry the scars for ever.

Of course, there were the rumours as well. People were looking for her. Her picture had been on the internet. There had been a YouTube video. Noone said anything directly to her, but Song knew they were talking about her behind her back.

She could no longer contact Li. The number she had for him was unobtainable. Lily was avoiding her. She had spoken to her when they first saw one another in a class. However, the conversation had been very stilted. Lily couldn’t meet Song’s eyes. Song couldn’t believe that Lily had come back to university when it had been her idea to leave in the first place. It seemed that Highbridge University was happy to have her back though.

Song also realised that she was bad news in the underground Chinese community. She couldn’t believe how quickly they closed ranks and cut her off.

Harry Zine had requested a Zoom call with her. He had started the conversation without even asking how she was.

"It is really important that you lay low at the university." He said "don't talk to anyone other than the teachers. All this will blow over very quickly."

Song wanted to say "What if I want to speak to someone? What if I want to share how that pig tried to rape me?" But of course she did not.

She was sure she had seen Jinni on campus on Monday. Jinni from the Purple Orchid. She had been part of the crowd waiting to go to class. She had run away as she was frightened to speak to anyone.

She could never speak. She had no voice.

She had wanted to be famous in America. Perhaps she was famous now but not for the reason she wanted.

Then the doorbell rang at her apartment. She went to answer it and a man she did not know stood there. He asked her to confirm her name. He then said "Consider yourself served with a subpoena to act as a witness in the trial of Barry Watkins for aggravated assault and battery."

Holding the package he gave her, she shut the door and fell down behind it. She began to cry.

What could she do now? She couldn't keep hiding and keeping silent. But how could she speak when her father and his lawyer were so against it? Noone cared about her.

Then she remembered someone who had loved her and cared about her. Someone who she had left and ran away from. Someone who she had not acknowledged on campus. But someone who she wanted more than anyone in the whole world. Jinni.

Taking her cell out she scrolled through the numbers. She still had Jinni's number. She had transferred it from her old cell. Sobbing she rang the number.

Jinni answered "This is Jinni. Who is calling?"

"It is Song" sobbed Song "please, please can I come to you?

Chapter 51

Jinni

Song returns…

When my cell rang and it was Song at first, I could not believe it. Then I became happy, then worried, then sad. My body was alive with emotion.

We agreed that Song should come to me as soon as possible. I knew she would be missing classes again, but at this point what did it really matter?

I paid for her airfare and took an uber out to the airport after the salon closed for our reunion.

While I waited for her, I rang Kevin and Ellie. I had confided in them before and I felt Kevin might know what to do.

Kevin recommended taking her to my apartment and he would investigate some things and come over later this evening.

When I saw Song at Arrivals my mood lifted and I felt my heart would burst with happiness. No matter that she brought with her trouble I knew that I would look out for and protect her for the rest of my life.

We hugged in Arrivals and both broke down into tears. It had only been a month or so since she was here last but it had felt like forever. There had been times when I thought I would never see her again.

We took an uber back to my apartment and I made us a simple salad while she brought me up to date on what was happening. It was obvious that she was traumatised by what had happened in Atlanta and it seemed she was not sleeping or coping well.

I was very hungry. I ate my salad quickly, but I noticed that Song only picked at her food absent mindedly. This is not how I remembered her but I did not say anything as then Kevin and Ellie arrived. Song remembered Ellie from the salon. I explained that

Kevin was a professor at the State University and I had spoken to him to ask if he would be able to help with Song's situation.

I noticed that Song seemed very nervous around Kevin. Perhaps he reminded her of her father. I sat next to her and put my arm around her to try to put her at ease.

Kevin said "We know you are in a very challenging situation, Song. You have been subpoenaed because Watkin's lawyers feel that your testimony will help reduce their client's sentence for aggravated assault and battery. Their story is that Watkins was trying to protect you. We can try to find out what evidence Watkin's lawyers have that you were at the Burger Bar that evening and in the alley."

At the mention of the alley Song flinched and put her head down.

"I was there they don't need to find out what evidence they have to prove it. I admit it." She said and she began to sob.

Ellie sat on the sofa at the other side of Song and took Song's hand. "I know this is very difficult for you Song" she said "Only you know what it feels like to be the victim of an attempted rape. Also, to be witness to such violence. However, I know I can help you. I want to introduce you to someone who can get you the support you need. Her name is Abebe Majola and she works with women who have been in similar situations to you. Will you agree to talk to her?"

Song nodded and started to cry. "Yes, if she will help me, I will talk to her. But it seems that I am just a burden to people now."

Kevin looked at Song and told her

"Abebe will help you. I am sure of that."

And then he went on

"If you give testimony at the trial and it comes out that you were at the Burger Bar then we have to find out how that will affect your immigration status.

It seems that your student visa is in good order as the time you were absent has been recorded as sickness. Your student visa allowed you to work on campus for up to 20 hours per week during the semester and full time during the breaks. I looked up what on campus means. It means either actually in university buildings or at a location the university approves. You worked at the Purple Orchid which is a nail salon and would not be approved, and Big Daddy's Burger Bar which also would not be approved. This makes for a difficult situation."

Song raised her head "But it is a lie that I was sick. My father's lawyer used that lie so that I could continue my studies. I wasn't sick I was working at that burger bar."

"But it will affect your student visa if this is exposed."

Song sat and did not speak for a minute.

"What will happen to Barry, the black man, if I don't speak in court to say he was defending me?"

Kevin considered this for a moment before speaking:

"He is facing a long prison sentence for aggravated assault and battery. The owner of the burger bar was very badly injured through the beating Watkins gave him. If there was no reason for the beating then the sentence would probably be the maximum."

Ellie spoke again then "Barry is facing up to 20 years in prison in Georgia."

Song sat and sobbed. Tears ran down her cheeks unchecked until I offered her a tissue. "If he had not been there….." she hesitated and drew in a shaky breath "that pig would have….would have" she couldn't bring herself to say the word.

"Senser would have raped you." Offered Ellie "Watkins saved you from that monster." Ellie was nearly in tears as well and she turned and hugged Song. I also turned and the three of us sat there in a group hug.

There was not much more said that evening, and Ellie promised to introduce Song to Abebe Majola the next day.

Song slept in my bed that night and as we lay together, I vowed I would never let her go ever again. After we had been sleeping for a few hours, I was awakened by Song letting out a scream and jumping out of bed. She was sweating and shaking all over and saying "No, no, no" over and over again. I got up and went over to her to try to calm her. I held her in my arms and stroked her back until she seemed to calm down. "It is okay darling" I said "you are here with me. You are safe here. Noone will harm you here."

Eventually Song was calm enough to get back into bed. I don't think until that moment I had realised how traumatised she was. Goodness knows what she had experienced in Atlanta. I held her stroking her hair and talking to her quietly until she fell asleep again. Her sleep was so fitful though. It was not long before she woke again and I saw her slip out of bed and begin to pace around the room. We were both very tired in the morning. I knew that I had to get her help. I rang my doctor and we made an appointment for that morning.

I went to the salon to open up and managed to move a couple of appointments around so that I could take Song to the doctor's office. My doctor diagnosed Song as having stress and depression and wrote her a sick note for university. My doctor also prescribed anti-depressant medication.

We sent the sick note through to the university after the appointment to explain Song's absence from classes. Then Song stayed at my apartment while I went to the salon. When I returned she said that a Zoom appointment had been made for 8 pm with Ellie and Dr Abebe Majola.

Song logged into Zoom while I prepared the food. I popped in and saw Ellie's face come onto the screen and then the face of an older black lady who had cropped her hair very short and wore no makeup. I had seen Dr Abebe Majola on Atlanta morning TV. I knew she was a no nonsense woman. I didn't see her as a future client of the Purple Orchid.

I could hear when I was preparing the food the conversation between the three of them.

Dr Majola introduced herself as someone who was working with and helping women who were illegal immigrants in America who had been the victims of sexual violence.

"I realise that you have a student visa, Song" she said "but if you admit what happened in the alley then there is a danger you will lose your visa and become an illegal immigrant or you will be deported."

Song said that was correct.

Dr Majola then went on to say "This is not an easy situation by any means. Before we go on any further can I ask how you, Song, feel after the incident?"

Song nodded

"Are you having any sleep problems?"

Song nodded "Night is the worse time. I have flashbacks during the day but at night I am tired and want to go to sleep. When I sleep I have nightmares and I am back there. I can smell the alley and Senser. It seems so real. I wake up screaming and sweating."

"Do you find you can concentrate during the day? When you are in class, for example?"

"When I am in class my mind wanders to that night. I hear the noises of the fight and hear Senser pleading. I see the blood. I feel fear about what would have happened if Barry had not come to save me." At this point Song broke down crying.

Dr Majola spoke in a comforting voice

"Song, first know you are not alone. Many women who have been victims of sexual violence suffer the same problems. You must know you are not alone. You have been suffering alone though since the incident. Attending classes and trying to act as if nothing had happened. However, many victims of sexual violence experience trauma that includes experiencing recurrent nightmares and flashbacks. There may be a difficulty in concentrating or sleeping. These are symptoms of deep-seated trauma.

I can get you help with a confidential group that meets in this city. Counsellors will help you to work through your trauma. The group will tell you that being believed and having a voice where people listen to you is essential for you to be able to get through the trauma you are experiencing. I believe up till now and coming here to Jinni's apartment no one wanted to believe you or discuss what really happened that night?"

Song nodded "My father's lawyer just told me to be quiet and not to tell anyone about what happened. My father didn't want to know anything. He just wanted me back in classes at Highbridge."

"You have to forgive yourself as well, Song" said Dr Abebe "What happened was not your fault. You had run away from college but nobody deserved to be treated the way you were treated. Nobody deserved that."

"But it is my fault" sobbed Song "I ran away. My parents were paying for me to go to university and I ran away. I let everyone down and now look at me."

"The counsellors will help you to understand what happened and to learn how you will be able to forgive yourself. Meanwhile you are now among friends and people who care for you and love you."

"My mother still loves me" sobbed Song "I know she does but I can't speak to her. My father wouldn't allow it."

"Remember we are not judging you Song" said Dr Abebe "We just want for you to get better."

I went over and held her hand. Her recovery was going to be painful and slow but I knew with our help she could recover. I was so happy she had done the right thing and come to me.

Dr Majola said that an appointment had been made for Song with a counsellor at the support group the next day and I felt this would be a very positive step. I also believed that Song would be brave enough to speak up for Barry Watkins in his trial. But what this would do to her future was frightening and uncertain to say the least. On this note, I received a call on my cell the next day from Harry Zine. I was at the salon and in the middle of a manicure when it came through. I called him back when my appointment finished to the back room of the salon where there is more privacy.

There were no pleasantries or formalities – he went straight in.

"I know Song is with you, Jinni" he said "Don't even try to deny it."

"Hold on, hold on" I said "You are correct. She is with me and she will stay with me until she can give her testimony at the trial. As you are no doubt aware she has been subpoenaed to speak at the trial of Barry Watkins."

"Yes I know about this." He said

"My doctor has signed Song off from her classes as she is suffering from stress and depression. She is now taking anti-depression medication. This testimony is going to prove to be very difficult for Song."

"I have already spoken to Barry's lawyer about her testimony. It has been agreed that there will be no mention of the fact that Song was working at the Burger Bar. This has no relevance to the aggravated assault and battery trial and attempted rape. The employment is the concern of the Immigration Services and not the Criminal Court. Therefore we will leave that out of the trial." He paused her for effect and then went on "I would like to meet with Song to help her put together her testimony."

"I am willing to concede that the employment is not relevant to this trial, but Song must say what she feels. Her voice must be heard in the trial. I do not want her to say a practiced piece that she has been given by you."

“Of course,” Harry said “Song will say what she feels is right, but I will be there to guide her on the legalities of what she is saying.”

I agreed to talk to Song. There were a couple of weeks before the trial and I was not going to rush her to make her statement. She had time to reflect and decide what it was best to say....

Chapter 53

Plans for Song's future

Professor Xingping Zhang had caught the midnight flight from Guangzhou to LAX and was now making his way to Highbridge University in a taxi. He was a troubled man. The contract he had negotiated with Highbridge had been so lucrative and had helped him advance his career in China. Now everything was threatened due to the behaviour of his only daughter. He could not contemplate why Song didn't want to study and pursue an academic career. His qualifications put him in the 1% of highly educated academics in China. Surely his daughter would want to follow in his footsteps. Yet all she did was run away and cause trouble.

He was due to meet his American attorney, Harry Zine at the university. Harry had rung him a couple of days ago to explain the latest situation. He remembered the conversation.

Harry said "As you know on the evening Song was arrested by the Immigration Services she was with a black man, Barry Watkins. Watkins says that he was defending Song when he was caught fighting. As I told you his friends have been using social media to try to find Song."

"Yes, I know about this" said Xingping Zhang "Why are you bringing this up again now? I hope that you have been successful in stopping this rubbish. I have certainly paid you enough to shut them up."

"The social media posts have stopped." Said Harry "But it seems an anonymous rich person has taken up the case and is paying for" here Harry stopped and coughed "Derek Lynes to represent Watkins at his trial."

"And – and – and what???" said Xingping Zhang "So what? Pay him off."

"I can't pay Derek Lynes off." Harry said "He is a very respected and prominent attorney. He also has deep pockets as he is being paid by a rich person."

"Why on earth would a rich American care about this case?" spluttered Xingping

"Who knows? It may be that the person comes from a poor background and it may be that they feel empathy for what allegedly happened at the burger bar." Said Harry "but who knows? Sometimes rich Americans like to take up causes to promote their own agenda. It could be an aspiring politician."

"The whole thing is ridiculous" said Xingping

"The issue is that Derek Lynes has tracked Song down and she has been served with a subpoena to appear at the trial of Watkins."

Professor Xingping said "What do you mean a subpoena? I am Chinese and don't understand your American ways."

Harry said "A subpoena is a court document requiring a person to appear as a witness in a trial. The person is required to take a vow that they are speaking the truth and then give evidence about what happened. If the person does not appear in court to give evidence then they may face imprisonment."

Professor Xingping Zhang put his head in his hands. "So Song has been handed this document?"

"Yes she has and she has signed for it making it official" said Harry "and to make matters even worse she has left Highbridge again. This time I knew where she would be and I tracked her down to the Purple Orchid."

"Can we not get her back?" said Xingping "I mean bring her back to Highbridge." He realised he was spluttering.

"The problem is that Highbridge want to speak to us both." Harry went on "They have a way forward but um I am not sure at the moment how that involves Song."

Professor Xingping had sat spluttering and blathering. This was horrendous.

Today was the meeting with the executives at Highbridge University. He was dreading it. He would have to put a brave face on and act as if all was fine in front of the Americans.

The taxi dropped him at the main reception and he could see Harry Zine was sitting there talking on his cell. Harry waved him over. He ended the call and said "They are ready for us. They said to go upstairs when you arrived."

The two of them walked upstairs to the Executive suite. The meeting was to be in Jerry Brill's office. Kirsty Wareham, the International Dean was already in the office with Jerry and stood up upon seeing them.

"Professor Xingping – Ryan. Good morning and welcome." She said "Harry, please come in and take a seat."

They sat around the table in the centre of the office. An admin assistant brought them tea and coffee. After initial pleasantries Kirsty got down to business. She first said that she was happy that the two universities could establish links and that Chinese students were able to come to Highbridge to study.

"We are very grateful to you Professor" she said "for these links."

Ryan (Xingping) nodded, he had a horrible feeling something much worse was about to be said.

Kirsty then went on to talk about recent events with Song "Her educational visa is in order." She said "However, there is going to be a trial in Atlanta and Song has to testify. We know that there is no suggestion that she bears any guilt for what happened in Atlanta, however we feel it is a lot for her to do. She is not in her own country and to have to give evidence at a trial may prove traumatic. Not least the surrounding publicity"

Here Kirsty paused for emphasis and then went on "As you know, Ryan, Song is not attending classes at the moment. She has a sick note from a doctor and is staying off campus. She is apparently suffering from stress and anxiety. She will not be attending classes until after the trial at least."

Harry spoke "Yes we are aware that Song is not attending class again and is signed off sick. My understanding is that will not affect her educational visa and that she will be allowed to repeat the classes she has missed."

Kirsty looked at Jerry and then said "It is not the requirements of the visa that are troubling us so much as the fact that Song is not um….." she paused for emphasis "settling into this university."

Jerry spoke for the first time "She has been meeting with her personal tutor and from these meetings it seems apparent that our style of teaching is not appropriate for Song's needs."

Jerry looked around the table and smiled at the other participants in the meeting. "We all have our own learning styles and here at Highbridge we have introduced an innovative way of learning into all classes. This involves group learning and presenting and an action oriented way of approaching studies. This innovative style is known throughout the education sector. In fact, whole conferences have been dedicated to discussing our style."

Ryan, himself an academic, seriously doubted that but decided it was best not to speak out. He felt dread as he knew where this type of speech was leading.

Kirsty said "We both know that this style of learning is often new and different for Chinese students who come here to study. In fact, we have discussed how this new way of learning presents new opportunities for them to experience a new culture and way of doing things."

Jerry took up the discussion then "As you know Ryan many Chinese students not only do well they excel in our system. Look at the results last year a Chinese student graduated summa cum laude and there were other students that also had excellent results."

Ryan had to agree, but he knew where this dual act was leading.

"Yet, sadly" said Kirsty "For some students this style and way of learning is just not right. It is not something they can adapt to. We have had a few who have really struggled to fit in with our ways of doing things."

"We are adamant our ways of learning are ground breaking and for the vast majority of Chinese students who come here, I truly believe." Said Jerry "it is a positive experience and they experience growth and understanding."

Ryan smiled a queasy smile – here we go, he thought.

"This is why" said Kirsty "We must consider your daughter Song and her future. Song is a student who has found this style of learning particularly challenging. We would like you to consider an offer for Song's future." She paused giving Ryan a chance to take this in. "I know that you wish Song to have a chance to study abroad. In this regard we have very close links with an Australian university – Woomeray Tech. They have a much more traditional style of teaching – in fact, it may be similar to the type of class Song would take in China. In addition, a professor at Woomeray is happy to have Song as an intern to help her with her research. A fabulous opportunity for her."

Ryan thought – Woomeray Tech. Was it even an accredited university? Out loud he said "I don't seem to have heard of Woomeray Tech. Can you tell me more?"

"Certainly" said Kirsty "Woomeray Tech is near to Alice Springs in the centre of the continent. It is a very quiet place, not near any of the large coastal cities. Perfect for study and quiet contemplation. I wish I had the chance to do my research in such a quiet and academic place!"

Ryan knew better than to ask how the college ranked. Of course, it wouldn't feature in the rankings of top Australian universities! This was an offer they were making so that Ryan could save face and

keep his links with Highbridge. But he had to take Song away and as soon as possible, he had figured that much out! It was humiliating, he mused. However, he had no choice.

"As you say" he said "Song has struggled with the style of teaching here. Perhaps some time at a more traditional campus in Australia may prove beneficial for her. I, myself, studied for a masters in Australia at RMIT in Melbourne. I have very fond memories of Australia."

Kirsty beamed at him "I really feel it is for the best for her. We can put you in touch with Dr Bruce Dingle who is Head of the Business School there so you can chat through what courses they can offer her."

"Certainly" said Ryan "That would be very helpful."

"Also, if you would like to chat to the other students who are here from China, we would be happy to set that up." Said Kirsty

"There is no need" said Ryan "They do write and feed back to me about their experiences here. There are so many positive and inspiring stories! I am looking forward to carrying our collaboration forward and sending you 25 more students in the fall semester."

So in that office and without being asked for her opinion Song's future was sealed. She would go now to Australia to study and meanwhile her father's links with the USA would remain intact and his own career would continue to blossom. He sat in the taxi on the way back to the airport looking at flight timetables as he would now go to visit his daughter who was staying with Jinni to explain to her what would happen after the trial.

Chapter 54

Ellie

Meets a feminist...

After the incident in Kevin's office, Ellie kept him to his word and was introduced to Dr Abebe Majola by Dr John Strickland. Ellie was very impressed with her. It seemed that she knew how to make her voice heard. Her research was very impressive. They chatted on Zoom and so it was Ellie who was the person who told her where Song was and arranged the meeting with Song. It was felt the meeting went really well and that she was able to help Song with the trauma she felt as a result of the incident in Atlanta.

After the meeting with Song, Abebe arranged another Zoom call with Ellie. She asked me if Ellie was doing research

"You seem very bright and you have curiosity which is always needed for an effective researcher."

"Kevin is the researcher, not me. I don't have a PhD. I peaked with a master's degree."

"You don't need a PhD, just a desire to find out. You should come along to one of my research group meetings. You might find that there is something you can do."

"I would love to come" Ellie said "I teach 4 days a week. I only have Friday free."

That was not a problem and it turned out the meeting was arranged during the lunch time so Ellie could go along virtually. So it was that Ellie joined the Zoom meeting of Abebe's research group. She was introduced to the group. The group started by discussing a paper they were presenting at a conference in Chicago on "The sexual exploitation of illegal immigrant women" Then Abebe went on to talk about a different case – an immigrant woman from a wealthy background who drops out of school and makes herself vulnerable. The group had not studied women in this category previously.

"How many women are there that have come over here on study visas and are struggling? Women that may have dropped out of university and have been abused. They no longer have a visa to live here so are effectively illegal immigrants."

The group were interested to find out more about women in this category.

One group member commented

"This seems like a far-fetched story to me. Perhaps this is a one-off case. There is so much done by the university to help international students. As you know, here we have systems in place to help foreign students – the International Office makes sure they have a mentor. This person helps the student and makes sure they know about all the services available. We have students here that do very well."

"But is this true of all universities? What about universities that may not be accredited? These still recruit international students."

"We want to hear the stories of women who have suffered sexual abuse and make sure their voices are heard." Said one woman

Ellie joined in then saying

"Certainly Song's story would be interesting. Perhaps she would agree to speak about her experiences – even if she did it anonymously."

It was a meeting she really enjoyed. That evening she spoke to Kevin about the meeting and the work the research group were doing.

"Why do you not offer to help them, Ellie?" Kevin said "You are obviously interested to find out more about issues in their area of expertise."

“I couldn’t be part of a prestigious research group.” she said “I’m not qualified.”

“Rubbish” said Kevin “I am sure they would love to have you help them. Also, you might find that the information you collect could be put towards your PhD. Ask if you can help. Even if you do something such as collecting information or evidence to start it would be a really good experience for you.”

Ellie nodded and agreed with him. He was right. Kevin was usually right. For Ellie to act as a research assistant would be a marvellous opportunity. She did not even care about being paid, She was just interested in finding out more about the topic.

Ellie thought about the best way to approach the situation. She decided to send an email to Abebe telling her how much she had enjoyed the meeting and asking if she could do anything to help the research group. An answer came back very quickly to say that they would be delighted to have her help them. Another meeting should be arranged some to set out how Ellie could help.....

Chapter 55

Jinni

Professor Xingping Zhang visits and decides Song's future...

There were two weeks before the Trial. Song had a sick note for the university and was staying at my apartment. She had been to see a Counsellor from a women's support group in the city which she had found to be really helpful.

During these two weeks, when I got home from the salon she would have made me a meal and we would sit and eat together and then she would massage my shoulders and comb my hair. Some nights she ran me a bath and I would lie luxuriating in the scented water and then she would climb in and we would bathe together, washing each other and kissing. I had never been more happy or relaxed.

After Song had been with me for a few days she received a message from her father. He was in Los Angeles at Highbridge University. He had been called to a meeting about her future and he wanted to visit and feed back about the meeting before flying back to China.

I was dreading his visit. Song seemed to accept it as inevitable. Professor Xingping Zhang arrived at my home on Thursday evening. Song had cooked and we first sat and ate together. Looking closely at him, I felt he had aged since I had seen him last. He looked weary and full of cares. He was a very troubled man. I appreciated that Song had caused him a lot of worry and stress.

After we had finished eating and the dishes had been cleared away, Xingping Zhang began to speak. We spoke in English as my native language is Thai and theirs Mandarin, but English was understandable by us all. I was grateful to Xingping Zhang for speaking in English so that I could join in the conversation.

"Please use my English name, Ryan as we will be talking in English. I have been to see the Deans of the Business School and the International Program at Highbridge" he said "they called me in to a meeting. My attorney, Harry Zine, went with me.

To cut to the crux of the meeting – Song, they do not feel you are fitting in at Highbridge with their teaching style."

Goodness me, it was hard not to laugh out loud, he was not kidding she wasn't fitting in! She had run away twice now and had really struggled from all accounts when she was there.

Song did not speak but sat with her head hung and her hair over her face. ?

I said out loud "I feel that it has been difficult for Song at the University. She would be much happier with me here working as a manicurist. I think we all know Song is not interested in an academic career." I felt confident saying this as when Song was missing Ryan had written to me and said he regretted pushing her into an academic career. If she was found then he would be happy for her to do what she wanted.

Song's head jerked up and she parted her hair and brushed it off her face. She looked defiant. "I did my best to make you happy, papa" she said

Ryan nodded and he said "We all know Song you struggled with academics at Highbridge. But thinking about this we have to acknowledge don't we that this wasn't the right environment for you, was it Song? It is not academia that is wrong for you. It was the style of learning – I believe this was something you didn't feel comfortable with? Presentations? Group work? This is not your style."

"That is true. It was not my style papa."

I could not believe what I was hearing.

Ryan then went on to say "For this reason, we all feel you would much happier at a more traditional university. One where they adhere to more traditional teaching methods. Reading text books and memorising passages. You would feel more comfortable in that atmosphere."

No, please no, he was going to transfer her somewhere. She shouldn't be at any university. She should be here with me in my salon and my home.

I said aloud "Perhaps Song would feel happier away from the academic life for a while? She is very welcome to stay with me here and work in my salon."

For a moment no one spoke and then Ryan said "I don't think you want to give up your academic career do you Song? You have always wanted to follow in my footsteps."

Song raised her chin and flicking her hair back said "Yes, papa. I always wanted to follow you."

I wanted to scream but that is not true – you know it is not true Song. You want to be with me.

Ryan said "We all have little" here he paused for emphasis "wobbles. I think that is the correct English word. It is part of growing up. But I know that you have the end in sight, Song. An academic career is calling you."

Wobbles – good grief how could he call what Song had done a wobble!! It was a clear cry for help from someone who was in the wrong place and wanted to break free.

Ryan went on "This is why I am so pleased to announce that Woomeray Tech in Australia are going to offer you a place on their program." He smiled now "This program is traditional and you will be working closely with a researcher there as her assistant."

I thought my eyes were going to pop out of my head – I wanted to stand up and scream. This couldn't be true. Australia? But of course it was highly likely that Highbridge University wanted her out of there before the publicity from the trial in Atlanta hit the newspapers and no other US university would take her. So her father had agreed she should go to Australia. All to save face for him and of course keep his lucrative contract with Highbridge

I looked at Song. She was still looking at her father and being brave. "Where is Woomeray Tech in Australia?" she asked

"It is in the outback" her father said "the nearest town is Alice Springs. It is also a peaceful and quiet place where you can concentrate on your studies without outside distractions. How lucky were we that Highbridge have been able to arrange this transfer for you."

He smiled and looked at both of us. I wondered if my mouth was gaping open.

"Song you do not need to take up this offer." I said "You can stay here with me and work in the nail salon. Or can you not go home to Guangzhou."

"You know full well that Song can't stay here, Jinni" said Ryan "She does not have papers to stay in the US if she gives up her academic visa." He softened his tone a little and said "I know you are fond of my daughter but she does not have a future in the US sadly. We have to think about the publicity from the trial in Atlanta. It is deeply regrettable that Song has to give evidence in this trial but there is nothing we can do about it. She will have to give the evidence. But then it is best she starts again with a clean slate in another country."

In another country? I wanted to scream. She is a person, not a possession that you can move around like a pawn in a game of chess. She has feelings and she loves it here with me. Why would you take her away from me?

"I could apply for her academic visa to be changed to a work visa if she stayed here. That would enable her to work in the salon" I protested.

"It is highly unlikely that that would be granted, Jinni" Ryan sighed "Now if she had finished her studies and had a PhD then she would be granted a work visa and could stay. But Song has few college credits, why would the US government grant her a visa?"

"We can try" I sobbed "She would be happy if she could stay here."

Song spoke for the first time "Jinni, I love that you care for me. I have been happy with you here. But my future lies with doing what papa asks me to do. My future is with my family and caring for my family"

This comment resonated with me. In Thailand we have the same feelings about family. Family is the most important. In Asian culture you would never disagree with your family in front of others. You would say "yes" even if inside you were saying "no". When we are growing up our family takes many decisions for us that are taken individually in Western culture. This includes what to wear and what to eat. When I first moved to America there were seemingly small things that shocked me, for example, I could not believe children in cafes and restaurants openly defying their parents refusing to eat what had been ordered.

In this case Song's father was asking her to move country again to complete her education. Why agree to something that would make her desperately unhappy? But I could see that her sense of family came first, before her sense of self. In Song's mind her family were the most important. All her life she would put family first. In Chinese culture, as in our Thai culture, we were brought up to believe that our parents took care of us when we were children, so therefore we will take care of our parents when they grow old. We would never put them in a care home or assisted living facility as is done in Western culture.

I knew that Song would never defy her family to stay here with me. Deep down I knew that I never would defy my own family if I was in the same position. Really it was amazing that she had defied her father by running away from Highbridge College. It only made it more obvious when you put this into the context of Chinese culture, how traumatic it must have been for her at Highbridge for her to defy her parents and run away. My heart ached for her and how her father could not seem to see that she was not academic and let her do something that would make her happy.

I knew that Song was going to go to Australia. Obviously it was felt if she was in the Outback in a place which was quiet and miles from the nearest big city she would settle down to her studies. If only I could believe this.

I know if you are reading this and you are from a Western culture it may be difficult to understand that Song would do as her father asks. It should be obvious to anyone that a university education was wrong for her. After living in America for a number of years I would ask her – which is best our Asian culture that puts family first and foremost or the American culture that puts being an individual first? If Song had been American then I know she would have stayed with me and we would have been able to find a way for her to work in the salon. But she was Chinese without immigration papers and had a strong sense of family. She had also been deeply traumatised by what had happened to her when she had run away and defied her father.

There was nothing I could do. The best thing I could do for Song was to continue to support her and be there for her. This time we would not lose touch. I would be online talking to her and encouraging her.

"Good girl" said Ryan "We can arrange for you to transfer to Woomeray Tech after the Trial. However it may take a while for a visa to be arranged and it is important you can leave this country and not have to go back to Highbridge. There may be publicity relating to the trial and it is better if you were out of the country. We will arrange for you to come back to China after the trial to wait for your visa to be granted so you can go to Australia."

I could vaguely see what he was saying – Song needed to be protected from any publicity from the Trial. Plus, I expect Highbridge would be terrified of the publicity around the trial.

I reached over and squeezed Song's hand. She looked into my eyes, and although my heart was broken, I smiled at her. "We will keep in touch" I said "Maybe I can get a few days off from the salon and come and visit you."

Song held onto my hand and I knew she was fighting tears "That would be so good, Jinni" she said.

Where would it all end for her? So beautiful and so misunderstood…

Chapter 53

Lila

Randi goes to Church and the New Orleans convention

At the salon change was also in the air for Lila. Jinni seemed to mean what she said when she visited Randi and perhaps she now regretted the way she had behaved. In any event she was warm and welcoming and showed an interest in Lila and her family. She also confided that Song was back and was due to give testimony at the trial of the man the social media posts had been referring to. It felt different at the Purple Orchid now. For the first time, Lila felt to be accepted and valued.

While Jinni's main focus was Song and the upcoming trial, Lila's main focus was her sister Randi. Slowly and with the support of Ronnie and Lila, Randi started to make a recovery. Staying with them she seemed to become more like her old self. She had called in sick at the Black Cat bar and spent the days cleaning their home and making them a meal for when they returned in the evening.

Each Sunday Randi went with them to church. She had promised Ronnie that she would go and each Sunday she was ready to go and joined in the singing and praying when she was there.

It was hard to say what the future would hold for her. She would not go back to her roommate and it was doubtful if she would go back to the Black Cat bar. She discussed joining Lila as a cleaner and she seemed to feel that would make a change from working in the bar.

She had been to the doctor and had been prescribed more anti-depressants. It didn't seem possible that she could manage without them at present.

Somchai had messaged at first, but Randi had been strong and had not seen him. His messages it seemed had become less and less frequent. Perhaps he would leave her alone and she would be able to get on with her life.

On Saturday it was the day of the New Orleans convention where the Brothers of Swing and the Institute for the Blind and Visually Impaired Jazz Band were playing. They were driving to New Orleans and had rented a small coach. There wasn't really room for Randi to go as the parents were accompanying the Jazz Band. But also Ronnie and Lila were not sure she would even want to go. It was a long drive and they had to be up to leave at 4 am. In the end Lila said she would stay at home with Randi. This was the first time Lila had not gone with the Brothers to one of their shows. She knew Adrienne was going, first as the mother of Alex the pianist, and second as she would be singing with the band.

It felt like a long day and Lila couldn't wait for Ronnie to return in the evening. It was late when he came in. He seemed in a good mood, but tired. Randi was already in bed and Ronnie and Lila sat on bar stools and discussed the day.

Ronnie said that Adrienne had sung the Toni Braxton song "Un-break my heart".

Lila felt this was a wrong choice for a Convention, but decided it was best not to say anything. Ronnie went on to say

"She nearly brought the roof down. The applause was deafening. God that woman has range. A little white woman who can sing like that. Wow!"

She makes me sick, Lila thought. What a great voice she has. Yuck. She was such a little mouse. It didn't seem right that someone who looked like that could have a voice like that! When she sang everyone listens. 'Then Lila felt guilty for her thoughts as she knew the Brothers had been struggling to attract attention and suddenly here was someone who could bring them the attention they wanted.

Lila knew she had to stop being such a jealous bitch and feel proud for them.

Ronnie also went to say that they had another booking as a result of the convention. It was in a city to the south of here in a theatre rather than in a bar/restaurant as was usual for them. They would be the warm up artists for a bigger well know band.

So Lila and Ronnie sat together toasting the success of the Brothers of Swing. Lila loved Ronnie so much. She was proud of him and wanted him to be successful.

All would be well, she knew. She moved closer to him and he put his arms around her.

Chapter 56

Lila

Promoting the Brothers …

Randi had started to go with Ronnie and Lila to their Church. It reminded Lila of their childhood. When they were growing up they went to Church and Sunday School with their parents. Randi dropped out during her teen years and Lila suspected had never been back. Lila on the other hand had always been an active member of a Church. Just one more way in which they were very different.

Randi had joined in the singing at the Church and seemed to be listening to the pastor as he talked. It was hoped that the service would resonate with her. The second Sunday she went to Church she went to the coffee and cakes after the service. Randi stood with Lila and Ronnie for a few minutes drinking her coffee. They had introduced her to the pastor. Seeing that he had come into the room for coffee Randi walked over to him and went straight into a deep conversation by saying

"I am struggling with your talk today."

The pastor looked at her.

"How are you struggling?"

"If God is supposed to be such a loving, caring God why is there so much suffering in this world?" She went on "There are children abused and starving. These people have to navigate life. Why would a caring God inflict this on the world."

The pastor paused for a moment and said:

"Those are very good questions, Randi. Questions we have all asked. God can use suffering to help us grow into better people. Hard times remind us that we need Him. Trials in this life can help us in order that our faith might be purified and proven."

Randi scoffed:

"I find this all a bit hard to take in, to be honest. Children are innocent, why should they have to suffer to come to the Lord? Why should anyone have to suffer?"

She paused there and then answered her own question

"I suppose they have to suffer in order to be stronger in their faith."

It wasn't obvious if the Pastor was getting through to her even though she had answered her own question. However, she asked if she could come with Ronnie and Lila again the next Sunday and she signed up for the church Whatsapp group where church members discuss the Bible. These were tiny steps but it seemed she wanted to welcome the Lord into her life and this might give her life a purpose and a future.

The next day Bruce the music director at the Institute for the Blind and Visually Impaired asked for a meeting with the Brothers. They were going to go along to the Institute at 5 pm that day. Lila went with them and they met with Bruce in the music room.

Bruce welcomed everyone to the Institute and they sat in a small circle. He had also invited Adrienne.

"I just wanted to say how wonderful it is that the Institute Jazz Band has been able to play with you guys. As you know this is the first term that the Institute has been open and teaching classes. The band members could all play their instruments before they joined the Institute but they had never played together. They have made enormous progress as a Jazz Band and much of this is down to being able to perform with you."

"We feel we also have made some real progress with our act" said Ronnie "singing with the Jazz Band instead of a backing track and having a female singer, Adrienne."

Bruce continued:

“As we come to the end of the first term of the new Institute, the Directors would like us to do a concert for all the parents and supporters. They are suggesting that we do this in the Newform Theatre in the downtown area. They would like the concert to feature the Jazz Band playing with the Brothers of Swing and Adrienne singing. This would be for a couple of numbers. You would choose what music you would perform -but it would be great if it could be a joint decision with the Jazz band.”

Bruce paused and then went on to say “If you would like to go ahead with this I will put your names on the publicity for the event.”

This was a very good opportunity for the Brothers and they agreed they would like to take part and thanked Bruce for the opportunity.

They now had two events coming up in much larger venues – both theatres. It seemed things were finally looking up for the Brothers of Swing.

Chapter 57

Jinni

Coaching Song for the trial....

At this time my thoughts were only of Song and the upcoming trial. As April drew to a close, Song and I only had a few days left together and I wanted to make the most of our time together. On Friday I left the salon in charge of my chief manicurist Julie and Song and I caught the train to the lakes area north of the city. The area was beautiful with softly rolling hills and wildflowers in the meadows. The meadows were ablaze with Black-eyed Susans, Prairie Verbena and Bluebonnets. There was a path around the lakes which we followed, talking all the time about our homelands and various adventures we had had while growing up. We never once talked about the future or the fact that we only had a few days left together. In my view Song had never looked more beautiful than she did on that day and I could see that she was smiling again and I hoped that she had been able to put some of the trauma of the recent weeks behind her.

During this time Song had to prepare for the upcoming Trial. Harry Zine himself visited us to help prepare Song. He had been instructed by Song's father to act on her behalf and to check her witness statement before she went to Court to be sure that she was not incriminating herself. Also, he told us he would help her with her preparation by discussing some of the questions she might expect to be asked by the prosecution and defence attorneys.

He spoke to Song in the evening when I was around. Although this was unusual it was what she wanted. She wanted me to be there while he went through the preparation.

Harry, Song and I sat around the dining table in my apartment. Harry was opposite from Song and I. Harry told Song that he had spoken to the prosecuting attorney and to the defence attorney in advance of her testimony.

“Let me explain about the trial and the charges against Barry Watkins.” Harry said “Harry has been charged with aggravated assault and battery which is a felony. Assault is defined under law as when an individual behaves in such a manner that it makes another person frightened they will be violently harmed. Battery is if the person actually goes ahead with the threat and touches another person violently. This is touching another person without their consent in a violent manner eg hitting someone.

The aggravated part comes from how serious the attack is. A battery is touching another in an offensive way – it becomes aggravated if the other person is wounded. For example,. The person suffers serious injuries such as broken bones or severe bruising etc. In the attack Eric Senser suffered a broken jaw, ruptured spleen, collapsed lung, broken leg and injuries to his left hip. These injuries certainly boost the charge from battery to aggravated battery.

However, to sustain a conviction in a trial it has to be proved that the attacker, in this case, Barry Watkins, acted maliciously and here I quote from the statute “without justification, excuse or mitigation.” What does that mean? Well it means he acted with intent, he meant to do harm. There are a number of defences that can be used to this charge which include self-defence. But in this case the main defence that Barry Watkins will use is that he did it to defend another person. He honestly believed that another person was in danger of being harmed, In this case, he believed that you, Song, were being attacked and he came to your aid. If he can prove that he can escape conviction.”

“Thank you for explaining that to us” I said

“If Song can explain that Senser was making unwanted sexual advances on her then the fact that Watkins was defending Song is a good defence.”

“It is very important to Barry Watkins that Song testifies” I said “Without Song how many years in prison is he looking at?”

"A minimum of 1 year, which given seriousness of the injuries I doubt, and a maximum of 20 years. I would estimate without Song's testimony he would be looking at about 10 years."

"You should go ahead and testify, Song. However, you should make your testimony as brief as possible. Although I know this might not be possible, it would of course be best if it did not come out in the court that you were working in the burger bar. If you are asked why you were in the vicinity of Big Daddy's Burger bar then tell them that you had gone there to eat ."

Song said "But that is not true. I would never eat the food that was prepared at that burger bar. It was greasy and not cooked properly. I was there because I worked there."

"I do know enough of court proceedings" I said " to know that Song would take an oath to say she is speaking the truth."

Harry sighed and leaned over the table "Song, you should not have been working in the burger bar. Eric Senser employed you as an illegal immigrant for cash paid under the table. If at all possible try to avoid mentioning this in your testimony."

"But isn't that the whole point?" Song exclaimed "Eric Senser employs women who don't have papers and then can make sexual advances on them and treat them like they are nothing. He knows that a woman who is working illegally in America is not likely to complain about his behaviour."

Harry Zine flushed slightly and then gained his composure "Song" he said "It is Barry Watkins who is on trial for beating Eric Senser. You are the mitigating factor for Barry Watkins. You can show that Barry came to your defence when Eric was trying to attack you. Eric Senser is not on trial here."

I spoke up then "You say Eric Senser is not on trial" I said "But why not? He should be on trial for attempted rape. He tried to rape Song. If Watkins had not come to her aid he would have succeeded, I believe."

Harry said “Yes that is true and that is why Song speaking up for Barry will be the defence he needs to avoid being sent to prison. But no one has charged Senser with anything.”

“Barry Watkins should be awarded a hero’s medal for standing up for Song.” I said

Harry’s voice became hard now. “Listen ladies” he said “We need to get this right. Under the legal system the court is only interested in hearing your testimony about the case that is being tried. It may be true that Eric Senser is a predator but that is for another court and another day. Don’t make your testimony a crusade against him – you must concentrate on talking about Barry Watkins and, if at all possible, avoid saying you worked at the burger bar.”

Song and I sat staring at him. We had got the message now but it seemed wrong that Senser would get away with his appalling behaviour towards women.

We thanked Harry Zine for briefing Song. I would be really glad when the trial was over as I was sure it would be a massive ordeal for Song. I squeezed her hand, she had to be brave and get through this..

The following night Dr Abebe Majola sent us a Zoom invitation. We set up the laptop on the dining table and there she was.

“How are you feeling now Song after meeting with a counsellor?”

“It has been very helpful” said Song

“I know you asked to meet with me” said Abebe “You said it was about your testimony at the trial. How can I be of help?”

I had not realised that it was Song who had reached out to Dr Abebe Majola when she sent the Zoom invitation. But I guess it made sense since Abebe had helped her previously to find a counsellor.

“Yes that is correct” said Song. “My father’s lawyer has met with Jinni and I to help me prepare my testimony. I am concerned about the direction he is suggesting." Song then went over our conversation with Harry Zine.

"I see" said Abebe "It seems to me you are concerned about other women who may work in that burger bar. I understand your worry that the owner may do it again and this time the person would not have Barry Watkins to protect them. Is that correct?"

Song started to cry. "It was so horrible" she cried "I had been so sheltered from the world living with my parents and at university. Even when I ran away I was lucky to meet Jinni and work at the Purple Orchid. But when I went to Atlanta it was as if a veil had been lifted from my face and I saw how cruel the world can be." She broke down and sobbed then and Abebe and I let her sob.

She then went on "I know Senser has attacked girls before in that burger bar. When I first started a woman came up to me on the sidewalk as I was leaving the bar and said to me "I know you are working there. You are a very beautiful girl. You should not work there. I just wanted to warn you about the owner, Eric Senser." I did not know what to do or say. I told her she was right, I did work there but I wasn't frightened. She then said "If you are working there my guess is you don't have working papers". She told me that she had a friend who was in the USA without immigration papers and who had worked there. Senser paid her very little money and always in cash. One day he told her to take the trash out to the alley behind the store. As she was leaning over the dumpster he came up behind her and raped her."

Song was now sobbing, her shoulders heaving and her nose running. I gave her tissues and felt my heart beating fast. Why oh why did she stay when she knew this? One telephone call to me or to her father was all it would have taken to get her out of this situation. But again there would have been the loss of face in admitting she had messed up. Making sure you do not lose face is very important in our culture.

When Song stopped sobbing Abebe said gently "At the trial Song it is your testimony. You have to say what you believe to be the truth.

You were in the alley at the rear of the burger bar by the dumpster when the attack took place, I believe?"

Song nodded "Yes I was taking the trash out."

"You need to consider very carefully how you will explain why you were in the alley at the back of the burger bar. It seems that Senser had asked women to go there previously and had followed them and may have attacked them."

"You also need to think about how you will feel in the future if you do not mention about Senser's appalling behaviour. Indeed, a clever attorney may well realise at the trial that things are being covered up and may try to get at the truth. You must therefore only speak the truth."

Song stopped crying then and nodded. "Thank you for your help Dr Abebe" she said.

I would be so glad when this trial was over. It was going to be so difficult for Song to give her testimony. I could only hope that she felt able to answer the questions that would be aimed at her and would be able to hold her own in court without breaking down in tears.

Chapter 58

Ellie

Helping Dr Abebe Majola

As April drew to a close and the date of the trial drew near, Ellie was 5 months pregnant and she and Kevin decided to tell more people. At present only his mother Jenni and her partner Niall knew.

Ellie decided to tell the ladies in the Purple Orchid salon. She told Jinni during her manicure and Jinni called Lila over from reception. She asked Lila to bring everyone a drink of iced tea and they raised a toast to the baby. It was a lovely moment and Ellie felt she was among friends in the salon.

At this time Ellie was also beginning to learn that helping Dr Abebe Majola was a way to make her voice heard. She had tried so hard to speak up using the internet and social media and although she had had some success and she had attracted a number of followers, overall it had been difficult. The big issue was that she had become angry by the responses people made to her posts. She then had had online rows with people. But also looking back at the number of people who had taken an interest in her podcasts and videos she had not felt to make an impact. There were only a few hundred people – at the most a thousand who had ever taken an interest in what she had to say.

Joining a research group was different. She know her role was only helping by checking out leads on the internet and doing a lot of the grunt work for the group. But she could see potential. If she earned their respect by doing the hard work at first, she might be asked to co-author papers and to present at conferences and other universities.

Dr Abebe Majola was a powerhouse. She was frequently asked to present on local TV and radio. Also, Ellie noticed the Daily Mail online had asked for her views on immigrant women and their sexual exploitation for an article they had written. Much of what she did was controversial but it seemed that when she spoke people listened even if it was to argue with her.

It was easy to see why there was such a big interest in Abebe's work. Everything she did was well researched. She would not present unless she had all the facts and these had been checked. Ellie realised now that she had tended to run off at the mouth after reading one or two articles and did not really have the research to back up what she said.

Abebe had been taking an interest in Song and the upcoming trial. Song was staying with Jinni before the trial. Ellie wanted to be able to go to Atlanta to watch the trial but sadly it fell on a day when she had to teach so she could not go. Then Kevin did the kindest thing ever. He asked the Head of Department if someone could cover her classes so she could go. It turned out that another member of staff was happy to cover for her if she would reciprocate in a couple of weeks time.

Ellie hoped that Song would speak up in the trial so that there would not be other women put into the position she had been. She was so pleased that she would be able to go with Jinni and watch the trial.

Overall these were happy times for Kevin and Ellie. He had mellowed quite a lot towards Ellie since she became pregnant and had stopped making her podcasts and YouTube videos. He was as excited about the baby as she was and they grew very close during this time. In the morning as they were carpooling to the university they would listen to the Jerry Levens commuter show on the local radio.

On Thursday they tuned in as usual and Jerry said:

"I just wanted to give a big shout out for the Institute for the Blind and Visually Impaired. In three weeks time the school will complete its first term in the premises in the regeneration area of the City. In recognition of this the Institute is giving a concert at the Newform

Theatre in the city centre. This concert will feature talent from the Institute and will include a set by the Institute Jazz Band. These are all blind or partially sighted musicians who have only just begun to play together this term. They will back up the Brothers of Swing who will be singing with them."

Ellie's ears pricked up at the mention of the Brothers of Swing. She remembered when she tried to help them. Niall, Jenni's partner, took part in a rally to get musicians to join a union so that they could be paid more when their music was streamed and Ellie had written a speech for him to make at the rally.

Jerry Levens went on

"Of course the Brothers of Swing are not pupils at the Institute. They are all sighted singers and as many of you will know have being playing gigs in this area for a number of years. I believe I have one of the brothers, Niall calling in to speak to me. Hi Niall can you hear me?"

Niall's voice came over the radio

"HI Jerry. Yes I can hear you. We are delighted to be singing with the Jazz Band at the Institute concert" he said

"Haven't you played with them previously? I believe you played with them during the Running Race?"

"Yes that was the first time we played together" said Niall "Previously the Brothers used to sing old standards with a backing track. It was Ronnie's partners idea to sing with a real band and to change the music. We decided to sing soul classics for the run."

"I do remember. People liked it as they said it made a great atmosphere for the running. Tell me though, how do the children play in a Jazz Band when they can't see? They won't be able to read their music."

Niall agreed with him and went on to say

"I've got Alex with me from the band. She is the pianist and she will tell you."

"HI Alex" said Jerry

Alex spoke out next:

"Well of course we can't read music so we have to memorise the tunes. This means we have to practice over and over again until we get it right. I don't mind the hard work though as I love to play the piano and to perform with the Jazz Band and the Brothers." She paused then "and with my mom."

"Oh yes" said Niall "we mustn't forget Adrienne, Alex mother, she has also sung with us. She has a brilliant voice."

"We are so looking forward to hearing you at the Concert guys" said Jerry "Remember the concert is open to the public and anyone can buy tickets from the Institute website."

The Brothers were really trying hard to be heard too. Singing with the blind Jazz Band had been a brilliant idea from Lila and it seemed they were beginning to be noticed in town.

It seemed that bigger things may lay in store for them in the future.

"Shall we go to the concert with my mom?" said Kevin

Wow that was a first! Previously he had not been too keen on hearing the Brothers of Swing! "Yes why don't we?" Ellie said.

Chapter 59

Los Angeles – The Beverly Hills Hotel

Matt Carey

Matt Carey, the musician, was aware that the trial of Barry Watkins was imminent. Matt had been paying for Derek Lynes bills to represent Barry Watkins, although this was a secret. Matt was in Los Angeles. This evening he had a concert at the Long Beach Arena and then he was flying back to Atlanta for his concert at the State Farm Arena. He had decided to stay at the Beverly Hills Hotel and sitting on the terrace of his room eating his breakfast he felt that had been a good decision.

Felicia, his assistant, was sitting with him briefing him on the day ahead. He wasn't really listening.

"Get me Robyn" he said to Felicia. Robyn was his publicist..

In a minute Robyn was on speaker phone. After initial pleasantries Matt said: "I want to make you aware that there is a trial next week in Atlanta of a brother accused of aggravated assault and battery. I have paid his legal fees, but I do not want any mention of this in the public arena."

Robyn seemed taken aback by this information, but Matt really was a law unto himself.

"Matt, if this is something to do with you I really should know" she said "you can be assured I will keep it confidential. But obviously we don't want anything in the press about aggravated assault and battery and I have to work out our exposure."

"The attack has nothing whatsoever to do with me." Assured Matt "it took place at a burger bar in South Atlanta. A brother beat the owner senseless while trying to save an employee from an attempted rape. However, I have history with that place and I wanted to help the brother. The owner is a piece of shit who employs illegal immigrants."

Robyn sounded nervous now – the mention of a sleazy burger bar that employed illegal immigrants and fighting terrified her. So far she had been able to keep Matt in the news with positive posts for his adoring fans. The online tabloids had run the following headlines during the recent tour:

"Matt Carey on dad duties in Piedmont Park" and

"Matt Carey looking for love with a down to earth God-fearing woman"

"Okay" she finally said "Do we think it is wise for you to be involved in something" here she paused for a moment "that has the sleaze factor?"

"The sleaze factor?" said Matt "What the hell you talking about girl?"

Robyn was trying to keep her composure

"Matt as your publicist I really don't think this is the sort of publicity you want. A sleazy burger bar, low life people and fighting. You are a very rich man we need to keep you out of trouble like that. "

Matt was silent so she blustered on

"I know you have said to keep quiet about this, but you have paid this man's legal fees. Is he aware of that?"

Matt was getting bored now

"Course he isn't" he said "I got Derek Lynes my attorney to represent him. You are my publicist – I just don't want anything leaking out – okay. That is why I have told you. The last thing I want is some screaming headline in TMZ that I have paid this man's fees and am in some way connected either with him or the shitty burger bar where the incident took place. You know what the Press are like. They will make a meal out of this."

Robyn didn't speak for a moment and then she said:

"This person, I am guessing can't afford to pay Derek Lynes."

"Of course he can't – he works at the Amazon depot."

"So it may very well be queried who paid the fees?" mused Robyn

Matt was finding it hard not to roll his eyes. How much did he pay her again? Why did she have to talk in such an affected poncy way?

"Robyn" he said slowly and deliberately "the message is that I didn't pay those fees even though I did. I don't want anything leaking out. I want it to be kept private."

"Okay I hear you" she said finally. She would make sure nothing leaked out.

Chapter 60

Atlanta

The Trial

The Trial had been set for 27 April 2023. Jinni and Ellie had caught an early flight to Atlanta and were at the Court House by 9 a.m. The trial was scheduled for 11 a.m. They waited outside until 10.55 and then were allowed into the court room for the trial.

The court was running on time and Barry Watkins was brought up from the holding cell. He sat with his lawyer Derek Lynes. He was wearing a suit which made him look professional.

Eric Senser was brought into the court in a wheelchair pushed by his long term partner Sonya. He sat in the first row behind the prosecution. There was no sign of Song.

The Judge started the proceedings by stating that Barry Watkins was on trial for aggravated assault and battery against Eric Senser. On day one of the trial the jury would hear opening statements from the state prosecution and also from the defence.

Angela Jones, for the prosecution first stood up and turning towards the Jury set out the details of the case.

"Eric Senser is a respectable business owner in South Atlanta. Together with his business partner, Sonya Gonzalez, he has owned Big Daddy's Burger Bar for the last 20 years. During that time Eric and Sonya have employed local people and been contributors towards the economy in the area. This was the first time that the burger bar has ever been featured in any legal proceedings.

On the evening of the attack Senser had been taking out the trash as the burger bar was closing at midnight when he was jumped by Barry Watkins. Watkins was in the alley at the rear of the burger bar. The alley was not well lit and Watkins had taken him completely by surprise when he set upon him. Eric Senser had suffered extensive injuries as a result of the attack by Barry Watkins. His injuries were listed as: broken jaw, ruptured spleen, collapsed lung, broken leg and injuries to his left hip. He had spent two weeks in hospital and was as yet unable to walk unaided. His recovery would be slow and painful. In fact his injuries spoke for themselves" said the prosecution and he went on to say he would like to avoid having Eric Senser called to the witness stand. To present the prosecutions case he would present evidence from the police and Eric's partner Sonya Gonzalez.

Derek Lynes, for the defence, then made his opening remarks to the Jury:

"My client Barry Watkins is a man of good character who has lived in S Atlanta for the last 10 years. He works as a fulfilment operative at the Amazon depot and is a regular attender at the South Street Tabernacle Baptist Church. Until the evening of this attack he had never been arrested or incarcerated. Watkins admits attacking Senser in the alley. However, today I will show you with the facts I present and a witness I will call that Barry Watkins had no intent to injure Eric Senser. In fact, Watkins was acting to protect another person when he attacked Senser."

The trial then began.

The police who attended the incident were then called. The policeman was named George Brown. He said that the police had been called by Senser's partner Sonya who said someone was beating Senser in the alley. By the time they arrived the perpetrator had fled. However Sonya identified him as Barry Watkins who was a regular customer at the burger bar.

George Brown said that such violence in South Atlanta was not uncommon. Sonya had indicated that it was possible that there had been an argument in the burger bar earlier in the evening between Senser and Watkins which may have led to the attack in the alley. However, he did not have any other witness who had come forward to say this was the cause of the attack.

Sonya indicated that Watkins lived in the "Green City apartments" a couple of blocks away. Brown said he had gone around to the apartments and was able to find out Watkins address by asking a youth who was outside smoking.

Watkins admitted the attack when the police visited his apartment.

The defence were then asked if they had questions for George Brown, the policeman. Derek Lynes stood and addressed George Brown.

"When you arrived at the scene at the burger bar were there any witnesses?" he asked

"There was Sonya Eric Senser's partner and no one else." Said the policeman

"The beating was by all accounts violent. Were there no other people, who hearing the commotion in the alley were willing to come forward?"

"There were a couple of people who were in the burger bar when the attack took place who we took their names and contact details. However, they were not able to help with what happened in the alley." Said the policeman.

"Very well" said Derek Lynes "you say you visited Barry Watkins apartment and he admitted the attack?"

"That is true" said the policeman

"Was there anyone with Barry Watkins when you visited the apartment?" said Derek Lynes

The policeman hesitated here and then said "Yes there was a Chinese woman with him. She could not show us papers. We called the Immigration Authorities and she was taken to a Deportation Centre."

"I believe this woman is named Song Zhang. Did you ask this woman if she was in the alley with Watkins when the attack took place?"

The policeman again hesitated “No we did not as we had no reason to believe she would have been at the burger bar. She gave her address as the apartment next door to Watkins.”

“Thank you. I have no further questions.” Said Derek Lynes

George Brown left the stand.

Next the Angela Jones, the prosecutor, called Sonya to give her evidence. Sonya went into the witness box and took the oath.

The prosecutor asked her to say her name and relationship to Eric Senser

“My name is Sonya Gonzalez” she said “I am the partner of Eric Senser and co-owner of Big Daddy’s Burger Bar for the last 20 years.”

“You work regularly in the burger bar?” said the prosecutor

“Yes, Eric is the cook who makes the burgers and I sit at the front on the till taking the money.” She said “We work very long hours. It is hard to make a profit nowadays.”

“Can you go through what happened on the night of the attack?” said the prosecutor

“It was a normal night at the burger bar. We were busy all evening. We close at midnight. As we were closing there were a couple of customers still sitting at tables finishing their food. I was tidying up and wiping down the cooking surfaces. Eric took the trash out to the dumpster in the alley behind the burger bar. After a couple of minutes Barry Watkins who was sitting finishing eating got up and left. When Eric did not return after a few minutes I got really worried. I went out of the shop and into the alley. He was laid on the floor and Barry Watkins was standing over him. Watkins ran away when he saw me. It was then that I saw how badly injured Eric was. Watkins had given him a real good beating. It was terrifying to see.”

“You say Watkins was stood over Eric. Was he beating Eric when you arrived?”

"He was kicking him as he lay on the ground" she said "It was horrific I will never forget that night."

"What did you do then?" said the prosecutor

"I rang the police and also my daughter to come and take Eric to the hospital." She said "the police arrived within a few minutes and took a statement. By then there were no witnesses to the attack. Just a couple of people who had been eating in the burger bar and came outside to see what was going on."

"Has Eric been able to return to his duties at the burger bar?" asked the prosecutor

"Not yet" said Sonya "It has been a very slow and painful recovery for him. He is still on sick leave."

"Thank you Sonya" said the prosecutor "No more questions"

Derek Lynes stood and approached the witness box

"Good morning Sonya" he said "I have a few questions for you."

"That is fine" said Sonya smiling and seeming to be confident about her testimony.

"I understand that you had staff working in the burger bar on the night of the attack." Said Derek

"Yes that is true. We had a couple of people in to help with plating up the orders and dishwashing."

"Can you tell us their names and if they were still there when the attack took place?"

Sonya seemed less confident now and hesitant "Thinking back I think the staff had left when the attack took place. Eric let them leave at 11.30. So there were not actually staff there at that time."

"I see" said Derek "Is it true that at the time of the attack you employed someone called Song Zhang to help you with various duties including front of house at the burger bar?"

Sonya was getting more nervous now. “mmm. Yes that is true. She only worked for us for a couple of weeks though”

“Was Song Zhang working in the burger bar on the evening of the attack?”

“mmm with all that happened it is hard to remember” said Sonya

“Try to remember” said Derek “I put it to you that Song Zhang was working in the burger bar on the night of the attack.”

Sonya said “Oh yes she was” and paused for a moment “I remember now.”

“What were her duties?” Derek asked

“She was front of house. Delivering orders and removing plates.”

“Is that all her duties?” asked Derek

“Yes “ said Sonya

“What about tidying up and emptying the trash?” said Derek

Sonya was wringing her hands and looking very nervous. She did not answer immediately.

“Just to remind you that you are under oath” said Derek

“mmmm. Well, yes she did help with clean up” said Sonya

“This included taking the trash out?” said Derek

“Yes, yes it would include that part.” Said Sonya

“I put it to you that it was Song Zhang who took the trash to the dumpster that evening.” Said Derek

Sonya glanced over at Eric in his wheelchair. He was staring at her trying to get her attention. His face was livid red and angry. She was terrified.

The prosecutor stood up “Objection. Leading the witness.”

“Sustained” said the Judge.

Derek changed tack slightly "Had Song Zhang left the burger bar by midnight - the time of the attack?"

Sonya had taken a tissue out of her pocket and was twisting it back and forth in her hand. "mmm I think she might have still been there." She said "I mean in the burger bar."

"Was she named by you as a witness to the attack when you spoke to the police? I can't see her name in the police report." Said Derek

"I was flustered and frightened" said Sonya "Eric laying there beaten and bruised. I was scared and forgot things."

"Did you forget that she was in the alley?" said Derek

The prosecutor objected and this was sustained

Derek said he would stop questioning for now of Sonya and he thanked her for her time.

The Judge then asked if the defense wanted to call any witnesses. Derek Lynes said he had two witnesses to call. The first witness was a doctor, Dr Mark Pell.

Dr Pell took the stand. He listed his qualifications as a qualified medical doctor who had worked in trauma suites and emergency rooms at two major hospitals. He was now a general practitioner in S Atlanta.

"I have called you to the stand Dr Pell" said Derek "As I understand you are Eric Senser's doctor, is that correct?"

"Yes that is correct" said Dr Pell

"However, you did not attend to Eric Senser on the night of the attack."

"Yes, Eric was taken to Grady Memorial Hospital and treated for his injuries. He was in hospital for two weeks and then released into my care." Said Dr Pell

“Can you tell us more about his injuries – explain about the severity of the injuries saying if they are life threatening or altering.”

Dr Pell consulted his notes “Eric’s injuries sustained in the attack were - : broken jaw, ruptured spleen, collapsed lung, broken leg and injuries to his left hip. These are serious injuries, but none of these injuries was life threatening or altering. Eric Senser is 53 years old and of previously good health.

The injury to the spleen was found to be a minor rupture. There was no need to remove the spleen. With bed rest it was decided that Eric would recover from this injury within a number of weeks from the attack.

In the case of a collapsed lung Pain and discomfort will diminish over time, but full recovery can take several weeks even after severe symptoms pass.

Surgery was not required for the broken jaw and it is felt that a full recovery can be made in a few weeks.

Eric has had his broken leg set and is wearing plaster which will come off after 6 weeks.

To sum up from meeting with Eric and reviewing his files I am of the opinion that with care and rest Eric should make a full recovery from all the injuries.”

Derek Lynes said “How long do you feel it will be before Eric can resume normal duties at the burger bar?”

Dr Pell said “I estimate a time of rest and recovery and it would be approximately 12 weeks from the date of the attack before Eric was able to resume normal duties.”

“However, just to be certain.” Said Derek “there is no reason why Eric will not be able to resume normal duties after a period of rest and recovery.”

“That is my belief” said Dr Pell

Derek thanked the witness for his time.

The prosecutor then got up to cross examine Dr Pell

“These injuries sound serious to me” said the prosecutor “Looking at these pictures which I have passed to the Jury that were taken on the night of the attack they look very traumatic and the result of great force.”

Derek jumped out “Objection. Leading the witness.”

The Judge agreed “Please ask your question” he said to the prosecutor

The prosecutor said “In your experience would it be normal for a person who had received serious injuries from an attack to suffer from mental trauma and flashbacks?”

Dr Pell agreed that this might be the case.

The prosecutor thanked him for his time and said he had no further questions.

Derek Lynes said he would like to call Song Zhang as a witness.

The court usher went out of the court and returned with Song. She was wearing all black and had her hair brushed back into a ponytail. She looked professional and serious.

She took the oath and then stood looking around the Court.

“Can I ask you questions in English?” said Derek Lynes

“Yes, of course. That is fine.” Said Song

“I understand that you were with Barry Watkins when he was arrested?”

“Yes that is correct.” Said Song

“Was Barry Watkins a friend of yours?” said Derek Lynes

“Yes, he lived next door and had been kind to me” said Song “I often chatted to him and visited his apartment.”

"How long had you been with him that evening?" said Derek Lynes

"I was with him at the burger bar earlier in the evening." Said Song. "I worked at the burger bar and was on shift that evening."

"Tell me what you remember about that evening" said Derek

Song was trembling as she stood in the witness box. "It was a busy evening at the burger bar. Barry Watkins came in late in the evening and was eating a burger as the burger bar was closing. I was helping with the clean up and I was asked by Eric Senser to take the trash out to the dumpster in the alley. I took the trash and went into the alley which was dark and poorly lit. I was leaning over the dumpster when I realised that Eric Senser had followed me into the alley. He came up behind me and he put his hands on me. He said he wanted to have sex with me. I tried to fight him off but he was bigger and stronger than me. He was laughing and saying "you know you want it." He was trying to rape me. This is why Barry Watkins attacked him. He attacked him to save me"

"I know this is difficult for you Song" said Derek Lynes "But did you give Eric Senser any encouragement. For example, you say he followed you into the alley"

Song was shaking "I can assure you I gave Eric Senser no encouragement. If Barry Watkins had not followed me then Eric would have attacked me."

"Thank you" said Derek Lynes.

The prosecution now stood and came over to the witness stand.

"You are making some serious allegations here" he said "First, you say you worked at the burger bar and was asked to take the trash to the alley. Second, you say Eric Senser followed you. Why would he do that if you were taking the trash out?"

"It was dark there and quiet. He could force himself upon me away from the eyes of his partner Sonya." Said Song "I am much smaller than him and he was forcing himself on me"

"I understand you made a statement when you were subpoenaed. But why did you not come forward to make any of these allegations when Barry Watkins was arrested?" said the prosecutor.

Song was shaking now and frightened. She put her head down for what seemed like an eternity. There was a hush in the court and then she spoke.

"To answer your question. I did not come forward earlier because I was an employee at Big Daddy's Burger Bar. I did not have papers to work in the burger bar. I am Chinese. I have an academic visa to study here in the US. This does not permit me to work off campus. I had run away from college as I was struggling to do the academic work and wanted to get away. After the incident in the alley I went with Barry Watkins to his apartment. The police came there. When they saw I could not show them papers they had me taken to a Deportation Centre. I got in touch with my father and my father's attorney worked to get my academic visa reinstated so I was not deported. We did not want to mention that I had been employed at the burger bar.

When I arrived in Atlanta I was told by other Chinese people that Eric Senser employed illegal immigrants no questions asked. Usually he had them in the kitchen washing dishes and doing chores but he wanted me to be front of house. There were rumors that he liked the young women. He had made sexual advances on women who were not interested, and his partner Sonya would pretend it did not happen."

The prosecutor jumped up to object – but the Judge overruled him.

Song stopped here to catch her breath. There was a hush in the court room and all eyes were on her. Song had her voice and she was going to use it.

"I felt it would not happen to me. I was not frightened and I carried out my job as best I could. On the night of the attack we had finished serving customers. Barry Watkins had come in for a burger and was seated at the counter. Eric asked me if I would take the trash out to the dumpster in the alley at the rear of the burger bar. I did as I was told. However, when I bent over to put the trash into the dumpster, he came up behind me. He had his hands all over me and was trying to pull my pants down. I tried to fight him off but he was stronger than me. I was now very frightened. I cried out for help. But no one seemed to hear me. Then Barry Watkins came into the alley. Later he told me that he wondered where I was as I had not returned after a few minutes. When he saw what was happening, he beat Eric Senser to stop his advances on me."

Song stopped here overcome by emotion. She was fighting back tears and was visibly shaking.

She looked at Barry Watkins sitting with his lawyer "That man is not a thug, sir" she said to the prosecutor "that man is a hero who came to my aid."

The prosecutor said "Is there any proof that you were working in the burger bar and that this story is not just a fabrication?"

Derek Lynes jumped up then and said "I have written statements from business people in the area and customers who have sworn that they saw Song working in the burger bar waiting on customers." He paused for a moment and then said "These have been put forward in evidence"

The prosecutor said "But no one actually saw you in the alley with Watkins and Senser?"

Song said "There were no witnesses except for Sonya. She saw that I was in the alley when she came outside. Barry took my hand and we ran away."

The prosecutor said "Sonya has sworn under oath that she did not see you in the alley."

Song lifted her head up and said in a loud, strong voice "I was in the alley that evening and Eric Senser had his hands on me. Barry Watkins acted to save me from this attack. That is the truth."

The Judge said "Thank you Song for your testimony. I think that is enough questions for now." Song was allowed to get down from the witness stand and take a seat.

Both the prosecutor and Derek Lynes presented their closing arguments to the Jury.

The prosecutor said that he wanted to reinforce the fact that Eric Senser was a respectable Atlanta business man. The injuries sustained by Eric Senser in the attack were severe and warranted the aggravated battery charge. He would be traumatized for some time to come. Although the injuries would heal, he would be mentally traumatised. Barry Watkins had given him a severe beating. There were no witnesses to what had happened in the alley. Song Zhang had not initially come forward. It was only when a subpoena was issued that she was willing to speak.

Derek Lynes then got up and facing the Jury began to speak:

"Barry Watkins admits that he attacked Senser in the alley behind the burger bar. This has never been in contention. The injuries sustained by Eric Senser were serious but his doctor has testified that the injuries were not life threatening or life altering. In other words, Eric Senser will make a full recovery.

Today members of the Jury what you must consider is WHY did Barry Watkins attack Eric Senser that evening? Barry Watkins is a man in his thirties, with no prior convictions. A man who is a member of a Church and a responsible member of the community. This is the question you must consider. Did Barry Watkins attack Eric Senser with INTENT and MALICE? Was this a motiveless attack?

The evidence presented today shows that this was not a motiveless attack. Barry Watkins was a friend of Song Zhang a Chinese woman who was working in the burger bar. When she did not return from taking trash to the alley, he went to look for her. There he found the following scene. Song Zhang was next to the dumpster with Eric Senser forcing himself upon her. Song was crying out for help.

Barry Watkins attacked Eric Senser to save Song Zhang from his advances.

Why did Song Zhang not present this evidence immediately? Why did she have to be served with a subpoena to give her side of the incident? Song Zhang was working illegally at Big Daddy's Burger Bar. She is a Chinese national who does not have working papers. Eric Senser was paying her cash under the table to wait on tables and clean up. If the Immigration Service had found out this would have serious consequences for both Eric Senser as the employer and Song Zhang as the employee.

Song Zhang decided not to speak initially in an attempt to have her Visa reinstated so that she could attend university. She was frightened of the consequences of speaking up. How would this affect her future?

I put it to you Members of the Jury that Barry Watkins acted in Song Zhang's defence and this was not a motiveless attack. Bearing this in mind I ask for the case to be dismissed."

The Jury went out to consider the case. It seemed like an eternity. Song sat with Ellie and Jinni while they waited. No verdict was issued that day. The next day everyone waited around for the verdict. Finally at 2pm on the second day they were called back into the Court.

The Judge asked the Foreman "Do you have a verdict?"

"Yes I do" said the Foreman

"Is the verdict a majority or unanimous verdict?" asked the Judge

"It is a unanimous verdict," said the Foreman

The Judge asked the defendant, Barry Watkins, to stand for the verdict.

The foreman said "We find the defendant not guilty of aggravated assault and battery. There was no malicious intent – he acted in good faith to protect a woman who was being attacked."

There was silence in the Court when the Jury announced their verdict. Jinni turned to Song and hugged her.

Barry Watkins who was standing next to Derek Lynes could not believe the verdict. It was too good to be true. He looked over at

Song with love in his eyes. She stood and went over and hugged him. They stood together hugging and holding each other.

Derek Lynes then implied that Barry should leave the courtroom as there were news reporters waiting outside looking for pictures and a report.

Derek Lynes walked out on to the court steps with Barry Watkins at his side and made a speech for the reporters

"Justice has been done today." He said "We would like to thank Song Zhang for her bravery and for speaking out in Barry's defence. Barry had only one thing on his mind that night in the alley behind the burger bar and that was to protect Song from a sexual predator. His brave actions stopped her from being violated that evening."

Barry then spoke for the first time "I want to thank Derek Lynes, my attorney, for believing me and for finding Song and especially for presenting my case to the Court. The truth has now come out. Senser is a dangerous man who picks on young illegal immigrants. He should be stopped. But most of all, I also really want to thank the anonymous brother who has paid Derek Lynes bills so that he can defend me and present this case. Thankyou. Thankyou. Thankyou.

Song did not want to be in the pictures and tried to hold back. However, the reporters were as interested in her as they were in Barry. As she came out of the court building and down the steps they rushed over to ask her questions. The local news were there filming. Jinni tried to hurry her away but Song stopped and looking at the camera said "What happened at that burger bar is a crime against women. Women who are poor and vulnerable and do not have working papers have been sexually exploited there. It should stop now."

Jinni, Ellie and Song left in a taxi that was headed for the airport. It was a bittersweet journey as Song would leave for her future in Australia and Jinni would head back to the Purple Orchid salon with Ellie.

Song Zhang who had followed celebrities and influencers and longed to be in the public eye was now in the news even as she boarded the flight home to China to wait for her visa to go to her new future at Woomeray Tech in Australia.

Chapter 61

Harry Zine

The aftermath of the Trial in Atlanta

The days following the trial were like something out of Harry Zine's worst nightmares.

The morning after the not guilty announcement he sat in his office in downtown Atlanta with the TV playing the local news. His PI Robert was sitting in the chair opposite him.

"A local burger bar has been exposed as a den of illegal immigrants."

The anchor woman was a blonde with perfect teeth and an orange fake tan. The camera panned from her to pictures of Big Daddy's burger bar where a number of people were stood outside.

"It seems that Big Daddy's Burger Bar in South Atlanta has been employing illegals for years and there were allegations today in court of sexual exploitation of women employed there." . "I am going over to our reporter at the scene – Bobbi Weston."

A black woman now took up the mic and said

"Here I am at Big Daddy's Burger Bar where a crowd has gathered." She addressed a woman stood in the crowd "Are you a regular here?" she asked

The woman said "I have been coming here for years. I knew something bad was going to happen. Eric and fat Sonya have been employing illegals for years. Everyone knew but kept their mouths shut."

A man commented "Close the place down. Eric and Sonya should be deported along with the illegals."

Harry reached over and turned the TV off. He looked weary and as if he had not slept. His usual immaculate appearance looked ruffled. His hair slightly greasy and his shirt crumpled.

"I have heard through the grapevine that that bitch Abebe Majola is going to go on "Morning Atlanta" later this morning to talk about the trial. Of course, I will be listening to her crackpot statements."

Robert made as if to answer but Harry went on as if he was talking to himself.

"The bottom line is I want to find out what our exposure is. It is only a matter of time before people start asking how Song was "rescued" from the Deportation Centre and reinstated at College. We are keen to keep Highbridge out of this" he stopped and twisted his tie loosening it. "That fucking girl. How could one Chinese student cause all this trouble? Why the fuck couldn't she just go to class and then fuck off home?"

Harry got up and started pacing "That was all it took. But no, she has to assert herself and run away. What a fucking disaster!!"

At that moment his PA opened the door and put her head around it. "The Dr Abebe Majola interview is just going to go live." She said "You asked me to let you know"

Harry sat down and put the TV back on "Oh there she is, fat ugly bitch spouting off again." He spluttered obviously furious.

Dr Abebe Majola was sitting in the studio opposite from Danny Brooks, a popular anchor man on Atlanta TV. She wore a simple dress and her hair was cut very short. Her appearance was that of a no nonsense professional woman.

"Hello Dr Majola" said Danny "We are pleased to have you on the show. Just some background for our viewers. Dr Majola is a professor at Georgia State University who is at present carrying out research into the sexual exploitation of immigrant women."

He then turned to Abebe and said "Wow!! What an explosive trial it was yesterday." He then turned back to the camera and said he was going to show some highlights for people not familiar with the trial.

After he had shown this, he said: "Your comments Dr Abebe"

"Immigrant women are vulnerable, especially if they are here illegally. When we think of illegal immigrants we may imagine that these are poor, vulnerable women who came over the border from Mexico. This case shows that there are other immigrants who can be exploited. Song Zhang was from a wealthy academic family in China and came here to go to university. Her troubles started when she ran away from university."

Danny said "Let me make sure I understand this – a foreign national here at one of our universities is supposed to stay on campus and study as their visa does not give them the right to work during the time they are doing their degree?"

Abebe nodded "Yes that is correct. They can work on campus or at a job approved by the university."

"Which university was she at again?"

Abebe said "Highbridge University in Los Angeles. It is a small private university."

"LA!! Wow! What the heck was she doing then working in South Atlanta at a burger bar?" Danny gaped at her. "There is no way the university approved that!! It is hardly commuting distance!! Come on people this is ridiculous. A student uses our education system to get into the USA and then goes rogue working at a burger bar."

"In this case the student, Song, was finding her studies difficult and she decided to drop out." Said Dr Abebe "It must have been a very traumatic time for her. Also, we must have empathy here. Although she had dropped out of university, she still had the right to be treated like a human being and not used and abused."

Danny dropped the pen he had been holding and addressing the camera said:

"This person should have been deported the minute she dropped out of school. Over the last couple of years over 8 million illegal immigrants have come to this country. We can't afford to take in that many people and support them. This person was supposed to be in school. Period. We have to have some standards."

Dr Abebe did not speak immediately. She rearranged the papers on the table in front of her and then she spoke

"We are also a first world country here in the USA. Arguably the most powerful nation in the world. If we cannot show empathy and understanding to the poor and vulnerable what does that say about us?"

Danny leaned over the table and carried on

"We are going to end up as a third world nation if we keep letting illegals live here. They will be taking over next just mind my words."

"You will never convince me" said Dr Abebe "and I hope you can't convince the viewers either. We need empathy and caring for all human beings or we are not a great nation."

On this the show went to the adverts and Dr Abebe's slot was finished.

"The fucking idiot let her have the last word" screamed Harry Zine. "This is an absolute unmitigated disaster. Highbridge College has now been named on the TV"

Harry knew that he had to act quickly. He composed himself and going to his laptop wrote a short speech. He had been keeping Highbridge College up to date with what had been happening in the trial and the verdict but Dr Abebe's TV appearance had moved things on a pace.

Dismissing his PI Robert, he rang Kirsty Wareham on the private number he had for her. At the same time he sent a link for her to catch up on the interview with Dr Abebe Majola. He mentioned the details of the interview and recommended she also watch it.

"I recommend that you make a statement now before reporters find you. That way you are not on the back foot. You must make it clear that Song is no longer a student and you have very good systems in place now to prevent this ever happening again."

Kirsty agreed with him that it was best to make a statement and get ahead of the press.

So it was that in the lunch time Atlanta news Kirsty appeared standing outside the main reception building on the Highbridge campus.

"I wish to make a statement about Song Zhang who until recently was a student at this university. Song came to the USA on a student visa to study business from her native China. Sometimes it can be challenging for students to settle into a new environment and we have systems in place to help overcome this. While at this university Song had a personal tutor who saw her regularly to make sure she was making progress and was settling in well. Despite this Song was not able to cope with the workload of an American university and dropped out. We were sorry to hear that she had been involved in an unfortunate incident in Atlanta. We understand she has now returned to her native China and we wish her all the best for her future there."

Harry was pleased that Kirsty had made this statement. It was damage limitation. He knew education was big business and that other universities would now close ranks and there would be very little if anything that would come out about other Chinese students that had dropped out and gone rogue.

"Of course" he said aloud "there is still that bitch Abebe – what would it take to shut her up?" She could still do damage. But it would be damage in general and not to his client and his case.

Calling Robert back into the room he sat back in his chair. "Hey Robert" he said "I have a job for you. Find out which fucker paid Derek Lynes bill. So far we have no clue whoever who this "Good Samaritan" is as this person has decided to keep stum. What an interfering fool. I need to know as that person is on my list" and here he smiled dangerously "for the future."

Chapter 62

Sonya

The aftermath of the trial in Atlanta

The not guilty verdict had been the worse possible outcome for the trial. Sonya had waited in the court room until she hoped all the reporters would have gone but as she came out pushing Eric in his wheelchair, it seemed she had been wrong. A black woman was waiting in the downstairs parking lot. She had a mic and a cameraman with her.

“What is your view on the not guilty verdict Sonya?” she asked, and with an appearance of concern “with Eric still in a wheelchair after the accident, it must have come as a shock.”

“You are goddam right it came as a shock” Sonya said “Eric beaten to a pulp in that alley. The court believing a lying Chinese woman.”

“Did you believe that she had the right to work in the USA?” said the reporter

“I wouldn’t have hired her if I didn’t” said Sonya imperiously. “We never hire illegals, we are decent business people.”

With that she moved away and helped Eric into the car. She got into the driver’s seat and set off for home.

The house Sonya shared with Eric was tiny and a couple of blocks away from Big Daddy’s Burger Bar. It was surrounded by a chain link fence and there was a sign “Beware of the Dog”.

There was no-one outside when they arrived and parking she helped Eric back into his wheelchair and into the house. He was moaning and carrying on about the trial and she helped him into the bedroom where she gave him two instead of one of his painkillers in the hope this would put him to sleep and he would shut up.

That evening the trial was featured on the local TV news. This included the interview with herself in the basement of the parking garage.

The local news featured another woman who appeared only if she could be in disguise. This included having her voice disguised. She stated in an accented voice:

“I am from Mexico. I came to this country illegally. I had to work to pay the agent who arranged for my crossing. I worked at Big Daddy’s Burger Bar. Eric Senser said he would pay me cash. At the end of my shift, I had to take the trash out to the dumpster behind the burger bar. One night Eric followed me and told me I could earn a little more cash if I was nice to him. He wanted me to have sex with him. I was very frightened. He was a big man and I did not like him at all. But my boyfriend was coming to pick me up from work and came into the alley. When he saw what was going on he beat Eric up. I had to leave the job. I could not go back.”

“Oh, for fuck’s sake” said Sonya out loud “Puta! You know you led Eric on. You were so greedy for a few extra dollars you would have done anything. I had to protect him from women like you for years.” She was shaking with rage. How dare this woman bring this up after what 5 or was it 6 years? Her boyfriend had been a wimp as well. He had tried to beat Eric up but it had been pathetic Eric had hardly been injured.

Sonya was tired of it now. She just wanted to get back to work and carry on as normal. She knew she would have to be a bit more careful who she employed but she would find a way around it.

The following morning, she got up and drawing the drapes back was horrified to see reporters outside the house. They were not on her land but were waiting on the sidewalk.

The house was too tiny to have a garage and her car was parked on the road. In any case Sonya usually walked to the burger bar. She walked out of the property purposefully. The reporters clamoured around her:

"A number of women are coming forward to say Eric attacked them. What do you have to say?"

Sonya bristled "It is all lies. These women are just on a bandwagon wanting publicity. Eric is a decent hardworking man. He is American to the core and reflects American values. How these people can attack a decent hardworking American is beyond horrible."

"Will you be employing illegals in the burger bar now?" another reporter asked her pointing a camera at her.

"Of course not" said Sonya feigning shock "We do not employ illegals. The Chinese woman was an honest mistake on our part. She lied and said she had papers."

She then stood back addressing all the reporters "You will have to excuse me now, I have to go and open the burger bar."

With that she set out towards the burger bar hoping they were not following.

When she got to the burger bar she saw a car parked outside. It looked vaguely familiar as did the man sitting in the driver's seat. She wondered how she knew him. She hoped it wasn't more reporters.

She let herself into the burger bar and began getting ready to open for the day. The burger bar had been closed yesterday for the trial. After the trial, when she got home, she had rung the undocumented Mexican workers she was currently employing and told them they were fired. She could not risk employing them at the moment. She fully intended to replace them when the furore surrounding the trial had died down. In the meantime, she called a friend who had a teenage daughter who was looking for work. Luckily this person, Janice, was available and could start immediately. Janice was American in case any reporters hanging around started asking questions.

After she had unlocked the door the man from the car came in and sat on one of the bar stools.

"Service doesn't start for another 15 minutes" Sonya said "but I can give you a coffee while you are waiting." He looked so familiar to her but she couldn't think where she knew him from.

"A coffee would be great." The man said. Sonya noticed he had an envelope with him that he placed on the counter.

Sonya went to the coffee pot and poured him a mug of coffee. She put the mug down in front of the man.

"Do I know you?" she asked "you look very familiar."

"You do know me Sonya" the man said "I have been here before. My name is Mike Pitts and I am from the US Immigration Services."

Sonya gaped at him. "Well Mike Pitts you will find nothing here. Just like you found nothing when you visited us before. As you can see there are no workers here. I have one worker at the moment, a woman called Janice, but she was born here in south Atlanta."

Mike took a slurp of his coffee and hesitated a while before answering "The thing is Sonya I don't need to find anything here. I already have all the evidence I need."

Sonya looked puzzled "Huh?" she said "What you talking about?"

"You see, Sonya, we have the Chinese woman, Song Zhang, on oath in a court hearing saying she worked here for cash when she did not have working papers. That is good enough for us."

"Rubbish." Sonya laughed out loud "You can't use that"

"It is not rubbish, Sonya, unfortunately for you. Not only can we use it if we want to - we fully intend to actually use it." Here he handed Sonya the envelope that was sitting on the counter. "This is a letter requesting you and Eric, if he is physically able, to attend the Immigration Services Office for an interview about your employment practices here at Big Daddy's."

Sonya started blustering and arguing but after a few minutes realised it was futile. After 20 years of employing illegal immigrants they had been found out and would have to face up to the consequences. She knew they could be facing a stiff fine or even prison time.

Mike left soon after this and after he had gone Sonya went into the restrooms and leaning against the wall let out a loud scream "Goddam you Eric" she yelled "disgusting, dirty man – you have finally ruined us!!"

Composing herself she came out of the restroom. She was slightly alarmed to see that Janice had not arrived in the burger bar. There was no one inside waiting for service. However, peering out of the window she saw there were a number of people on the sidewalk. She could see Janice at the back of the group. It looked like she was being prevented from getting through.

Sonya opened the door and shouted "What the hell is going on?"

A woman said "We don't need scum like you and Eric around here – you are giving the area a bad name."

"Fuck off my property" yelled Sonya – she was beginning to feel just a bit scared. Eric was still not well enough to come back to work and she was on her own. How dare these people stand in front of the café and behave in this hostile way?

"If you don't go now I'll call the police on you" Sonya screamed "Janice – come through now." She pointed out Janice standing smirking at the back of the small crowd. "Can't you see that she is American? We only employ American citizens here."

"Janice run away while you can. They are filthy scum and we don't want them in South Atlanta" screeched one woman

The crowd moved aside so Janice could walk past and into the burger bar. Sonya and Janice then began preparing the lunch service. It was very quiet though. It seemed very few people came in although there was a crowd outside. The same happened at the evening service. Sonya was furious. Finally, at 8 pm she rang the police and complained about the crowd loitering outside the burger bar.

At 8.20 pm a policeman came and dispersed the crowd. He came into the burger bar where there was a sole customer sitting on a bar stool eating a burger.

Sonya did not think to say thank you. Instead she went into a long tirade about how ridiculous it was that people were outside her burger bar "carrying on" as she put it. The policeman left soon afterwards.

By 8.50 pm the crowd had returned and to add insult to injury at 9 pm a local TV news crew turned up. The presenter stood with the crowd and a camera man began to film the crowd outside.

By now Sonya was beyond herself with rage. She felt like she was going to explode. She had never in her whole life been this angry before.

Without thinking she stormed outside and began shouting "I am being victimised." She ranted and raved "this should not be allowed to happen in a decent God-fearing community. I have worked hard for 20 years and this is how I am treated."

That evening her face and the crowd outside Big Daddy's appeared on the local news. The newscaster said this is what had happened in the aftermath of the trial.

That day the burger bar only sold four burgers all day. It was hardly worth keeping open so Sonya closed early at 10 pm and went home to Eric.

The next day she arrived to find there was spray paint across the new paint on the front of the burger bar "Scum" "Rapist" it said.

For the first time Sonya felt that she might be beat – sitting inside she finally broke down in tears and sobbed for what had been and what might have been. When Janice arrived she had stopped her tears. She sent Janice to the store for whitewash and then she left

Janice cooking the burgers while she went outside and wiped the front of the burger bar down. At least Janice had returned she said to herself and tomorrow was another day.

"People will forget Janice" she said returning with the mop and bucket "we must carry on as if nothing has happened. Eric will be back in a couple of weeks. That will make a big difference."

Janice nodded turning a burger over. She wasn't listening to a word Sonya said. She was thinking about the concert she was going to later. Matt Carey was on at State Farm Arena. She couldn't wait.

"No matter what happens, or just how bad
It seems today, life goes on, and it will be better tomorrow."
Maya Angelou

.

Chapter 63

Matt Carey

The Aftermath of the Trial in Atlanta

Derek Lynes had rung Matt Carey, the celebrity who was paying his bills, as soon as the verdict was announced and had kept ringing him with updates as they unfolded.

Matt had now returned to Atlanta for the end of his tour as coincidence had it. He was going to appear at the State Farm Arena.

"Do you intend to out yourself?" asked Derek Lynes "as the person who paid Barry Watkin's bills?"

"No I have no intention of outing myself." Said Matt Carey. "I feel it is best if it remains that there was an anonymous person who paid your bill. Did you also find Barry somewhere to live?"

"We found him a small efficiency in the area he is familiar with and he is beyond delighted. He couldn't go back to his rental as Tomas his roommate had sublet the room to someone else."

"What about his job?" asked Matt "Didn't he used to work at Amazon? Can he go back?"

"Yes, that has worked out for him as well" said Derek "he is back working for Amazon.

Derek also reported that a woman had spoken to Dr Abebe Majola that Eric Senser had raped her a couple of years ago. The circumstances were the same. An illegal immigrant working for cash and sent to take the trash out to the alley. The women felt she could come forward as she had been able to apply for amnesty and was now no longer in the USA illegally. Dr Abebe Majola had encouraged her to go to the police and make a complaint."

Matt had enjoyed watching the TV news and seeing the aftermath of the trial. He would have loved to have been a fly on the wall to witness Sonya's screams but he didn't need to witness them to know the world of Eric Senser and Sonya Gonzalez was finally unravelling.

Matt remembered the grease and grime and fear at Big Daddy's. Employing the most vulnerable and using and abusing them. Eric getting his sexual kicks and Sonya turning a blind eye.

Being able to sing had been Matt's out from this sordid world. He was blessed.

Matt knew that he had had an abundant life and he wanted to give something back.

He helped himself to a whiskey and raised a toast.

"This is for all the vulnerable people across the years who had to suffer at the hands of that pair and had no voice to stand up to them."

He said this out loud to no one in particular. It was worth every cent he had spent on the lawyer.

That evening when he sang in State Farm Arena the crowd went wild. In the cheap seats Janice was up singing and dancing. But not far behind her if you looked carefully, you could see a large, black man with a beer in his hand and a smile from ear to ear. He was on his feet singing along and dancing, loving every moment of this evening and his new-found freedom.

"Know yourself. Never forget where you come from, and
Reach back to help someone else come forward too."
Alpha Alexander

"People say, "what is the sense of our small effort?"
They cannot see that we must lay one brick at a time,
Take one step at a time. A pebble cast into a pond
Causes ripples that spread in all directions. Each one of our
thoughts, words, and deeds is just like that. No one
Has a right to sit down and feel hopeless. There's so much work to
do."
Dorothy Day

Chapter 64

The Aftermath of the Trial at the Purple Orchid

Jinni

The weeks following the trial in Atlanta were some of the most difficult in my life. This related both to my business and to my personal life.

After the trial Ellie and I stood with Song on the steps of the Court House and she spoke to the news team who were filming us. I was proud of her for speaking up for other vulnerable women. She had been to hell and back but was now thinking of others and was prepared to speak up for them.

Looking at the cameras she had said "What happened at that burger bar is a crime against women. Women who are poor and vulnerable and do not have working papers have been sexually exploited there. It should stop now."

We took a taxi to the airport. I held her hand on the way there and we promised to keep in touch. She could use Zoom in China and we were going to use it to talk regularly. We set up a date for our first meeting in the taxi.

I could sense that Song was happy that the trial was over and that now she couldn't wait to see her mother again in China. I wondered if they would force her to go to the college in Australia. Deep down I knew they would. Even though her father knew she was not academic he would still force her to study for a degree.

We lingered as long as we could at the airport and then Song had to go to International Departures and Ellie and I to domestic departures. I tried to smile but the tears still came as I waved good-bye. Ellie put her arm around me and we walked together to the gate for our flight.

Over the next couple of days details of the trial hit the TV stations across the southern states. I don't believe it went nationwide but it certainly was featured here. It seemed strange seeing myself with Ellie standing on the court steps. Dr Abebe Majola was on TV as well, putting forward her views. There were scenes of crowds outside Big Daddy's Burger Bar complaining about employing illegal immigrants. I know this sounds really naïve but watching TV I felt everyone was on our side. They would see that what happened at the Big Daddy's Burger Bar was a crime against poor, vulnerable women and they would want justice. Yes, and not only that, they would see that justice had been done.

Oh my dear, how wrong could I be!

On the Saturday morning, I got on the train to go to the salon as normal. It was busy but I found a seat and was flipping through social media on my cell phone when this woman, who I had never seen before in my life, came up to me.

"I know you." She said "I saw your face on TV. Go back to your own country scum!! We don't need you and your type in this country Chinese scum."

I was horrified and struck dumb for a moment. I could sense other people were looking. What should I do? My heart was beating fast. This woman's face was contorted by hate.

"I have as much right to be here as you" I said "I am not Chinese – I am Thai, but I have papers to be in this country."

"Yay right" she raised her voice now "Its people like you that are destroying this country. Taking jobs away from Americans – go back to Thailand where you belong we don't want you here!!"

I had to get off the train then – I was conscious of the fact everyone was looking at me. I was visibly shaking and near to tears. It was terrifying.

I got to the salon and opened up. Lila followed me into the salon.

"Are you okay Jinni?" she said in a concerned voice. I told her what had happened.

“Don’t’ worry about some nutcase on the train, Jinni” she said “some people are mental cases. Do you want to sit down for a moment to pull yourself together before your first appointment? I can make you a cup of green tea?”

“Thanks that is very kind, but I am sure I will be okay” I said seeing my first appointment coming through the door. She was a regular of mine and I worked on her manicure and we chatted about her upcoming cruise to the Caribbean. As she was leaving I noticed my second appointment had not come in. Lila was on reception and she seemed slightly agitated.

“um Jinni” she said “your 10 am just cancelled.”

“Do we know why?” I asked

“Mmmm she didn’t really say” said Lila awkwardly. “But the thing is there are a lot of cancellations today.”

I was beginning to get the message, though it felt very wrong.

“Thank you Lila” I said “we will do our best to give the best manicure in town to the customers who do come in.”

Despite my attempts at bravado it was a very quiet day in the salon with numerous cancellations. In an attempt to make things better I put an advert on social media “1/2 price mani/pedi to first 30 people to book this week.” I put a number on for people to phone in. That should help things I felt.

The weekend was uneventful. I had dinner on Saturday evening with my very good Thai friends who wanted to know about the trial and how things had gone. Noi said “Song was so lucky to have your support, Jinni. I do hope none of this affects your business.”

I smiled and brushed the comment off.

On Monday morning I caught the train without incident but as I was walking through the Walks shopping centre to my salon a woman stood in my way.

"I know you" she said "you are here illegally and employ illegal immigrants in your shop. I saw that Chinese girl on TV. People like you disgust me taking jobs away from Americans."

I did not have time to respond before she spat on me. This was worse than the incident on Saturday. Turning I ran in the opposite direction. I felt sick and frightened. I leant against the wall and, using a tissue, wiped the spittle from off my face. I then strode in a determined fashion towards the salon.

Monday was just as bad as Saturday. People cancelling appointments for no apparent reason. We did have some takers for the ½ price mani/pedi but overall, it was quiet. The salon used to be so busy with every chair taken. I told myself it would blow over in a day or two. People had notoriously short memories.

I was so wrong. It seemed people now associated the Purple Orchid with illegal immigrants. In fact, people were saying I was an illegal immigrant. They wanted me out of their town. How could I ever get over this?

Lila found me sitting with my head in my hands in the little back room.

"It's pretty bad isn't it Jinni?" she said "people assume you were employing illegal immigrants because of the trial and your involvement."

"I shouldn't have gone to the trial. I should have kept a low profile. But I love Song and I wanted to support her. I don't know how I can come back from this."

"It will get better, Jinni" said Lila "Just wait and see"

At that moment I couldn't believe her – I felt all my life's work was going to be lost. It was one of the lowest periods in my life....

Chapter 65

Ellie

The aftermath of the Trial at the Purple Orchid

After the trial Ellie was excited about working with Dr Abebe Majola and helping her with her research. She had been to another meeting with the research team where it was decided to expand the research to look at women who might drop out of university and be in the States illegally. Ellie was going to do some of the leg work.

One thing was obvious, someone had paid Barry Watkin's legal fees. His attorney was very good and probably cost a lot of money to hire. Ellie liked to think it was one of the celebrities she had written to. Of course, she had no proof it was her that had put this in motion. If she was being honest, she found these American celebrities very strange – why would someone pay Barry Watkins bills and then not communicate with the person who had sent the message informing them of his plight? Also, why would they not say in public that they had paid the fees? Surely this would be good publicity. The celebrity would look like a "Good Samaritan". Wouldn't it be good publicity? It all seemed very peculiar. One thing was for sure, Ellie certainly wasn't going to confide any of her thoughts to Kevin who would tell her to get a life and stop being so stupid.

Ellie was busy teaching. If anyone at the university had seen her on the Court steps after the trial it was not mentioned. Kevin and Ellie had some enjoyable commutes back and forth talking about the baby and their future. All seemed well until the Friday.

On the Friday after the trial Ellie was due to go to the Purple Orchid for her nail appointment. She was a bit surprised that Lila rang her first thing to get her to confirm her appointment. This was new and unusual. Her appointment was at 1 pm and she got to the salon in good time. She was a bit shocked walking in as it seemed empty in the salon. Usually it was a buzz of gossip and laughter. Today it seemed eerily silent and only two of the seats were taken.

“It’s very quiet isn’t it?” Ellie mentioned to Lila who was on reception “Usually its very busy on a Friday.”

Immediately she said this, Ellie saw the expression on Lila’s face and she looked horrified. At first, Ellie didn’t know what she had said. Then she began to realise something was very wrong. She spoke quietly “what is wrong, Lila?”

Lila looked close to tears “It’s the aftermath of the trial” she whispered

Oh no. It started to dawn on Ellie slowly - people were linking Jinni with the trial and the illegal immigrants.

Ellie was shocked. She had expected the vast majority (if not everyone!) would have been on Jinni’s side and felt that justice was done. Yet it seemed that they thought Jinni had been supporting illegal immigrants.

“Where is Jinni?”

“She is working on a manicure.” Said Lila

“Can you give me your cell and I will ring you tonight?” Ellie said. She felt like an uncaring fool. She had never given a thought to the fact that people might turn on Jinni. She felt she was so insensitive. She just wanted to do all she could to help Jinni now she knew.

Julie gave Ellie a manicure so she did not have a chance to speak to Jinni, other than to smile and wave.

That evening she rang Lila.

Lila said

“Every day people ring in cancelling appointments. Yesterday apparently someone was stood outside telling people not to come in as foreign illegal scum worked in the Purple Orchid and it should be shut down.

People say they remember Song working at the Purple Orchid in November and December of last year. Then she disappeared. They say now that all the staff are illegal immigrants."

"What rubbish!" Ellie said "Obviously you are American!! Oh, Lila this is a disaster! Jinni has worked so hard to build the business up and it is her pride and joy."

"People are like sheep" said Lila "when one person says something then everyone else joins in."

"We have to be able to help Jinni." Ellie said: "Let me think how we can do this."

Ellie gave this a lot of thought but it was very tricky. If they spoke up for Jinni then it was true she had employed Song when she did not have papers. How were they going to get round that?

Ellie was so deep in thought that Kevin asked what she was thinking about. She decided to tell him.

"Now listen here, Ellie" said Kevin "Jinni is a good business woman and she doesn't deserve to lose her business but really we have to keep out of this. People can get very nasty if they feel a place is employing illegals to work there and who knows what might happen."

"But the point is Kevin, Jinni doesn't employ illegals – all her staff are American. She is Thai but has working papers. We have to help her, where is she if she doesn't have friends?"

"Get off the soap box, Ellie" Kevin said "And go and help Abebe with her research. You don't have to do anything. Keep out of trouble. You are pregnant and shouldn't be getting yourself wound up like this. You have to think of the baby."

Kevin always had Ellie's best interests at heart. But the thing is Ellie never listened especially when it was about a friend. Jinni was her friend as well as her manicurist and she couldn't just stand by and let her business fail could she?

Soon she had an idea and was texting and messaging …

Chapter 66

Lila

The aftermath of the trial

The days after the trial were very difficult in the salon. The trial was not shown nationwide but it was certainly shown across the southern states. At first when Lila saw Ellie, Jinni and Song stood on the Court steps she thought how brilliant. She wanted to stand and applaud. But it is funny what people will cling to – many folks felt they recognised Song from the Purple Orchid when they saw her stood with Jinni. They then jumped to the conclusion that the Purple Orchid was a hot bed of illegal immigrants. This view wasn't helped by the fact that Jinni is Thai and they felt she did not have working papers either.

The salon went from being really busy to being virtually empty. People were rude to Jinni outside the salon and one woman spat on her! It was awful.

For the first time in her life Lila felt helpless, she did not know how to help.

However, she had not bet on Ellie who was amazing! When she found out she started making plans to help Jinni. They talked on her cell, and through messages and texts.

Ellie first got an appointment with a reporter from the local newspaper "The Pinnacle". Lila and Ellie met this person in a coffee shop in the downtown near the Purple Orchid. The reporter was a young guy who looked about 12. They bought him coffee rather than the other way round. Lila still felt this would be a disaster as looking at him didn't instil confidence. He also kept sniffing and snorting and saying "yay, yay, yay". However, the next day the following appeared in the online Pinnacle

> Opinion Piece: Hero salon owner exposes sexual exploitation in Atlanta.

Jinni, the owner of the Purple Orchid nail salon is a brave woman, To help protect her friend Song Zhang, she has helped expose a burger bar in Atlanta where the owner was sexually exploiting illegal immigrant women. Song Zhang, a Chinese woman who had run away from university and was working in the USA illegally was being attacked by the owner of the burger bar who was trying to rape her. Barry Watkins, 33, attacked the owner to protect Song and was subsequently prosecuted for aggravated assault and battery. This week in a nail biting trial in Atlanta, Barry has been cleared of the charges when it was proved he was protecting Song.

Eleanor Watson, 35, said in Jinni's defence "I am a customer and friend of the owner of the Purple Orchid, Jinni. Last autumn Song Zhang worked briefly at the Purple Orchid when she had run away from university. At the time Jinni did not know she didn't have working papers. When this came out Song ran away to Atlanta with disastrous consequences. Jinni never gave up on her friend and has stood by her throughout her ordeal and the trial."

Lila Matthews, 48, who is a receptionist at the Purple Orchid said "Jinni is from Thailand but has papers to live and work in the USA. She does not employ illegal immigrants. All the staff are Americans by birth, including myself."

WE should celebrate a hero in our midst not tar her with the same brush as the owner of Big Daddy's Burger Bar.

Lila liked the way it was written – it should be a different spin on what had happened.

Then Jerry Levens, the presenter of the "Commuter Show" on the local radio station took up the story. He asked if he could interview Ellie and Lila on his show which had a very big audience in the city.

Ellie really held forth on the radio about the trial and the issues that women who are vulnerable and poor and have no-one to speak up for them face.

Then it was Lila's turn to speak:

"I just want to say that Jinni is running the Purple Orchid nail salon legally and until the last couple of weeks it has been a thriving business. Please, please do not put her into the same category as Eric Senser, the owner of Big Daddy's Burger Bar. Jinni does not employ illegal immigrants. Come in and see – the manicurists are American. Jinni is Thai but has working papers. I was born in Louisiana and I am proud to say I work at the Purple Orchid."

Jerry agreed "This is a big shout out for the Purple Orchid nail bar and for Jinni who stood up for her friend and helped expose the sexual exploitation of women in S Atlanta. I want to give a shout out as well for Barry Watkins, if you are listening, you are a hero man. You have my vote."

Then Lila jumped in and said "Thank you Jerry for your vote of confidence. There is so much to be proud of in this city. We have the new regeneration area and the Institute for the Blind and Visually Impaired. Also don't forget to get your tickets for the end of first term concert at the Newform Theatre on May 27. The Brothers of Swing will be singing with the Institute Jazz Band."

Jerry laughed – "Yes a big shout out" he said "for the Brother of Swing and the Institute Jazz Band. See you at the Newform Theatre on May 27."

When Lila went to the Purple Orchid after the radio show Jinni came up to her and hugged her. She had tears in her eyes. "Thank you for supporting me" she murmured. "I am so lucky to have you as staff."

Things weren't really that much better though. It was hoped that Jinni had deep pockets and could ride out the boycott of the salon. They could only hope it would get better in the future. Jinni had also confided that she was going to develop another premises in the regeneration area. It was a time of great uncertainty for the salon and for her….

EPILOGUE

May 27, 2023

The concert

The Newform theatre sits on Kennedy Boulevard between the downtown and the regeneration area. It can seat 300 people and has an imposing façade, but is really beyond its best days. On May 27, representatives from the Institute for the Blind and Visually Impaired were there all day getting ready for the concert which started at 7 pm. It was a sell-out.

The concert started on time and had several parts to it with the students performing different vignettes. A poem by the first-year students, a song by the second years and a short play by the seniors.

The headline act though was the Institute Jazz Band playing with the Brothers of Swing. Adrienne joined them. Adrienne sang a couple of classic tunes ending with a duet between Ronnie and Adrienne 'Cheek to Cheek'. The audience loved this and there was a standing ovation.

In the audience Ellie and Kevin sitting with Kevin's mother, Jennie, were all on their feet applauding.

Lila felt like a proud mother watching the Brothers – they were on the way to stardom she was sure! Next to her Randi was smiling and applauding. Sitting next to Randi was the pastor who Randi had asked to join them at the concert and he was on his feet applauding as well.

Across town in the back room of the Purple Orchid Jinni sat drinking a SangSom, which is a strong Thai rum. She was drinking from a glass and the bottle was on the desk. She had meant to go to the concert and knew she should have gone to support the Brothers of Swing but time had got away from her. On the salon's music system she had Chinese songs playing – "Letting Go" by Tanya Chua. She only played Chinese songs nowadays. A spreadsheet had been printed out and was in front of her with figures and workings –by the side of this was a note she had written and which had the number of a bank. On her laptop was a screen where she was drawing up an advert

> "Ali will be at the Purple Orchid on Thursday 1 June 2023.
> Beautiful nail art – ½ price – Book your appointment now
> Ring 900-600-7342 and ask for Jinni."

Jinni slurped her drink and then she moved on to another screen on her laptop and into Zoom

A beautiful face came onto the screen smiling and waving. She could hear birds singing and see beautiful flowers in the background. A voice spoke "I'm in the garden with mother and its hot."

Jinni smiled "Good evening my darling. I've been waiting all day for this. It is lovely to see you."

Printed in Great Britain
by Amazon

49831038R00155